CANDLELIGHT REGENCY SPECIAL

CANDLELIGHT REGENCIES

The Gypsy Heiress

LAURA LONDON

A CANDLELIGHT REGENCY SPECIAL

Published by
Dell Publishing Co., Inc.
1 Dag Hammarskjold Plaza
New York, New York 10017

Dell ® TM 681510, Dell Publishing Co., Inc.

ISBN: 0-440-12960-5

Printed in the United States of America

First printing—March 1981

The
Gypsy
Heiress

Chapter One

It was impulse, and the ache of pity that made me stop to free the fox. Father would have warned me to pass it by. "No, Liza, let be. That one belongs to God," he might have whispered, and my grandmother would have made a hand sign, a secret sign from the ancient language and told me, "Leave the mokada jook for the poacher. Shoo! Fox is a dirty beast!" But four years had passed since Father was buried in the pretty churchyard on a sunwashed hill in Greece. Grandma had seen her last sunset three weeks ago, and now there was no one to scold and guide, to love and laugh with, and to sit with under the black night skies watching the sparkling stars that held in each the heart of an angel.

The fox had already been in the trap for some time; from my high perched seat in the wagon I could see the ragged path cut through the roadside underbrush where the fox had dragged the trap in her struggle to escape. The creature was near exhaustion, though her spirit was strong. As I approached, she bared her teeth and growled a warning, so I stopped where I was and sat on the sparse grass beside a mound of wild lilies. I sat with my legs together, as was proper for a gypsy maiden. She was wise, the fox, and stopped the rumble in her throat to show her approval for my respectful attitude. The clouds shifted in the heavens as we sat, and golden spikes of sunlight pierced the leaves of the overhanging oak. I could feel the speckles of heat across the width of my cheekbones and was glad for it and for the many layers of my bright cotton skirts that kept the spring soil's damp from my legs. After the fox had time to take my scent, I began to talk to the frightened animal softly in Romany.

It took an hour, more perhaps, until the fox trusted me enough to let me come close and work open the rusted jaws of the trap. A fallen branch from the oak had been caught accidentally in the metal teeth and had prevented the trap from doing its ugly work. To my joy, I found the fox's leg was not broken, only much scratched. The fox, the mokada jook, leapt away at once and disappeared into the underbrush.

My heart was light for the first time in three weeks as I stood brushing the forest floor from my skirts. The crashing of a man's boots through the nearby thicket came so swiftly that I had not time to turn my face toward the sound before a heavy hand fell upon the back of my neck and jerked me around.

"So! A stinkin' gypsy brat! You're the one's been settin' these traps, are ye? By Ged, ye'll learn before you're much older what justice we've got here for poachers. Where's the rest o' ye?"

My accuser was a short man of middle age with the body of a boxer. The fine quality of his woolen frock-coat and breeches advertised his prosperity; the professional fit bespoke his superior status. His anger-reddened features might have been pleasant if he were in a softer frame of mind; there was nothing of the bully about him, only the righteous outrage of an honest man confronted with a thief. Had I been any young English girl, a farmer's daughter perhaps, or a hand at the local fulling-mill, the man might have seen my fear or waited to hear my plea of innocence. But I am a gypsy, and it needed only that to convict me of all crimes. Grandmother said it was the lot of the gypsy to be despised by the non-gypsies, the gorgios; it was God's will. I tried desperately to view the man

10

only as a manifestation of the Divine Plan and to think of something to placate him. My hesitation was too long, and the man shook me with ruthless impatience. The trap fell from my trembling fingers, leaving a deep scratch across my palm.

"Don't ye ken the King's English, wench? Where are they, eh? I haven't heard that there was any such vermin camped hereabouts."

"There are none, sir," I said, and immediately regretted my words. Grandma had warned me more than once about letting a man know I was unaccompanied in a secluded place. So carefully guarded had I been that this was the first time I had ever had the opportunity to use that knowledge—the first time, and I had failed.

As it happened, the man didn't believe me anyway. He called me a sly little liar and a devil's daughter, and, encasing my wrist in a hand so calloused it bit like iron, he pulled me toward the woods.

My fear was as deep as the ocean's hidden valleys; I struggled, although it stained my dignity. As I tried to twist and fight, the man paid no more heed to me than he might have to the bucking of a spring lamb being led to the market. Minutes ago, I had been a free being, seeking to share my freedom with a trapped animal. Now it was I who was trapped, as though the creators had ordained that I must trade my liberty for hers.

The man strode implacably through the underbrush, deflecting branches that swung sharply back to whip my cheeks. The pain of it shocked open my mind, which had been so locked in grief since the death of my grandmother, and I began a torrent of explanation that fell worthlessly upon the man's broad gray back.

"You'll have your hour in court, wench," the man growled, preoccupied. "My only task is to get you there."

He pulled me into a clearing, where a large brown, Roman-nosed horse was cropping the grass in the radius of an iron spike which held its tether. Wordlessly, the man tied my wrists together with one end of a long rope, and

11

held the other end as he untethered his horse and mounted.

With a quick, flipping motion, he gave the rope which held me a few twists around his own wrist, and heeled the horse into motion. I had no choice but to follow, my tied arms stretched before me like the tongue of a wagon.

Though the man held his mount to a walk, the horse's long legs moved too rapidly for me, and I had to train my gait to an uncomfortable half-run in order to keep pace. The sharp, iron-clad hooves cleared the ground no more than a wagon wheel's width from me; I feared the large creature might find me an irritant at its heels and strike out. And might not the man, through an impulse of cruelty or forgetfulness, put spurs to his mount and urge him to a speed beyond my means?

I took little comfort in the reflection that dragging might be a more merciful death than I would meet through the English courts. I knew how poachers were punished. Men, women, and children alike were whipped and pilloried, followed by imprisonment in vile cells rampant with deadly gaol fever. And prison was for Englishmen born. I was a gypsy, and me, they would hang. Who had not passed the crossroads and seen wretched corpses dangling from the gibbet? There seemed to lie a great crevice at my feet. Arivell, the beng, the God of Darkness and Death lay at wait in it, his awful jaws yawning open to swallow me as he had my parents and my grandmother.

The road became sun-dappled as the track widened and the trees overhead began to part. We were leaving the forest. At another time I would have been filled with the delicious joy of visiting a new place, but the misery of my situation clouded my view as the wall of silvery-barked ash trees was left behind.

After crossing a clear, shallow stream filled with darting minnows, the man turned his horse down a grassy corridor through an orchard of snowy, blossoming apple trees, growing in neat well-attended rows. The heady scent was almost overpowering with each step under the blossoms, bringing into sharper focus the smell of the horse which

12

pulled me along. The corridor led onto a sloping avenue bordered on both sides by monkey-puzzle trees. The close-cropped grass was like a carpet, made for walking, but I still stumbled, if only because I was trying so hard not to stumble. There must have been some pity in the man, for though he gave a disgusted snort, he stopped his animal when I lost my footing a third time, waited for me to get up, and then moved on more slowly.

After half a mile, the man dismounted and led the horse and me up a slope that ran with daffodils like a spill of butter and cream. As we reached the crest, I looked below into the dip of a natural amphitheater.

A shock of recognition came as I gazed at the focal point of the dramatically diving greensward. It was Edgehill Hall! Indeed it could be none other—the historic home of the Earls of Brockhaven. I knew its façade well from a book of etchings my father kept, *Great Houses of the British Isles*. My family had carried few books; life in a wagon did not lend itself to the gathering of material possessions. Those they did carry I had read again and again. *Great Houses* had been one of my favorite volumes, for the stately homes had seemed fairy castles from a dream peopled by fine and noble lords and ladies of courage and intelligence. I knew it wasn't so, of course—Grandma had said they were evil gorgios like the rest of them, who starved and ill-treated their servants and threw gypsies off their meadows.

But Edgehill Hall it surely was. It was one of the few mansions built in that uniquely English cousin to the Continental Gothic, the Perpendicular style. Its great symmetrical façade was awash with the sunlight reflected from its many and generously proportioned windows. They said of it, "Edgehill Hall, more glass than wall."

I shyly asked the man, "Sir, are you—can you be Lord Brockhaven?"

He looked back at me over his shoulder, the angry frown deep as though he suspected me of mocking him. "What do you know of Brockhaven?"

"Nothing, my lord," I answered, wishing I had held my

tongue instead of making him more angry. "Only I've seen the hall in a picture book. I . . . I never knew I was passing so close."

"Or you might have been more careful with your traps, eh?" said the man harshly. He stared hard at me. Then his expression lessened in severity, perhaps in reaction to something he saw in my face. His lips twitched as though a humorous thought had touched his mind.

"No, I'm not 'my lord.' I'm his game warden, and a far different stamp of a man than he. Come on with ye."

As we neared the Hall, I saw in greater detail the cluster of outbuildings which sprouted in the late day shadow like mushrooms in the shelter of a massive stump. The buildings were architecturally matched to the Hall, of the same design and stone, though on a smaller and functional scale. Each building was surrounded by a planting of early bulbs—columbines, poppies, and pinks—which ran around the square of the building out to border the flagstone walks connecting each with its nearest counterpart. A pillar of steam rose from the laundry and wafted over a huge succession house filled with the shiny green leaves of orange trees, planted to provide yearlong fresh fruit to the inhabitants of the Hall. There was a bakehouse, a dairy, a brewhouse, and a number of small pretty cottages, and, at the end of the row, a stable block with a blacksmith shop and a carriage barn. A group of children were playing at skips underfoot three scurrying, aproned servants. The action stopped when they paused to stare at the man on horseback and me, his captive. The smallest of the children, a boy, broke and ran screaming to his mother, who sat spinning by an open doorway. He hid behind her skirts, pointing and screaming.

"Gypsies, ma! Gypsies! They've come to steal me away!"

The woman lay down her spindle, and in an affectionately scolding tone said to the boy, "Hush you, James. Be a man! You can see Mr. Stewart has her tied up with a rope so she won't be stealing away anything."

An older woman stepped out of the bakehouse. She was

14

dressed in a crisp white uniform, and covered in flour up to her elbows. She kneaded a pillow of white bread dough as she said: "A gypsy, is it? Folks'll have to be watchin' their property again with *them* about. Has she been thievin', Mr. Stewart?"

"Poachin'," said the man gruffly. He seemed strangely vexed as he looked back at me.

"Are ye going to take her in the wagon to the gaol in Chipping, sir?" asked a youth who sat idly on the icehouse stoop, chewing on a strand of straw.

The game warden scowled uneasily at his questioner. "Aye, but what business is it of yours, layabout?" He swept his questioners with a scowl as black as a summer thunderstorm. "If ye've all stared your fill, remember the lesson of Lot's wife and be about your business! I've the situation well in hand."

It was a measure of the game warden's authority that he was obeyed at once, even by the straw-chewing youth who rolled his eyes expressively at the bakery maid and sauntered off toward the dairy.

After that, the stares became surreptitious. Usually, such scrutiny made me self-conscious, though Grandmother said that a gypsy should meet the stares of peasants with contempt and secret amusement. Now, I was too distressed to care.

"John! Afternoon, my good man!"

The voice was youthful, male and heartlessly cheerful. I looked up to see a young man dressed at the height of fashion riding toward us on a Thoroughbred horse that might have sold for upward of a hundred guineas. Evidently the beautiful animal had been worked hard, for its sloping shoulders were shining with sweat.

The rider was twenty, perhaps a little older, with clear gray eyes sparkling from the exercise, and cheeks reddened from the wind. It was a handsome face, well-boned, but there were haughty edges to the mouth which time had not yet softened.

"What have you got there?" said the youth, spurring his horse toward us.

"Poacher, sir," answered the warden. So the younger man was not the Earl, or Stewart would have addressed him as "my lord." "Caught her by the forty-acre forest near the valley road, and I'll be taking her into town."

The younger man gave the warden a look of humorous reproach. "You promised to let me have first pick of any new fillies at Edgehill."

Stewart watched warily as the youth, with one hand on the reins, edged his horse in front of me, and gently lifted my chin with the butt end of his riding crop. He smiled at me in an intense way that I found rather frightening; however, it emboldened me to plead my cause.

"I wasn't poaching, sir!" I said. "There was—I saw a fox, a trapped fox as I was passing by the forest in my wagon, and I only sought to free it. I hadn't thought at the time, but I realize now that I can prove what I'm saying." I swung around and looked up at John Stewart. "Sir, if we could go back to that place where the trap was set, you would see shredded fox fur and signs of blood, and you would believe me when I say I couldn't have been setting the trap, but that it had been there for some time." I read a new uncertainty in the warden's face, and looked desperately back to the young man. "I beg you, sir."

The youth gave a subtle smile as though he found it amusing that a creature of such little importance should plead so hard for its life.

"Such passion," he said. "Perhaps you could convince me." He leaned over and cupped my cheek in his hand. "Would you try, my little nymph?"

Alarmed by his tone, I took a step back. He smiled again at my reticence as one might smile at the quaint antics of a squirrel, and looked at Stewart, saying, "Bring her to the house."

Stewart looked distressed. "Master Robert, you know I cannot. You ought to know better than to ask."

Master Robert returned look for look with a haughty stare, though his gray eyes twinkled. "Do you say 'cannot' to me, John? God, that would be a first."

"There's my reward for spoiling you," Stewart said

glumly. "Now you're in your manhood, you upbraid me for it. I'm taking the gel to Chipping."

"You won't, John. You'll bring her in the house as I asked," Robert said matter-of-factly, with impenetrable self-confidence. "Don't be a prude, man," he said, softening the words with a persuasive smile.

It was clear that John Stewart was upset. "I'm a Christian man, Master Robert. You know that."

The youth backed his horse several paces, with a gleam of unholy amusement in his eyes. "Why, certainly I know that. That's why I'm not asking *you* to be brought to the house. See that in one-half hour she's in my . . ."

"Reading room," interrupted Stewart firmly.

"A dainty compromise, John," spoke the young man over his shoulder as he cantered the horse toward the stable block, "and as good a place to begin as any."

I won't let them see me cry, I thought. I won't. I must keep a clear head and find some way to escape. But when Stewart led me into the big house through the wide corridors of the kitchen complex, the possibility of escape seemed as hard to imagine as sharp peppers in May. I suffered the chafing of the rope on my wrists and followed my captor down the halls.

As I looked about at the hushed, beautiful surroundings, the very concepts of flight, terror, and escape seemed an intrusion from the outside world. Plush exotic carpets muted our footsteps and all further sound of our progress down the halls, which were hung with gorgeous, brightly colored tapestries. The ceilings were brilliantly frescoed. At points in the hallway were tables set with gold vases filled with arrangements of fresh flowers, the tables themselves carved and gilded by masterful hands. To buy a simple, rough-hewn table was ten shillings at the least. I could scarcely imagine anyone possessing the fortune to own even one of Edgehill's tables. This was opulence far beyond what I would have thought possible in a dwelling; it seemed more luxury than would be available to kings or princes. An anxious tightness arose in my throat to match the binding constriction on my wrists.

17

The wide glass panel in the reading room overlooked the south lawn. The walls and plaster ceiling were blue, with ribbing picked out in white. Fine paintings adorned the walls, treasures of their kind by Van Dyke, Hopner, and Reynolds.

Without looking at me, Stewart summoned a footman, directed him to stand watch over me, and untied the rope from my wrists. Coiling it into a loose loop around his wrist, he stomped from the room without another word. The footman, a freckle-faced, fair-skinned lad of eighteen, looked embarrassed but determined to do his duty. He warned me not to try any of my gypsy tricks on him, not to put my greasy fingers on any of his lordship's tables, and not to sit down. I was left with nothing to do but stare disconsolately out the window, rubbing my wrists to restore circulation, and watching a family of deer from the estate herd grazing under a clump of beech trees far down the lot. I noticed a fiery pain throbbing on my palm where the trap had cut me.

I thought sadly of my wagon with its clean varnished sides, and my horse, Yojo, in his brass-studded harness, still hitched to the wagon. He was thirsty by now, I was sure. He would roll his great shoulders uncomfortably under the leather collar, and turn his head to nicker at Kory, the stallion, that I had left tethered to the wagon's back rack. I knew my two horses. They would lift their ears at each strange sound, and look for me, only to be disappointed. I stood as I was for a long time. The deer wandered out of sight into the beech trees. The footman shifted position uncomfortably, and shadow from the branches of a large oak tree touched the stone base of the house.

I was beginning to wonder if the young man called Master Robert had forgotten about me when I heard footsteps in the hall, and he entered the room. Dressed in clean buckskins and a crisp white shirt, he gestured his dismissal of the footman, who left with relief. Robert smiled at me, but before he could speak, I said, "Has your warden found the fox fur? Am I to be freed?"

I could see my long-term fortunes were of little concern to him; my sensitivities piqued no interest. But as much as my words were capable of surprising him, they did so. It simply had not occurred to him that I might still wish to leave.

"I doubt if Stewart's gone to look at your fox trap. The prize bitch in the Squire's hound pack has begun to whelp, and the Squire has sent for John to play midwife." He walked leisurely over to me, and leaned against the window frame. He was very close, the gaze of the gray eyes caressing my face. "Please me, and I won't let them hurt you."

I wasn't certain of his meaning, but found my suspicions too terrible to voice. "I am afraid, sir," I managed, "that I would find you too hard to please."

He grinned. "Why?"

" 'Tis evident, sir. I'm so different from you."

He captured one of my braids and threaded it slowly through his hand. "*Vive la différence,* my pet. Since Adam and Eve in the garden . . ."

I was beginning to feel sick and shaky. "That's not what I meant, sir. I refer to the difference in our *degrees.*"

"King and pauper, admiral and Latin master—you'll find, my dear, that we're all the same underneath the sheets."

It was impossible to insulate myself from his meaning. My knowledge of this aspect of the male character was limited to incomplete scraps culled from my reading and tart comments from my grandmother. The thought of increasing my knowledge at these callous young hands was as terrifying as John Stewart's prison. My mind cast wildly for some way to deny him without causing him to deliver me up to the Chipping gaol.

More than once I had seen my grandmother exploit superstitions of the gorgios to protect herself. "If you let me go in peace, sir, I shall put a spell for good fortune on your name."

"Do you do hocus-pocus, my pet? How charming. Why you worry? I've already told you I'd let you go without

19

harm." He caught my remaining braid in his hand; his gray eyes were pitiless. "After I'm done with you." He pulled my face to his by the braids; I tried to pull away, wincing in pain from the hard ache of my hair yanking at my scalp. He bent as though to kiss me. I gave a cry of fear, which startled him enough to slacken his grip, and I was able to tear myself loose and run for the door in an unthinking panic, tugging inefficiently at the brass doorknob. Without looking behind me to see if Master Robert were following me, I finally opened the door and tried to leave the room, only to collide with someone attempting to enter from the other side.

I felt the warm, steadying pressure of a hand on my shoulder as I gasped for lost breath and looked up through a mist of tears to see the man who had accidentally prevented my escape. He was tall, a few years older than the man who had tried to kiss me, and there was a physical resemblance between them that could only have been familial. There was a hardness to his body, accentuated by a jacket and breeches that covered his slim hips without a crease. The breeches seemed to flow in perfect line into the tops of highly polished boots of black leather. The face was strikingly handsome, lean, and aristocratic, and framed by dark, glowing hair that curled naturally in a manner that hairdressers have tried unsuccessfully through the ages to pleasingly emulate. His eyes were deep blue, and had in them the crystalline quality of an early spring sky.

I later learned that many young English maidens could have put a name to that dazzling face. But as my contact with the British aristocracy, or in fact with any aristocracy, had been nonexistent, no spark of recognition informed my mind as I stared at him. I hardly knew whether to class his arrival as an improvement in my situation or a decay. Those intimately familiar with the man would surely have advised that it must be the latter.

As I was eventually to know, it would have been too much to have said that the blue-eyed man's reputation was a stench in the nostrils of every decent citizen. The man

20

had his defenders. To those detractors who charged that he had not an amiable bone in his admittedly graceful body, there was the refutation of Lady Jersey, who claimed that he had once kept her company in a garden alcove for a period of no less than ten minutes and made conversation that, if it was not precisely amiable, was at least free from his customary, biting rudeness. Perhaps the record length of the contact was due to a heavy rain that prevented his leaving the shelter; perhaps a liberal dose of Lord Jersey's brandy accounted for the relatively mellow tenor of his conversation. Say what you would, he was *not* as black as he was painted.

The largest block of his critics came from those gentlemen gifted with pretty wives and mistresses, for there seemed to be a lamentable tendency for such ladies to fall headlong in love with the man after receiving even the smallest trace of encouragement—a crooked smile from the shapely lips, or the most minor courtesy. Fathers were brutally torn. Should they present their daughters to him in the remote hope that it might be their daughter to win his heart and enormous fortune? Or should they hide their girls when the fellow was about out of the horrifying, but far more likely possibility that his erratic fancy should alight on the damsel with every object in view save marriage? No one had ever accused him of having an excessive regard for public opinion, and he had overstepped the limits of respectable oat-sowing times out of mind. Still, he was too rich, too well-born, and too highly placed to be shunned, and the only hostesses who proclaimed to their acquaintances that they would *never* have that man in the house were hostesses who were as sure as Sunday that he wouldn't have come anyway.

All ignorance, I could see only the unmistakable mark of cynicism sketched on the otherwise pristine features, as though repeated disillusionment had tarnished his vision of the world. If he felt as much as a wheat grain of kindness toward me, it was not apparent in his face. He was staring at me as though I were an oily rag left by carelessness on the reading room floor. His hand dropped from my shoulder and rested on his long thighs as he spoke.

"It appears honest John Stewart was right."

"Oh, dear," said Robert, his gray eyes suddenly filled with laughter. "What did he say?"

"He said he was afraid he'd inadvertently assisted in a rape."

It was a hard word for me to hear. I felt the sting of blood in my cheeks, and glanced quickly at the younger man. There was defiance in his face, though only a trace, as he stared affectionately back at the man in the doorway.

"Do you object, big brother?" he said.

The older man ran me up and down rapidly with a contemptuous look. "Our tastes always were different." The look stopped on the cut in my hand; the man's eyes clouded enigmatically, his frown deepened, one eyebrow was lifted. To Robert, he said, "Must you maim them first?" He caught my hand. I tried to jerk it away, but he held it fast. "Hold still," he commanded sharply. I still struggled, and he caught my chin firmly in his other hand and looked into my eyes. "Hold still," he repeated deliberately. I felt burned by his gaze, and took in a sharp breath, but held myself quietly while he uncurled my fingers to look at my wounded palm.

Robert, watching this tableau, spoke softly. "I hadn't noticed that."

For the first time his brother appeared to smile, a sparse curl at the edge of his lips. "I believe you. It's in character." Without looking up from the wound, he asked me, "On what did you cut yourself?"

I swallowed. "The trap. I had stopped to free a fox . . ."

"I've already heard your story," he interrupted. "John Stewart left me a note. You weren't catching a fox; you were letting it go. Very original. If the wound goes septic, you'll probably lose your hand, you know."

"I shan't," I contradicted, a good deal shaken. "My grandmother was a healer, and she taught me some of her skills. I shall put a poultice of mold on it, and after three days adder's tongue boiled with olive oil."

"Wonderful. Filthy it up with a lot of herbs. Until medical science has the time to figure out which folk cures are helpful and which are lethal, if you get an injury on my land, you'll have it treated my way. Come over in the light."

"The light?" I asked, confused by his words. I had imagined I was to be turned over at once to the distressing ministrations of a disapproving maidservant. "And . . . you did say—*your* land. Surely you cannot be Lord Brockhaven!"

"Why can't I be Brockhaven?"

"I had thought," I said, "that an earl would be a much older man."

I heard a crack of laughter from Robert behind me.

"*I* had thought," replied Brockhaven, "that a gypsy would speak wretched English. Why is your speech so pure?"

It embarrassed me that he had noticed, though I ought to have expected it. My use of Grandmother's tongue, the Romany, was clear and perfect and yet somehow my father's refined English had been the dominant influence on my speech. I dreamed in Romany, I thought in a mixture of English and Romany, but when I spoke aloud, my English sounded as though I'd been raised in a Sussex manor house instead of under the tin roof of a gypsy caravan. It was the only part of my father's legacy that I regretted, for it irrevocably proclaimed my mixed blood.

"I was taught," I said, and hoped he'd ask no more.

He didn't pursue the matter, merely giving me a look saying clearly that mine was exactly the kind of stupid answer one could expect from a weak-witted rustic. After propelling me to the window, he examined my hand once more in the sunlight before picking up the lid of a flip-top bureau. Holding my hand over a built-in basin, he began to clean my wound with a stream of water from the matching china pitcher. In a lower drawer there were linen napkins, bleached to a blinding lily white. In a sharp ges-

23

ture that would have brought palpitations to his house-keeper's conscientious heart, he rent one of the immaculate creations in half and probed carefully at the torn flesh on my palm.

I had expected to suffer terribly from this procedure so I was amazed when the gentleness of his touch reduced my pain to a soft sting. I had almost begun to think that I had perhaps misjudged his harshness when he pulled a crystal decanter from a shelf in the bureau and, holding tightly to my wrist, poured a flood of brandy on the injured hand.

I gasped, paled, and swayed on my feet. Hard young arms caught me before I could fall, and Brockhaven lowered me to an upholstered chair with more efficiency than tenderness. Helpless, I drooped my head against the wing and closed my eyes. He fashioned a comfortable bandage from a folded napkin, laid it on my palm, and wrapped it snugly around my wrist. Summoning my strength, I forced myself to recover and, fighting the dizziness, rose to my feet with the help of the chair arm. I faced Lord Brock-haven.

"It had to be done, I know," I said, in a strained voice. "Thank you."

Whatever values Lord Brockhaven possessed, sentimen-tality was not among them. "I would have done the same," he said, "for an animal." He turned to walk from the room, stopping when he reached the door to give his brother a smile's shadow. "Even without a bloody palm, I find her none too appetizing. Doubtless, you'll tell me that your tastes are different than mine, but if you want my ad-vice, give her a bath first."

As he reached for the door handle, I cried out, "No! Oh, please no! Have pity, my lord! Let me go!"

Brockhaven eyed me sardonically and then suddenly he paused, his gaze dropping to the gleaming gold chain that circled my neck. Though it was an unusual chain, with tiny crossbars set in each link, he might not have noticed it if his attention had not been drawn there by my habit of touching it nervously in anxious moments. His eyes sharp-ened as he looked at it, as though the chain had touched

24

off a spark in his mind. To my surprise, he crossed the room in a swift stride and slid his finger behind the delicate goldwork where it lay at the base of my neck. He lifted it to expose the attached medallion, which had fallen behind the cloth of my bodice. There was a change in his expression that I could not identify. What emotions moved him, I didn't know, but there was little doubt that he recognized the medallion. It had been a gift from my father; I knew it was valuable, and yet, it was hardly enough so to excite the interest of a man like the earl with his many fabulous possessions.

Robert had come to stand beside his brother.

"She stole it, of course," said Robert tensely.

Afraid of being accused of yet another crime, I was quick to reply to the accusation. "I haven't! It was my father's!"

"Your father's," Brockhaven repeated thoughtfully. "Incredible."

"Her father stole it," suggested Rob, looking questioningly at Lord Brockhaven. "Alex, it can't be."

A grim smile crossed Brockhaven's features. "That's easily checked." He turned back to me with a thoughtful, studying gaze and reached up to my face, the side of this thumb stroking my cheek. "What's given the color to your skin, brat? Was it the sun . . . ?" His searching fingers traveled down to my neck. "Or was it your parents?"

I hadn't the faintest idea why he had developed this frightening interest in my parentage, my skin tone, or my medallion. The most alarming possibility was that the medallion might hold some secret significance of which I was unaware. When I had asked my father the meaning of the figures in the tiny coat of arms engraved upon it, he had made a conspiratorial wink at my grandmother, and said it was his, that he was making of it a present to me and that that was all I needed to know. I could see that my father had been wrong.

The rounded neckline of my blouse was of the kind that could be tightened or loosened by means of a drawstring.

25

Still watching me, Brockhaven looped the tied end of the string around the tip of his index finger.

"How are you made where the sun doesn't touch?" he said.

I was stiff with distress, but still managed to back away from him.

"Take her arms, Rob, and hold her." My arms were clamped in an implacable grip.

Then, ignoring my frantic misery, Brockhaven drew the strand toward him to release the drawstring's knot. My blouse slid down with the swift silence of a falling cloud to bare my shoulders and came to rest tenuously on the tips of my breasts.

The cramped quarters of a traveling wagon would afford little privacy were it not the way of the gypsies to exercise discretion in personal matters. Modesty of dress assumed a heightened importance and for me to be so exposed before a stranger was so mortifying that it amazed me that the shame did not strike me dead on the spot.

In my ear, I heard Rob's voice. "That," he murmured, "is lovely."

If Brockhaven agreed with his brother, there was nothing in his expression that said so. Little beyond clinical detachment was to be seen on his face. He stroked the snowy surface of my breast. The sensation made me shiver involuntarily.

Brockhaven said, "It happens also to be white."

Not knowing where the path of his thoughts were leading, I tried instinctively to block it.

"I come from a light-skinned family," I said defensively. "Some gypsies are light, some dark. It's the same with the English."

"Yes," he agreed. "The same." He looked away from me and gazed out on the stretch of greensward that lay outside the window. Then, as though recalled to the mundane tasks at hand, he turned back and retied the string of my bodice, drawing it up with the same brisk, adult efficiency one might use to tie a child's nightshirt. When it was done, he looked at my face again and said abruptly, "Who fathered you?"

My heart refused to take a rhythm, my mind to form a defense. Lord Brockhaven's eyes sharpened as he observed my agitation.

"Don't you know?" he asked in a tone calculated to insult.

I was stung into answering, "My father was the best of honorable men."

Brockhaven's smile was mocking. "And has this paragon a name?"

"Taisio." My answer increased the ironic twist to Brockhaven's lips.

"A gypsy name," he drawled, his blue eyes scanning my face for each nuance of feeling. "But had he another?"

He had, of course. I had heard my grandmother use it to him twice, no, three times, in moments of anger. It was a gorgio's name, an Englishman's name, and those three slips of my grandmother's tongue had been the only spoken acknowledgment in all my growing years that my father had not been born a gypsy.

Children learn in more ways than the direct teaching of their parents. I had always wondered why I traveled alone with my grandmother and father without friends or family. To ask was to be called a silly lambkin, along with the mock-indignant query as to whether or not they were good enough company for me. Then one night, sitting around a fire made with rain-damp wood, Grandmother had talked to me as she so often did of the Romany ways. She happened to say that if a gypsy girl ignores the wiser counsel of her father in choosing her husband from among the Rom, and instead seeks a gorgio as her mate, the tribal elders will mark her forever as an outcast. It was weeks before I picked that lesson from the many and applied it to my own situation. And when I did, the recognition came gradually and without a shock, and I accepted it as an inescapable tenet of life. My mother, who had died at my birth, had been cast out for choosing my father, and Grandmother, rather than be parted from her daughter, had chosen to be exiled from the tribe with her; later, she had raised her grandchild. I knew less of the gorgios, but though my father never talked of it, I wondered if he too had been cast out of his family for taking a gypsy bride.

All this I knew, and yet I had never spoken of it. My impulse was to hide it from Lord Brockhaven as one conceals a blemish from critical eyes. I shook my head, denying that other, thrice-heard name of my father's.

Robert walked in an arc in front of me, regarding me in the way a gypsy assesses a horse for sale.

"She's lying," he said. There was a controlled excitement in his tone. "You can see it in her face. What do you think she knows?"

"Very little. That's why she's so afraid," said Brockhaven. To me he said coolly, "Sit down."

A gypsy maid with the smallest pretentions to virtue would never consider sitting alone with male strangers; if she was able physically to stand, it was clearly a mistake to increase the intimacy of the situation by sitting. I stood as I was.

The Earl of Brockhaven was not accustomed to having a direct command disobeyed, and it did nothing to sweeten his temper. White and blue flames flickered in his eyes. In two rapid strides, he closed the space between us and clamped his hand on my upper arm. He was a full head taller than me, so I had to put back my head to look at his face. When he spoke, his voice was neither loud, nor harsh, but there was an edge of suppressed temper to it that few would have cared to ignore.

"There appears to be a defect in your hearing that I hope will be corrected by the time I repeat myself." He paused. "Sit down."

I did as he commanded, though I moved like a sleepwalker.

Brockhaven leaned back, resting the heels of his hands on a highly polished mahogany desk.

"You are aware, I believe," he continued, "that whatever the theory of British law, in the practice of it I may do virtually whatever I want with you, including giving you to my brother. If all I want from you is to have my curiosity satisfied, then it would be in your best interests to do so. I want your father's name."

I could only hope that if I told him this one thing, he would let me go in peace. Our gazes held position like two carriages meeting on a narrow bridge. Finally I gave in, and cracked the tension with a single word.

"Compton."

I heard Robert take a quickly indrawn breath. "Compton. My God!"

"His first name," Brockhaven rapped sharply.

I had not anticipated such a forceful reaction. My voice shook as I answered him. "Compton is all I know."

"Does she have the look of him, Alex, do you think?" said Robert.

"Perhaps . . . I only saw him once, you know; and a child's memory?" Brockhaven shrugged. "Some years ago Lady Mary showed me a miniature, too, but it was a poor likeness. The girl's eyes are the same. Fragile. Emotional."

I turned my face, distressed that he could so easily penetrate the mysteries of my spirit. Unhappily, I asked him, "May I go?"

Brockhaven's lips formed a grim line. "No. Where's your father?"

"He died five years ago."

The brothers exchanged glances.

"Your mother?" asked Brockhaven.

"She died when I was born."

Robert frowned and threw himself into a chair opposite me. "All those years," his voice puzzled. "Why do you think he never came back, Alex?"

Brockhaven indicated me with a glance. "What of the little one, Rob? You knew the old Marquis! Would you have come prodigaling home, expecting him to dangle your half-bred brat on his knee?"

Rob shrugged. "Infants are easily abandoned; they have such a difficult time following one home."

"It would seem that Compton had a conscience," said

29

Brockhaven dryly. He looked an inquiry at me as I murmured "Marquis?" in a bewildered voice.

"Marquis of Chadbourne," he said. "Do you know the name?"

I shook my head no.

"Do you have brothers and sisters?" he asked. I shook my head again. "Any other family?"

"My—grandmother died three weeks ago. She was the only one."

"Who's had the care of you since then?"

"I've been alone, traveling with the wagon, with the horses, as we'd always done. Why do you care?" I asked. "Why does it matter?"

Brockhaven went to the bureau and returned with a small glass of wine which he held out to me.

"At the moment, my interest in you is . . . Historical would be an appropriate word. If that changes, I'll let you know."

"I don't understand you," I said helplessly, not taking the wine.

"Nevertheless, that explanation will suffice for now." Brockhaven lifted my good hand and curled my fingers around the glass. "Drink. So you won't swoon a second time."

This time I had no illusions that he would be indifferent to my disobedience. I took two sips of the mellow wine, feeling it warm my fear-wearied body. No, he was not the man to let me faint, not until he had finished his endless questioning. How dearly I was paying for my charity to the mokada jook. Poor creature, perhaps it *was* an unlucky animal, as Grandmother had said, like the cat and the snake.

Robert leaned forward slightly. "But why did you travel here, of all places? Have you been here before?"

"Never. In spring we usually go north to the horse fairs where Grandmother sets a tent in the crowd and tells fortunes. But this year Grandmother changed our route." I stared into the wineglass. "It was after the day we polished the harness brasses. She was very tired and went early to bed. She'd never done that before. Ever. The next morning she changed the route and said we should come this way."

Brockhaven took the glass from my slack fingers and set it on the side table. "Grandmother died, and I followed the route. But it ended at a river not a mile beyond here." My face changed, the melancholy replaced by terror. "Does it end here because I'm to be hanged?"

Some measure of my agony may at last have touched Brockhaven, for he took my hand, spread my fingers using his own, and with exquisite tenderness touched his thumb along my palm.

"Don't be foolish, gypsy girl," he said, his voice amazingly shed of its earlier harshness. "You can see you have a very long life line. Surely your grandmother has told you that?"

"She did, but it was a joke," I said, wondering how he knew enough to identify the life line. "Gypsies don't tell the fortunes of other gypsies. 'Tis only a trick to make money from the greedy gorgios who wish to see the future hidden for them in God's heart."

The earl's blue eyes shone suddenly with the tolerant amusement he might have felt toward a nipping puppy. "Have you teeth, then, little rabbit? I'm glad. You won't be so easily eaten alive." He closed my fist in his own. "Where's the money come from since Grandma died? I don't care what it was; just tell me the truth."

My blood began to throb under the skin covered by his fingers. "I sold one of the gold pieces Grandmother had hidden under the wagon's loose floorboard."

"Did you sell anything else? Your body, perhaps?"

It was an insult past bearing. Even exhaustion could not rob me of the energy to tear my hand from his and stand erect, though I could feel tears shimmering on my eyelashes.

"No!" I said, "Oh, no! Never! For you to suggest such a thing is . . ."

He cut me off. "Yes, yes. I've trampled your honor in the dust. Spare me your phrases of adolescent melodrama. Your answer might have been otherwise if you'd had time to run out of gold pieces. It's as well for you that you didn't. It's easier to present an unwanted heiress when she's an innocent girl. The more seasoned you are, the more likely they are to think we've staged your appearance."

"Who are *they*?" I cried in helpless bewilderment. "Staged what? I don't understand what you mean!"

"I know." He gave me a smile that would have brought more than one celebrated beauty to her knees. "Relax and trust me." One glance at my answering expression made Brockhaven's smile twist into a grin. "Very well, don't trust me. The fact is that you have no say in the matter."

And that I found, to my indignation and distress, was the sum of what he intended to tell me. The earl took a seat at a small writing table, set a sheet of paper on its mirror-bright varnished surface, and began to write. Without looking up, Brockhaven addressed his brother.

"Rob, I'm going to ride into Chipping tomorrow to talk with Chadbourne's lawyers."

Rob started to laugh. "God, you're quick. Who *are* Chadbourne's lawyers?"

"I don't know, but I'll find out when I get there." He dipped the pen again and continued writing as he talked. "I'll leave the girl with you. Keep her locked up when you're not with her, or she'll probably run off and we'll have the very devil of a time finding her. And don't tell anyone why she's here."

"Servants'll talk." Rob leaned one hand on the desk.

Brockhaven sighed, sat back, and looked at me with his detached, appraising stare. "Damn. That's right. We'll simply have to let them think that she's here as your plaything."

Robert threw back his head and laughed. "Under lock and key. Oh, my shattered reputation."

Brockhaven smiled at his brother. "Never mind, child. You'll be acquitted when I get back and we've placed her in the hands of her guardian."

"Who do you think that will be?" said Robert.

32

Brockhaven gave a smile indicative of inner satisfaction. "I don't know. All I know is that it won't be Vincent."

Robert looked at his brother with understanding in his gray eyes. "And how surprised cousin Vinny will be, won't he?" He picked up the sheet Brockhaven had been writing on, and read it before handing it back. "Just hurry back to Edgehill before the girl takes it in her head to scream out the window and the whole county finds out she's here. *I* don't want to be the one to introduce the wench to Vinny and Bella."

"Oh, no, my dear. I reserve that pleasure for myself," said Brockhaven, his lips curved into a smile. "If the chit gets hysterical, I'm sure I can rely on you, Robert, to find some way to hush her."

Chapter Two

Having lived my life in the open, close to the sky and the earth, not having slept, eaten, or passed my time in a building of any sort, being closed inside four walls was a suffocation for me. It would have been difficult for me to adjust even if I had willingly come to live there; to be imprisoned was almost beyond bearing. Only fear that violent means might be used to quiet me kept me from throwing myself against the door and sobbing to be released.

Back and forth I paced the floor of the small room. It was a pretty enough prison, its windows hung with white cotton curtains printed in red dots. A neatly made bed stood in the middle, but I was used to sleeping on a feather mattress laid under my wagon. There was fresh water on the table in the pitcher and basin set, but I was used to the bracing sweetness of cold spring water. And when a disapproving maidservant brought me a dinner of lamb and boiled potatoes, the taste was unfamiliar. I couldn't swallow more than a bite, hungry though I was.

I had time and more to ponder all that had transpired in the reading room. There was little doubt that Brockhaven had conceived the incredible notion that I was in some way related to this Marquis of Chadbourne, who seemed a man of cruel and tyrannical disposition. No two qualities would have been further from my father's nature. Bizarre coincidence must be responsible for any similarity that existed between me and the girl that the Earl of Brockhaven thought I was. And why had the Earl refined so much on the scraps of information I had given him? While Compton might not title as many folk as Smith or Miller, it was hardly what one could call a rare name.

I pulled the medallion from my neck and studied it. It was old and rather crudely carved. On its face a Saracen in flowing robes held his sword aloft as he danced between a pair of bushes heavy with roses. On the back were scratched two words: "on alone." I knew it was gold and therefore of value, but I had always assumed that there must have been hundreds, maybe thousands, struck from the same mold.

By the time the mighty gorgios' lawyers had pursued these scanty tidbits of evidence, they would likely inform the earl that I had nothing to do with any marquises and Brockhaven ought to do his civic duty and turn me over to a sheriff without delay.

These joyless musings were interrupted by the arrival of a footman and the housemaid, who came to clear away the dinner tray. The good woman observed at once that scarcely a bite had been taken. Her expression grew even more disapproving, and she read me a stern lecture on the disastrous effects on the body of skipped meals, punctuated by grim examples of skittish young women who had refused their dinners and woke up the next morning with every hair shed from their heads and eyelashes sparer than hairs on a pig's butt!

I was not sorry when the maid was distracted by a glance out the window.

"Look there!" she said, shaking her head in dismal satisfaction. "Clouds are stackin' up like hay piles in September. It's sure to turn colder so we'd best be layin' in a fire."

The accompanying footman was dispatched to procure firewood, which he agreed to do though pointing out to the room in general that it really *was* the *under*footman's job to bring wood. The maid took the opportunity to explain to me that I was lucky to be incarcerated in a Christian household where the inhabitants felt bound by the laws of charity to provide a fire for *all* company, be they thieving heathens or no.

The firewood was brought, the tinder procured. All went well until the maid tried to open the flue so the smoke could escape up the chimney. Apparently it had been several seasons since the chimney was cleaned, for the flue refused to open as much as a single inch. The maid banged up the chimney at the offending flue with her broom handle but to no avail. She handed the broom in disgust to the young footman and, when he faired no better, she stepped back and proclaimed that someone ought to summon the estate carpenter. The long-suffering footman heaved a sigh and was off again to return some half hour later with the carpenter and his apprentice, a likely lad of fourteen summers.

The carpenter was a man thin to the point of gauntness with skin like old saddle leather. He carried with him an aura of importance befitting his elevated station in life. Bending at the waist, he gazed solemnly up to examine the flue. Barely, if ever, has a flue been surveyed with more serious attention! At last the carpenter turned to his expectant audience, smiled condescendingly at the maid's broom handle, and announced that a shovel was what was wanted here. With a confident nod, he sent his apprentice off to fetch that article, much to the relief of the footman, who felt he'd already done more than his share of the legwork.

The apprentice returned with the shovel and the prideful expression of one who has successfully completed a vital mission. Then the carpenter banged at the flue in exactly the same manner as the maid and the footman before him, only longer and with more force. At last the flue gave with a loud bang, and the carpenter had just time to give a triumphant smile before receiving on his head a bushel of soot.

The maid wore a tragic expression and spoke not a word for the entire hour it took her to clean up the mess.

When I was left, finally, to my own devices, impulse drew me to the window, and I threw open the sash. I breathed deeply of the cool night air that rushed past me to fill the stale vacuum of the room, and gazed out at the stars—thousands of them—and the sharp black line of the hill to the rear of the manor. Three stories below and to the left, down the dark stretch of wall, I saw a long yellow rectangle of light from the kitchen's open door that stretched onto the lawn and threw a low yew hedge into relief. There was a buzz of conversation and clinking crockery. The servants were having their supper.

A mastiff big as a pony came sniffing near the kitchen door and then sat up, begging. A large leg of mutton came flying out of the door to be snatched into its huge jaws, then carried off silently into the night, leaving the court-yard deserted.

Escape! If ever there was a good time, this was it, with the servants happy at their dinner, and enough noise to cover any sound that I might make. Plan after plan worked its way through my despairing mind. Once my father had told me of an African princess escaping the slave hunters by climbing from a cave on a rope woven from her braids and petticoats. I could only sadly conclude that either the princess had possessed longer hair than I did or wore more copious petticoats.

Everything else considered and rejected, there was one avenue left that appeared to offer some hope. About four and a half feet below the window an ornamental stone pediment protruded at least six inches from the wall. If I could climb out the window, take a footing on the pediment, and find handholds among the rough stonework, I might be able to inch my way to the next window. I was sure that room was vacant, for I'd heard no noise from the room and no light played through the window. If luck was with me, slowly, cautiously, I might make my way to the door and freedom!

It was too frightening a thought to give myself time to consider. I mustered my courage quickly and sat on the window ledge, then lowered myself to the pediment. I tried gradually to place my full weight on it, but not gradually enough for, with a sudden crumble, the pediment fell away beneath me, leaving me dangling in the darkness!

Shock saved me, causing my fingers to clench and grip the window ledge. I gasped as I felt my weight pulling on my stretched arms, and my injured hand throbbed. I tried to reach with my feet to the remaining pediment, but there was no foothold close enough. I tried to pull myself up, without success, and my elbows were painfully lacerated by the stone building face.

Suddenly I heard the door to my room bang open and Brockhaven's voice uttering a sharp oath. His footsteps came rapidly to the window. I felt his steely grip on my wrists as I was lifted upward, the window ledge scraping across my stomach as I was hauled over it like a sack of potatoes.

Once inside, he dumped me unceremoniously on the floor in the billows of my own brightly colored skirts.

"You don't have to quake at my feet like an injured moth," he snapped. "I'm not going to beat you. What in God's name did you think you were doing? Waiting for a winged gypsy spirit to carry you to the ground?"

Choking back tears as I rubbed my hands against my burning midriff, I said, "We don't have a spirit that carries people to the ground. I was trying to climb to the next window and escape."

"I'm happy to have that point cleared up. I might not have been able to fathom it on my own. And you've opened your palm again as well."

"It ought to be packed with honey," I said, grasping at any excuse to shift the focus from my failed escape.

"Oh? I thought mold."

"Mold for a new wound, honey later that day, bares off the fever, drives poison away."

"I've always enjoyed folk platitudes," commented Brockhaven in a tone which indicated the opposite. He closed the window with a loud crack and then slid an arm around my shoulders, another under my knees, and lifted me gently to the bed.

I was light for him; I could feel the strength in his arms. As before, his touch sent an odd flare of warmth through me. It embarrassed me and I shivered, turning my face away as he brought a linen towel from the wash stand and sat on the bed beside me, rebinding my hand.

After a moment's silence, he said, "This must hurt like the devil. Do you want laudanum?"

"No, thank you."

The room was quiet again except for the snapping of the fire, and through its flickering light I stole a glimpse at the man beside me. His head was bent slightly to his task. The hearth's flames touched the shining dark hair with tongues of red, and the skin over his taut cheekbones glowed golden. He looked up, as though sensing my scrutiny, and met my gaze with sapphire eyes. "What's the matter?" he asked, watching me.

"I'm . . . not sure what you mean."

"You look as though you expect to be eaten alive." His fingers left my wrist and lightly explored the pulse in my neck. "And your heartbeat is hard. Are you afraid I'm going to try to bed you?"

If my heart was quick before, his words doubled its pace as the blood raced to color my face. My experience with the male gender was too limited to allow me to meet his bluntness with anything like poise. I was too uncomfortable even to tear my gaze from his, so I stared at him, made a nervous cough in my throat, and reflected that if I said yes, he was as likely as not to tell me I was flattering myself. Yet how could I say no when the real reason for my unease was his disturbing nearness?

"I don't know," I said, and received the sardonic look I had been expecting.

"You don't know if you're afraid, or you don't know if I'm going to bed you?"

I had to swallow before I could find the voice to answer.

"I don't know why you would have wanted to ask me that question."

"Don't you?" One corner of his mouth turned up.

40

"Well, well, we are an innocent, aren't we? Poor Daisy. What would you do it I did try?" His face held a mocking expression as he looked at me.

"I would fight to protect myself," I answered in a shaking voice. I was aware, terribly aware, of his hand resting against my throat.

"Very impressive. Do you happen to know how to fight off a man?"

"You know that I cannot, for I was helpless when you had Robert hold me so that you could . . ." My voice was thick with suppressed tears. "I know I'm at your mercy. Does it please you to have me say it?"

Brockhaven's mood shifted with disconcerting suddenness. He made a careless shrug and put his hand back to my bandage, repinning it with one short, fluid stroke. "You seem to have a novel idea of the things that would pleasure me, little rabbit," he said, his tone reverting to the matter-of-fact. "You're not only at my mercy, you're at anyone's mercy. Or don't you realize that *any* young woman in a reasonable state of health and passable good looks who travels around by herself in a wagon would soon become privy to any number of attacks she wasn't able to fight off? For the time being, you're much better off here with me."

I studied his face. "Because your interest in me is purely historical?"

"Precisely, my child. Relieved?"

"It's not that."

"What then?" he said.

"When you called me my child, just now," I told him, "you sounded like a priest."

"Good Lord! A manifestly false similarity."

"That's what *I* thought," I said, struggling to lift my head. After acknowledging my remark with the trace of a smile, he slid his arm under my shoulders and lifted them to position the pillow under my head.

"You're weak as a monkey," he observed. "And no wonder—they tell me you won't eat."

"Is that why you came to this room? To make me eat?"

41

I asked curiously. It was incredible that he would know if I'd eaten, or care.

"It's fortune that I came in when I did," he said dryly, "or you'd be lying below in a hundred pieces, leaving someone with the unpleasant chore of scraping you bit by bit into a coffin. Yes, I came to make you eat."

My spirit came splashing back. "Is your plan to do that by glowering at me and describing my corpse between each bite?"

"I don't *glower*," he said irritably. "Why won't you eat?"

"I don't like the way the food tastes," I said bluntly.

Sweetly, he asked, "What's amiss? Doesn't it have enough garlic in it?"

I drew my brows close together. "Gypsies have other flavorings besides garlic."

"And I'm sure"—the earl's dulcet tones dripped with sarcasm—"that there will be some time in the future, albeit possibly the far distant future, when I'll be fascinated to hear what they are."

"You have contempt for the ways of the gypsy?"

"Not at all. Beyond gold teeth and sad violins, I don't know anything about gypsies." When he'd laid me on the bed, one of my long braids had fallen across his knee. He lifted the glossy fall of hair and began, absently, to unbraid it. "Enlighten me—what *would* you eat?"

I cupped my cheek in my sore palm, and again turned my head sideways on the pillow, dragging my gaze away from his graceful fingers straying in my hair.

"My situation is so distressing," I said. "How could I eat?"

"It's easy. You open your mouth, put in the food, and masticate. If you weren't too distressed to eat, what would it be?"

I thought it over. "A gooey, perhaps."

"A gooey. Splendid. What is it?"

"There are different ones. Some are like pudding, some are like pie. Grandmas's favorite was oatmeal pounded with goose's blood and suet."

"I'm afraid I haven't laid in a stock of goose blood. Can you think of anything a little less revolting?"

"You may say what you like about the food my people eat." I turned back indignantly to face Brockhaven. "What of yours, pray? Do you know what I was brought with my supper? Horrible, slimy, slippery things that the maid said are soft cooked eggs!"

My words amused him. "Very well. No eggs. What else did your grandmother make?"

"Stew, with fresh herbs," I said, "and crisp greens."

"Thank God for that. I was beginning to fear we'd have to gather eel's tongues at midnight. I'll see what they can do belowstairs." He got up from the bed.

"I . . . my lord?" I hesitated. "At my wagon there are horses . . ."

"And you didn't want to stress that earlier, in hopes you might be able to sneak off and gallop into the sunset? Don't worry, Stewart's already had them brought to the stable and fed. Was the stallion your father's?"

"No. Mine. I trained him myself."

His eyebrows rose. "You have highly original methods. Stewart says he's a mankiller. He almost took the arm off one of my stable boys with his teeth."

I was genuinely concerned. "I'm sorry! Probably, my Kory thought someone was trying to steal him."

"Don't let it trouble you. The boy will be fine." His hand dropped to briefly touch my shoulder, then my cheek. "And don't try to run off on me, will you, rabbit? I'm not going to let anyone hurt you."

I was not sure if it was fear that made me tremble, or his touch. "I'm not the person you think I am! I know that I'm not."

His expression was enigmatic. "If we discover that's true, you're free to go. Content?"

They were the words I had been waiting to hear, and I couldn't understand why they brought me no joy. "Content," I answered him, but for some elusive reason there was a certain lack of conviction in my voice.

Chapter Three

Apparently Lord Brockhaven had little confidence in my assurance that I wouldn't try to repeat my escape, for he assigned the dour-faced maidservant to spend the night in the room with me. A truckle bed was set up for the maid, Betty, who arrived at bedtime bearing a branched candlestick surrounded by reflecting globes of a kind to make more light, and a basketful of torn pillow covers to mend. I offered to help, and though she refused, the offer must have softened her as she left off her mending long enough to brew a cup of herbal tea to help me sleep. She even brought me one of her own nightdresses and a pretty cotton cap to put over my hair, but I could not help looking askance at the garments—it was so much warmer to sleep in the petticoats I already had on. Why did gorgios bother with the impractical chore of changing clothes to sleep?

Betty made her own preparations for bed, clucking at my eccentric ways, and then knelt by her truckle bed and pointedly said her prayers aloud, enunciating each word in a clear, ringing tone, hoping, no doubt, that they would have a good effect on my heathen manners.

It was noon, perhaps later, the next day when there came the sound of a tentative knock at the bedroom door. I had spent the morning with Betty at such unexciting occupations as folding table napkins and polishing the spoons of the one hundred and forty-four silver place settings, which afforded me far more time than I liked to ponder my fate.

Since the knock perhaps signaled news, I lifted my head expectantly as Betty crossed the room and pulled open the door. To my surprise, Betty's reaction to the visitor was one of strong condemnation.

"What," cried the maid, "in the name of all creation are you doing here?"

On the surface of it, I could see nothing to excite Betty's disapproval for there didn't appear to be anything havey-cavey about the young girl waiting to enter. The shapeless woolen cape that swathed her figure had nothing of the disreputable about it; such garments are worn often by women well-moneyed enough to afford something warm, yet too poor to afford something pretty. Looking closer, though, I realized that the colorless cloak was no pair with the elaborate cluster of ringlets dressed into her soft brown hair. It was the kind of hair arrangement that took professional skill. Only if she had the many arms of an octopus could she have done it on herself.

Other than the hair, she was not what the gorgios extol as a beauty. Her mouth was wider than the copperplate ideal, her nose turned up puppy-fashion at the tip, and though her complexion was clear, it was neither dimpled nor white as new snow. Here was no lady who risked her health by taking minute amounts of arsenic daily to pale her skin.

A mediocre portraitist might have portrayed her reposing image as plain. I found her subtly taking and when she looked past Betty to me and smiled warmly, the animation made her lovely. The girl pulled off her cloak in a gesture that announced her intention to stay, and beneath the cloak, in astonishing contrast, was a beautiful and obviously expensive honey-colored muslin gown.

"Don't fuss and f-fuss, Betty, dearest," she said in a melodious voice which carried the hint of a stammer. Later I was to learn that this hesitation in her speech had persisted despite (or perhaps because of) her governess' strenuous and sometimes brutal efforts toward its eradication. For myself, I found the stammer an intriguing and not unattractive accent to the rhythm of her words; in time I grew not to notice it at all.

To return to our first meeting: after her first words and rather to my surprise, the brown-haired girl kissed Betty quickly on the cheek and continued, "Here I am, so what of it? I must talk to the gypsy girl."

Betty returned the cheerful kiss with a severe look. "Must be talkin' to the gypsy girl indeed! Have your wits gone beggin', Lady Ellen? Where's your maid, Patty? Never let me hear she's let you come here."

"Well, she has," said Lady Ellen with a teasing note. "In fact, she's h-here with me guarding the backstairs, ready to whisk me off in a moment if someone comes."

"The back stairs?" exclaimed Betty. "Well, then, who's watching the main stair, may I ask?"

The brown-haired girl gave Betty a bright smile and encouraging pat on the hand. "You, I hope. You needn't, of course, if you don't care to, and if Lord Brockhaven or his brother should happen to come and find me here, then I shall simply . . ."

I was fated to rest in ignorance of what Lady Ellen *would* have done, for Betty had fairly leaped from the room and whisked the door shut behind her. Evidently Lady Ellen thought the sentence had done its work, for she showed no inclination to finish it. She said to me, "Hello! I'm so happy to meet you! I know you must think my arrival very strange, but you see, I've come here to rescue you. Not that I'm at all sure you *want* to b-be rescued. You see, I'm not sure why you're here, which has a great deal of bearing on things. So, do you need to be rescued?"

I was rather overcome by this astonishing offer, but it had a good effect on my spirits.

"I'm not sure," I replied. "Perhaps you'd be so good as to advise me?"

"Oh, yes," said Lady Ellen, turning pink from gratification. "I love to give advice, but I'm r-rarely asked for any.

Shall we sit together on the floor? Oh, what's this you're doing—polishing silver! I shall help you!"

She sat on her knees, lifted a spoon, dunked it in the pot of polish and began to buff it with the soft cloth Betty had abandoned. I sat beside her, tossing my braids to the back so that their length wouldn't brush on the tarnish-soiled newspaper.

"I beg your pardon . . ." I began, "but would you mind . . . that is, do you live in this house?"

"Not today. T-today I snuck in," she said, looking rather pleased at this accomplishment. "For the month I've been staying with Mrs. Perscough, four miles to the north. Five of her sons (all under the age of eight) have been taken with the measles, and as I've already had them, I offered to stay and help keep the boys entertained while they recuperated."

It seemed to me a charitable zeal approaching saintliness for anyone to undertake the prolonged entertainment of five boys under eight, *especially* if those boys were suffering from the peevishness of spirit natural to anyone recovering from serious illness. I began to express my respect, but the lady with the brown ringlets would have none of it.

"I'm not so saintly as you think," she confessed in a frank way, "because, you s-see, I had an ulterior motive for my offer. I've lived at Edgehill for the last two years since my father died, with my stepmother, Lady Gwendolyn. She takes care of the domestic details that Lord Brockhaven doesn't care a pin about and in r-return, he makes her quite a splendid allowance. Frequently, she goes traveling, now that she has the money, and she's happier than she's ever been before in her life. She married Papa when I was ten, after my own mother died, and really she's been a dear to me, so I'm glad things are better for her. Poor Papa! I don't wish to defame his memory, but he was so . . . well, one that never likes to leave the house and his cozy study for *any* purpose. I'm afraid our social life was nearly nil. You, I suppose, have been everywhere . . . ?"

48

"Oh, no," I said, distressed by the sadly wistful note in her voice. "Not *everywhere*. Only in Great Britain and—and parts of Europe." Seeing that my remark had failed in its intended effect, I turned the conversation to its original course. "Was it to do with your stepmother that you went to stay with Mrs. Perscough?"

"Yes, it was. Last month Lady Gwendolyn received an invitation to stay with one of her great friends in Sussex. To tell the truth, I did what I could to get out of going along, b-because her friend has twin boys who are a year older than me and their favorite game is to make fun of my stammer."

I was incensed. "How wicked!"

"They don't mean to be unkind," said Ellen with a forced smile. "I truly believe they don't. It's as much my own fault, for I can't seem to bear for them to see it hurts me, so I laugh along and t-try with all my heart not to let my stammer show. The problem is that the more I don't want to stammer, the more I *do* stammer. Around men, I'm hopeless. A blithering fool."

How great was the warmth of my feeling toward this girl who had taken it upon herself to befriend me. Me, a gypsy, despised by most of her race! I hastened to comfort her unhappiness.

"But to stammer is a gift from the God of All Things, Lady Ellen. Surely you must know that? Among my people, it would be said that you are blessed, and therefore loved by the fairies. Somewhere in the world, at every moment, there is a new babe struggling to make his first word. When a fairy sees this, she flies to you, whisks away a word, and gives it to the baby so that he can say his first precious word. What could be more lovely than to have given speech to so many tiny souls?"

It was obviously the first positive thing Ellen had ever heard about her stammer, and she was moved almost to tears. We just smiled at each other for a moment and then I asked, "Why is it that you couldn't have remained at Edgehill in Lady Gwendolyn's absence?"

Much later, when I knew more of her world, I wondered how Ellen had kept herself from laughing at my question, for it must have seemed foolish to her, but there was not a trace of condescension in her gray eyes as she said, "My stepmother is an aunt to Brockhaven and Robert, but I'm not related by blood at all. Lord Brockhaven is a much-talked-about man, and if I was to be here unchaperoned, society would treat it as an appalling scandal, I assure you. The Beau Monde is like that. Suspicious. And with Brockhaven being such a rake, he can't come within ten yards of a woman without being rumored as her lover. That's why Betty didn't like me to be here, and I don't suppose Lord Brockhaven would like it much either."

"Then I wonder—how did you hear of my situation?"

"Joey Copeil, the third underfootman at Edgehill, told the story of your arrival to his brother, Bob, the cobbler. Bob told his wife, who told it to Mr. Bumper, who carves wooden chickens to sell to the travelers that come in the spring and summer to see Edgehill. Mrs. Bumper told my maid, Patty. First I heard that Lord Brockhaven had c-caught a gypsy on his property and intended to send her to jail. I didn't think it for a minute! The laws against poaching are barbarous, and Lord Brockhaven would *never* give anyone up to them."

"Has he a reputation for kindness?" I asked, not quite able to believe it.

"Oh, no, no, no—did I say that? He isn't *kind,* but he's . . . good." From her expression I guessed that certain sinister memories intruded into Lady Ellen's consciousness. "Well, he's not precisely g-good either, and if you would ask any of the neighboring landowners, they'll tell you that he's the most arrogant man in their acquaintance. You see, that's how he acts with his peers—but there's not a man in this county who treats better his dependents. There are occasions when he's displayed the greatest sensitivity toward his social inferiors."

"And there are times," I said, "when he hasn't."

Pretty sympathy filled Lady Ellen's brown eyes. "That's true as well . . . have you been cruelly, cruelly used?"

I gave a sudden smile and held up a finger. "Only one 'cruelly.' What other rumor did you hear?"

"I heard that you were being held here against your will, harem-style. That I knew was a falsehood, because it would be ridiculous for Brockhaven to force his attentions on anyone when women *attack* him on the streets begging to be his mistresses. Or at least," she added conscientiously, "one did. Last season a dancer from the ballet whisked her gown to her waist right there at Vauxhall Gardens and made a heartfelt declaration of her affections. I wasn't there, of course, but people talked of nothing else for days on end."

I couldn't forbear not to ask, "What did Brockhaven do?"

"I don't know, but it must have been very shocking. Even Lucia Perscough, who tells *everything*, would not repeat it to me. One can pretty much assume, though, because Lucia did admit to seeing the dancer riding with Brockhaven in Hyde Park one week later. Of course, that was nearly a year ago and it's quite blown over. Brockhaven runs through his mistresses at a shocking pace. And his brother Robert is, if anything, worse, but I can't believe he'd have to lock anyone up either. You see, that's why I had to see for myself. If there is any way that I can serve you, I will! Tell me *everything*."

Feeling rather undone by the voluminous request from such a sympathetic listener, I said in a shaky voice, "Thank you, Lady Ellen! May a thousand hedgehogs make their homes in your garden."

It was then that I learned that gorgios don't value hedgehogs as they ought, for it was clear from Lady Ellen's surprised expression that she failed to understand the goodwill intended by my blessing. I taxed her with it and she admitted, to my shock, that she had never made use of a hedgehog and worse, had never met anyone who had! I was astounded, for what could be more succulent than the flesh of the hedgehog cooked in clay? And the fat—why, there is nothing more effective for the treatment of all ailments of the skin, from boils to dandruff to removing calluses of the foot. I changed the subject quickly so I would not show my new friend how appalled I was at her ignorance.

"May I begin by asking you if you have heard of the Marquis of Chadbourne?"

Lady Ellen appeared to be intrigued. "Yes! He owned Chad Hall and his lands march with Lord Brockhaven's property, or at least they used to. The old marquis is dead and his granddaughter lives on the property now."

"His granddaughter? Then . . . did the marquis have sons?"

"Yes, indeed. There were two. Martin was the youngest. He died some years ago of a diseased liver. His daughter, Isabella, married a cousin of Lord Brockhaven's and they live in Chad Hall."

"Robert mentioned them, I think! If it is the same people you mean, he said something about not wishing to introduce me to them."

Lady Ellen puzzled over this while she selected another spoon to polish. "How very odd of him, to be sure, for I can't imagine why . . ." She rubbed thoughtfully at a tarnished spot. "Ah, well, where was I? The two sons of the marquis. I know very little about the elder son, who would be Isabella's uncle. They say he was bored with the deadly respectability of being heir to a great title, and he ran away from home before I was born. Made a dreadful misalliance, if I remember correctly, with a gypsy girl." She stopped suddenly and stared at me with new-found knowledge exploding in her eyes like Chinese candles. "Are y-you the Marquis of Chadbourne's granddaughter?"

"That . . . that seems to be what Lord Brockhaven believes."

Lady Ellen's almond-shaped eyes opened wide. "You're a m-missing heiress? A *gypsy* heiress! It's beyond anything! Good heavens. Why, then you're . . ."

We were interrupted by the sound of running feet from the hallway, and Betty burst into the room, explaining, "Master Robert is coming up to speak with the gypsy girl—I heard him talking to one of the footmen on the lower landing! What would he do should he find you prowling in a bachelor household, Lady Ellen?"

"I don't know—do you think he would try to seduce me?" said Lady Ellen, looking hopeful.

"He's more likely to take you over his knee, give you twenty whacks with the hairbrush, and send you about your business like he did Julie Aldgate, that dizzy friend of yours he found sneaking into his bedchamber last fall."

"That's what I'm afraid of," said Lady Ellen. She bounced to her feet, sending a shower of silver spoons flying in all directions, and dove under the bed. I just had time to catch sight of Lady Ellen's gray-hooded cloak flung on a chair and throw it under the bed after her as the masculine footsteps neared the door.

Robert entered and said good afternoon to me and to Betty, who was still breathing heavily from her own run down the hall. Before he could say anything else, he stared at the floor beside the bed. Following the line of his gaze, I saw with dismay the tip of one of Lady Ellen's prettily made riding boots protruding from underneath the bedspread. He raised an eyebrow, and asked me calmly, "Did you know there's someone underneath your bed?"

The someone under the bed exclaimed "Oh!" There was a pronounced rustling of material, and a small figure cocooned in gray wool wiggled from under the bed and cannonballed from the room, whacked hard into the opposing hallway wall, and took off down the corridor at a run. Betty looked flustered and said, " 'Twas one of the maids, sir, dusting the underside of the bed."

"Which one of my brother's maids is it," asked Robert blandly, "that does her dusting in fifty-guinea riding boots?" I joined Betty in an intent examination of the floor.

"It wasn't Julie Aldgate," Betty mumbled.

"Then we'll let it pass. But, Betty, don't let whoever she may be run tame in here again. I've no wish to be challenged to pistols at dawn by any red-faced, ale-bellied, irate papas from the local squirearchy. Now," he said, his gaze turning full on me, "our gypsy captive. I am here out of pity for what I thought was your solitude. How would you like to come with me to the sunroom and let me teach you to play chess?"

Pride held me back a moment, then I said yes, because the loneliness and the closeness of the small chamber were a weight on my soul, the more so after the pleasure of Ellen's visit.

I was not sure that I trusted Robert, and I had little interest in chess, as my grandmother had taught me that cards and board games were the devil's invitation to idleness and folly. Yet neither my distrust nor my disinterest were strong enough to deter me from seizing the chance to escape my confinement, even if it would be only for a short time.

The sunroom was high-ceilinged, with long, arched windows that let in slanting pillars of sunlight. A chessboard as wide as a barn window was laid out in the middle of a deep blue and scarlet Persian carpet and beside it was a round mahogany case.

"Come and sit on the rug," invited Robert as we entered the room. "You see? Gypsy-style. Did you ever play before?"

"No," I replied. "My grandmother said such things were a waste of time."

"Oh, yes. It wastes time—but elegantly." The mahogany case was set on a spinning platform; he moved it around to the latch, and opened it to remove and display in his hand an elaborately carved chess piece. "My father had the set made as a present for my mother. This is the queen, carved in my mother's likeness."

I took the piece and examined it closely. The little ivory face was beautiful and it had long hair curling down its back, but even in this miniature figure, the artist had managed to portray an aura of haughtiness and self love.

"My father, naturally, the king." Robert removed another piece from the case and held it at arm's length. "It's a futile thing, vanity. Here he stands, immortalized in ivory and no higher than your ankle. Grotesque. There's a

54

lesson in it, though I can't think what it is. Vincent could, probably."

"Vincent?" I questioned, taking the ivory king in my hand.

"My cousin, Brockhaven's cousin. You'll meet Vincent—you can bet on his becoming conspicuous as soon as he hears about you."

Robert's tone was not cordial, so I asked curiously, "Will I like him, do you think?"

"I imagine." Robert's expression conveyed nothing. "People generally do." As though the subject bored him, he shifted my attention back to the chessman.

"The castle pieces, as you can see, are based on Edgehill, which, thank God, my father never got a chance to inherit and ruin. And the pawns—it was my father's idea of a jest to have them made in my brother's image. Alex was three years old at the time. Fortunately for me, I hadn't been born yet."

I set down the king and gently lifted one of the pawns. It was a handsome little boy with curly hair. "How proud he looks," I said softly. "But sad, as though he'd scraped his knee and doesn't want anyone to know. What happens to the pawns in the game?"

"They're the discards that the other pieces trample at will," said Robert. "Now let me tell you about the queen. That's where the throne's power really lies . . ."

In spite of myself, I began to follow Robert's lively instruction. He described the way each piece could move and had barely begun to explore with me the subtleties of the game's strategy when he was called away by a lackey, who came to announce that Mr. Stewart said Mr. Robert ought to come and talk to the two bricklayers who were laying the foundation for the new buttery. There was a quarrel going on, it seemed, on whether there ought to be a second door, and, though Robert protested that he knew nothing and cared less about the design of butteries, he excused himself to me and went anyway, ordering the footman to remain outside the door, saying with a grin that it was to guard me from temptation.

Left to my own devices, I moved the pieces experimentally around the board, handling each one with great care, while the sun touched on my back like a great warm hand. Following an impulse, I lined the chess pieces in a row and lay down beside them; with my cheek on the floor, they looked almost like real people, down to the rings on the queen's hand. The shifting, swirling dust motes in the beam of sunlight looked like a magic dust that would impart to them the gift of life; and come alive they did, in the dream I had as I fell into a light sleep.

I was being held prisoner in the tiny castle; the queen was standing guard outside the door. I had been dragged to the castle behind the ivory horse and my legs were sore from walking. The pawn astride the horse was John Stewart and he kept turning back to look at me, his ivory face impassive. I was frightened——of the queen, of the horse, and most afraid of being small. But then the king appeared, walking regally toward me through the sunbeams, and helped me from the window of the castle; and we danced together. The king had the features of the Earl of Brockhaven and as we danced my tiredness and fear began to drain away. His hand was steady on my back, and there was in his eyes a concern as deep as the black night that surrounded us, the silver stars reflecting their shimmer in the sparkling fabric of my gown. The stars became brighter, and my rapture increased, until finally the light was so intense that I had to blink to protect my eyes from the glare.

As I opened my eyes, I found myself looking into a blinding fog of sunlight. I blinked again to clear my vision, and saw the Earl of Brockhaven sitting in a chair before me, his chin resting in one hand, his long legs stretched out before him.

"It must have been a beautiful dream," he said.

"The chessmen . . . came to life." I struggled to sit up and looked about me, not sure if the dream had ended, and took in my hands the little ivory king. I looked back at Brockhaven and said, stupidly, "You're back."

"As you see." He stood and lifted the chess piece from

my hand. "It's my father's likeness. Did Rob tell you? The carver flattered him, of course. He'd put on weight by then. Drinking. And my mother"—he picked up the queen—"never looked this virginal."

Robert might have spoken of his parents without affection, but Brockhaven's tone was so embroidered with distaste that I stared at him, shocked.

Tentatively I asked, "Your parents . . . they are dead?"

"Long dead."

"Then how can you speak of them so unkindly when they brought you into the world, cared for you . . . ?"

Brockhaven began to replace the pieces in their mahogany case. He gave me a short smile and said, "You think all parents care for their children? Tell me, how did *yours* keep you so protected from the world, traveling around in a wagon?"

I turned my head away. "It's easily done when you are an outcast and of mixed parentage. Gypsies look down on you. Gorgios look down on you."

The room was silent for a minute, and then Brockhaven said, "No one will look down on you again. You stand to inherit a large portion of one of the most coveted estates in England."

There was a moment of numbness. I shook my head.

"It's perfectly true," he returned calmly. "Your grandfather was the Marquis of Chadbourne; your father was his oldest son, Charles Compton. If you had been a boy, you'd be a marquis. However, there are no male heirs in the line, so the title dies. But you get the bulk of the fortune."

"How can that possibly be true?" I whispered. "How can I be the person you think I am? What proof can you have?"

He was about to answer me when he was interrupted by the sound of a loud barking beyond the door of the sunroom, a loud barking accented by the rising clamor of a high-pitched female voice and layered on an undertone of male voices. Some sort of altercation was evidently taking place in the hallway. Brockhaven snapped shut the mahogany case, threw open the sunroom's double doors, and called sharply, "Caesar!" The barking stopped abruptly. "Rob, take him out. Thank you. It's all right, Fitzmore, you may go. I'll handle it now."

"Handle it! Handle it!" There was a rustle of skirts, and the woman's voice grew louder. "How can you talk about handling things, at this, of all times! Was it really you who sent that dreadful little man . . . that—that lawyer"—the word was spoken with bitter contempt—"to my house? To tell me I'm to be cheated out of my fortune by some base, filthy gypsy?" She reached the threshold of the room and pointed an accusing finger at me, demanding, "Is that *her*? No, don't bother to answer! I can *tell*!"

For a moment we stared at each other. The look of hatred in her eyes was so strong that I am forced to admit it influenced my opinion of her, but even that prejudice could not prevent me from acknowledging to myself that she was the archetype of English beauty, such as one might see on a bottle of facial cream. She was blond, alluringly so, with the green eyes so admired by the poets, and cheeks as pink as apple blossoms. She was the kind of beauty you can imagine riding in a city park surrounded by adoring males, her bonnet tipped coquettishly to one side and tied under her ear in a perfect bow. It was a measure of the lady's strong distress that her pretty hat was squashed flat on her head and secured under her chin in a careless knot.

A man came through the door behind her, a cinder-blond, gray-eyed man who carried himself with a studied air of elegance. He appeared not exactly calculating, but the tension around his eyes indicated a well-rehearsed and intelligent self-control. I found nothing in that to criticize. I mention it because it was such an extreme contrast to the near hysterical beauty at his side. The man gave Brockhaven an expressive glance which was, I thought, meant to convey sympathy and a fellow-feeling of solidarity. Brockhaven's response was to stare coldly through the man, and close the door with a flip of his wrist.

"Why don't you temper with age, Bella?" he asked the blond girl scathingly. "Spare my servants your tantrums, or I'll give them orders to admit you by the back door."

"Don't! Don't be a beast to me, Alex! You know I can't bear it," she gasped. "This is some vile trick you've contrived with this—this . . ." Trying to find a synonym degrading enough to fit my character seemed to spend the final coin of her dignity. She flew at him sobbing and threw her fists violently against his chest. Brockhaven looked down at her with distaste, though he made no move to stop her, and finally she wore herself out and collapsed against him, whimpering pitifully.

"It's not true, is it Alex? Alex, *dear* Alex, tell me it's not true. A silly jest to scare me, isn't it? Say it is! Please say it is!"

Many men would probably have loved to have been the recipient of her clinging embrace, but Brockhaven did not appear to be among them.

He roughly clamped his hands on her wrists and pried her off his slim person, holding her at arm's length while she cried and hiccuped.

"Tendrils, Isabella!" he said sharply, shaking her wrists. "Dig them into your husband, not into me. The girl's your cousin. You can scream and cry a fortnight if you choose; it won't change the fact."

Her lips were so taut with fury that she could barely manage her words. "I shall fight this with every legal means at my disposal."

Brockhaven let go her wrists. "Do," he assented cordially. "A pretty fool you'll look, but then"—he took one of her golden curls and lifted it in his hand—"you always were a pretty fool."

The lady glared at Brockhaven with a frightened pout and retreated to the side of the blond man, her fingers fluttering like nervous sparrows against the fabric of his cravat.

"Vincent, he can't do this to me. Can he?"

The man enclosed her hands in his, pressuring their movement to a standstill, and said patiently, "I've tried to explain, my dear, in the carriage on the way over, that this is not Alex's doing. He merely discovered what might be an orphan member of our family and quite rightly took steps to restore her to us." The man gave Brockhaven an even smile, his lips curling upward at the corners like a piping wave. "Your lawyer's been with us, as you can guess. It's quite a romantic tale, is it not? The discovery of an heiress to Chad! And to think *you* were the one to find her. It's enough to boggle the imagination."

"Particularly if one's imagination is susceptible to boggling," remarked Brockhaven indifferently. "I take it you've been informed that there's no doubt to her identity? Not only does she have the medallion, but we found a Glussy Bible under the floorboards of her wagon that contained a record of her birth and identified her as Compton's daughter."

There was an ill feeling inside of me, worse than the day when I'd become seven and accidentally poisoned myself by chewing on a leaf of spurge that I had mistaken for chickweed. I'd always known, though I'd never done more than glance at it once, that my father had written my birth in the Bible, because Grandmother said it was not the gypsy way to value such records; birth papers were for the thick-skulled gorgios who would forget the names of their own children if they did not write them down.

My frightened gypsy soul hammered against my heart, crying its wish to flee from the pain and the prison of my gorgio-tainted blood and escape to the wind and the road and the forest. Such was the battle to stop the devouring fangs of panic that, when at last I won control, there was little left inside me but a wasted emptiness. As if my lips were some great distance from me, I heard them utter, "No, no . . ."

As through a fog, I saw the man, Vincent, approach me, delivering a gentle smile to my stricken heart. "Forgive me," he said. "How thoughtless we've all been! I'm sure that if I were in your place, I'd be looking twice as lost. My name is Vincent Randolph and I'm married to your cousin, Isabella. That makes us relatives of some sort, don't you think? Permit me to extend my hand as your friend."

He lifted my limp hand and pressed it warmly in his.

"Almost," said Brockhaven from behind him, "one can hear the swell of an angelic chorus."

Vincent glanced back at the earl before giving me a reassuring grin. "Sentiment embarrasses Alex. You never mind him, and we'll be as syrupy as we please. Come and shake hands with your cousin, Isabella." He made as though to draw me toward his wife, but the beauty pulled away.

"You're out of your mind, Vincent. It's obvious the girl's an imposter."

Vincent said her name softly. "Isabella."

A quiver coursed through her, and she spun in a circle where she stood. "I don't care—I hate her. I hate her! I wish she was dead."

Lord Brockhaven spoke an oath under his breath and said, "Do something about her, Vincent, or I swear I will."

The lady beat a hasty retreat behind a wide-backed chair, which told me that she was no stranger to Lord Brockhaven's temper.

"Don't you dare talk to me like that, Alex!" she rapped out explosively. "As though I were a lap dog that's chewed the drapery fringe. Why should I touch that filthy gutter-snipe? My cousin, indeed! Look at her! Our plow horses have better tended hair and her skin's as sun bitten as a Turk's. She disgusts me, with her ragged skirt and bare feet. And if you take head lice from her, Vincent, don't think you can come to my bed with them."

They were certainly not pretty words, but they were closer to what I had learned to expect from a gorgio, and they did have the virtue of being honest. I admit, however, that her last remark was far from what I had been taught was the correctly respectful way to speak to a husband. Vincent stood very still beside me, and I wondered if he was hiding a great anger or if Grandmother had exaggerated the subservience women offered to their spouses. Or perhaps English women are more outspoken than gypsies.

Brockhaven's voice cut through the numb, racing pattern of my thoughts.

"No matter how you'd dress the chit, Isabella, the quality of her manners puts yours to shame."

It was clear that the lady didn't like his remark one little bit. "And yours!" she said vengefully.

"And mine," he agreed, looking back at her with maliciously sparkling eyes. With lowered brows, she watched him for a moment, the blue lace that covered her bodice swelling and dropping slowly with her long, deep breaths. She gave Brockhaven a glance of acid mockery, tossed her chin, swept up her skirt, and came to stand within a yard of me. Making a faint curtsy, Isabella inclined her head and in a majestically cold voice, she said, "Cousin."

Vincent gave a delighted laugh, his face holding a good deal more satisfaction than the occasion seemed to warrant. He put one arm around me and one around his wife. Though the gesture was kindly meant, I felt a stab of anxiety, for it was an ordeal to be claimed as kin by strangers, be they however good-willed.

"There now!" he said. "We've cleared the first hurdle. Shall we sit down like the shining examples of civilized folk that we are, and talk through our situation? Will you offer us tea, Alex?"

"By all means," replied Brockhaven. "A family party taking tea at Edgehill. Let's play the thing to the hilt." Instead of pulling the call bell, as I'd seen Robert do when he wanted to summon one of his servants, Brockhaven went into the hallway and gave instructions to a footman.

Vincent took my arm and led me to the chair that his wife had so recently used to shield herself from Brockhaven, and gave me an expectant look that I had come to realize means that a gentleman wants you to sit down so he can do so himself, as it is the English way that ladies must sit down before the men. It is the opposite with gypsies. I sank into the chair, feeling as though I had no more bones than a cloth doll, and Vincent sat with his wife on the short sofa.

Brockhaven came back into the room and ran a sardonic glance over his company. "Cozy," he observed. He took a seat opposite Vincent. "I suppose you'll want to look at the Bible."

Vincent dismissed the Bible with the wave of his pale, large-boned right hand. "Leave that for the courts. Your lawyer is convinced of the document's authenticity; let it stand like that for the present." His voice was grim, but perfectly self-possessed. "To proceed! It appears that Liza stands to inherit the lion's share of what we thought was Isabella's estate."

The numbness in my chest grew so heavy that it became an effort to breathe. No wonder Isabella hated me, if she thought that I had come to take away her home. Vincent's kindness was even greater than I had supposed, for if he had spoken truly, then only the most generous man could greet my arrival with anything touching cordiality. Ellen *had* called me a gypsy heiress, but I had not thought that she meant I was heir to more than a great English name. I'm not sure why my eyes turned with such haste to Lord Brockhaven—for confirmation perhaps? He wasn't looking at me, but somehow I knew from his expression that Vincent's words were soundly based. Brockhaven regarded his cousin through half-closed eyes, a strange fire glowing in their depths. If he was enjoying his cousin's chagrin, he gave no sign. Neither was there an effort to convey sympathy. His lips moved only slightly as he said, "If you thought the estate was Isabella's, then you've been unwise. Her long-lost, though unforgotten uncle, or his offspring, might have appeared at any time to vest their claim."

"After twenty years," Vincent said gently, "it seemed— shall we say—unlikely."

Brockhaven made a thin smile. "Yes. We've all suffered, haven't we, from the unlikely." He transferred his gaze to Isabella, who had been sitting plucking with unmindful agitation at the armrest of the sofa. "As Bartholemew probably told you, you'll hardly be starving. Liza gets the land

and the income from the portion of it used in agriculture, but your trust fund—enough to keep an Oriental caliph in luxury—is still yours. And should you desire it, you have the use of the house for life."

Isabella's eyes were dilated and glistening. "But she gets the land . . . the land."

Brockhaven shrugged. "If you manage your income well, you can afford to buy more—and Vincent can still have his empire."

There could be no doubt that Brockhaven's words were a baited challenge. They might have been a threat had Brockhaven allowed that much emotion to color his voice. I had learned from Ellen that Brockhaven had no reputation for punctilio, but I could no longer ignore that this was something more. What Lord Brockhaven felt for Vincent was, at the very least, a long-held, if strictly disciplined, animosity. My discovery filled me with an urgent disquiet. Without understanding why, I was filled with the dread of a rabbit trapped in a cowyard, to be trampled without design or malice because she wasn't fleet or clever enough to avoid getting in the way. I'm not surprised that Vincent looked at me with compassion. I'm sure I bore a stricken expression.

"Poor child," he said, "you look bewildered. Had this not been explained to you? I didn't realize! What a shock for you! Permit me to clarify what we've been saying. Your paternal grandfather has left fifteen thousand acres of land for you, possibly more. We won't know the full sum of it until the courts have examined the nuances of the will."

"Fifteen . . . thousand? It can't be!" I heard the hollow whisper of my thoughts. "I don't want it. Can I give it back?"

Vincent was amused. "That would be impossible, my dear, believe me. And even if it could be done, we could never permit you to do anything so detrimental to your interests. In a day or two, you'll begin to grow used to the idea . . ."

"Please, I don't *want* to grow used to the idea," I said

wretchedly. "People must live on the land. I wouldn't understand what to do for them, or how to care for the things that are there. I couldn't! I wasn't born to that kind of life, and it's as far from what I know as *my* life would be to you."

The young man tilted his head back, as though he was beginning to really see me. To my embarrassment, his eyes began to gleam with tender admiration. He said slowly, "You are a woman in a million, do you realize that? That your initial thoughts should be for the families who live on the land!"

"Oh, don't, Vincent!" snapped his wife. "It's plain to see that the twit's stupider than a mule." She glared at me. "It's not who lives on the land, you ninny-tinny gypsy, it's the income from the land. Enough to buy every shabby gypsy wagon in Europe and enough left over for tick soap, which is the first thing that I intend to buy for you as soon as the court appoints me as your guardian."

Brockhaven leaned back in his chair, the long, sensuously muscled line of his leg stretched before him, one ankle resting on the other. "The court won't appoint," he said. "Chadbourne left a codicil to his will naming a trustee, should the estate pass into the hands of a minor child."

"How like the old man." Vincent's eyes narrowed at the corners, curiosity laid naked in his face. "That hadn't occurred to me, I'll admit." He turned to me. "I don't want to speak ill of the dead, but in time you'll learn that your grandfather was something of a tartar—hence your own father's running away, never to return. Not expecting him to return, I'm afraid that none of us put much attention into the clauses of the will that concern you, and I couldn't tell you who he might have appointed to have the care of you. Never mind. Mr. Bartholemew, the lawyer, will know, and in the meantime, I want you to make your home with us! Isabella and I are your family now, my dear, and that bond is going to ease us through every difficulty that we meet." He gave me a quick smile as though we had sealed a bargain. Then he turned to Lord Brockhaven. "Alex, Isabella and I won't forget what you've done for us in discovering Liza! I'm fully sensible of the trouble you've taken in this matter, and there's no reason for you to be burdened further with the child. Liza will accompany us when we leave this afternoon."

There was a certain quiet authority in Vincent's bland voice. With each calm word, I felt as though the air was being squeezed slowly from around me, and each breath I took refreshed my lungs less than the one before it. It was insane, this beginning of a feeling that I didn't want to leave Edgehill. This house had been a prison, and that for scarcely a day. Nor is it the gypsy way to nourish sentimental feelings for any location. As a race, we are well-hated in every country in Europe, and so we are trained from infancy to move on without regret or sorrow. Dread filled me as I waited for Lord Brockhaven to agree with his cousin. No one was more amazed than me when he did not.

"Sweet Vincent, so eager," Brockhaven said, with the glimmer of a smile. "It grieves me to disappoint you, but I'm afraid, as Liza's guardian, I can't allow you to remove her from Edgehill."

There was a moment of astonished silence before Vincent snapped, "What nonsense is this?"

Brockhaven slowly uncrossed his elegant legs. "Chadbourne left the trusteeship in the hands of his trusted friend, Lord Brockhaven."

Again the emotional silence, this time broken by Isabella, her skin white with wrath. "He couldn't stand you! Why, I remember the day he told me he'd rather see me dead on my feet than married to you. When Grandfather wrote his will, there were four men between you and the title of Lord Brockhaven. No one expected you to inherit Brockhaven's title and fortune—no one! Grandfather would never have wanted you to have the charge of one of his grandchildren."

"Then it's a pity," Brockhaven said, giving her a bright mocking glance, "that he didn't have more foresight than to list the trusteeship in the name of Lord Brockhaven without bothering to specify which one."

Vincent, I could see, was watching Lord Brockhaven with the wary appraisal of a man trying to disarm an intruder with a loaded pistol. In a reasoning tone, he said, "Alex, Liza can't stay here, you know that. Let's not argue."

"Why not?" said Brockhaven with a malicious sparkle.

"Because the girl's suffered enough already. She must be frightened from her wits as is! You have no love for me—all right." Vincent shrugged. "You never have returned the affection I've tried to express for you, but this time . . . Alex, don't punish the girl to hurt me." The man left the couch and paced a circle on the Oriental carpet. "Can we discuss this privately?"

"I don't think so," said Brockhaven, the emotion shuttered again from his face. "Say what you think you have to and then get out."

Vincent paled. "Damn," he said softly. "Why do you have to make everything so difficult? You don't mean any of this. You don't want that girl."

Brockhaven rose from his chair with lazy grace and strolled to stand behind me. I twisted back to see him, still not able to believe that he could be serious about assuming my guardianship! He looked down at me with a withdrawal as complete as it might have been if I had turned into a vase. Last night, in the attic room, he had seemed like a man—a dangerous man, it was true—but human. Now he had become again like the beautifully made demon god, as careless in kindness as in cruelty. He dropped an idle hand to stroke my hair where it lay on my shoulder, the diamond signet at the base of his finger winking like a firefly against the darkness of my hair.

There was a certain genius in Brockhaven for manipulating the mood of those around him as he willed. "Knowing me as you do, Vincent, why would you think that I might *not* want the girl?" he said in a tone fine-tuned to the faintly suggestive.

"No!" Isabella cried out through pinched lips. "Take your hands off her, Alex! I can't bear it, I told you that I

67

can't!" I think she might have flown at Brockhaven had
her husband not caught her forcefully to his side. Neither
Vincent nor Brockhaven was the kind of man who allows
anger to letter his features, but I didn't need that to know
Vincent was very angry. The fire in his eyes met the ice in
Brockhaven's, and I wondered what subtle barb had been
concealed in Lord Brockhaven's words to provoke such
feeling. Surely something more than concern for my wel-
fare had brought Isabella to the point of tears.

"Your insinuations don't amuse me, Alex," snapped
Vincent.

"I live to amuse you, Vince," said Brockhaven, lifting
his hand from my shoulder. The back of his hand brushed
my cheek and I felt the cold of his diamond as it passed
over my skin. "Didn't I just play one of your favorite
tunes—so that you could dance?"

Isabella flung herself from her husband's arms in a gesture of nervous irritation. "Yes, yes! There you have it,
Vincent! Alex has got the better of you again, hasn't he?
You *promised* when you married me that you'd take care
of my property, and it's come to this! What good have you
done me? When Grandfather turned senile, I wanted to
have him declared incompetent, do you remember? I knew
he was dangerous, the way he didn't trust a soul and
blithering on and on about his runaway son. But would
you let me have him put away? Oh, no, not *you*. You
were too afraid of what people would say. Look what's
come of it! That dreadful codicil to the will, a nasty gypsy
brat to shame us all, and Brockhaven in control of my
land." She looked away from her husband's stony face in
disgust and rounded passionately on Lord Brockhaven.
"Oh, Alex, why did you let me marry Vincent? I wish
you'd kidnapped me, carried me away, ravished me! My
father would have had to give in then! You're the only
man I know who would have had the stomach to help me
get rid of Grandfather before it was too late."

"Very possibly," said Brockhaven, "but don't cast yourself on my chest again, because only one of us enjoys it."

Vincent's firm lips had become a grim line set like a sea

wall against the bitter tide of his wife's intemperance. Unlike Lord Brockhaven, Vincent hadn't elevated the mastering of self to a high art, but as I had guessed, he was well able to shed an inconvenient emotion had he reason. Another man might have been distracted from the thread of his interest. The only attention Vincent dealt his wife was a glance that seemed to file her as unfinished business and might have hid anything from compassion to disgust. Then, as though her outburst had never been, he readdressed Brockhaven. "You've carried this far enough. You know, I know, and God knows that with the girl's breeding it's going to be hard enough, *hard enough* to have her accepted into her rightful place in society."

"Vincent, in his unfledged innocence," Brockhaven said mockingly. "When we publish her bank balance, the ton will swarm around her like worms after buckthorn."

"Perhaps," said Vincent, his temper at last beginning to shred, "but even *you* will admit, Alex, that with Gwen away, there's no female here to chaperon her, and if it becomes known that she's been living here unchaperoned with you and Robert, there's not one respectable household in this county or any other that will allow her to set one foot past the door, regardless of whether or not you're her legal guardian. You might as well put a sign on the girl saying 'whore' and march her down Bond Street."

The door opened with an emphatic click and Robert sauntered in to catch the tail of Vincent's angry comment. Robert smiled around the room with ludicrously exaggerated good humor and chirped, "I wish someone had told me you four were in here talking smutty. I'd have come back much sooner. Why are we going to parade Liza around like a whore?"

Since Vincent was standing so much as my friend, I am ashamed to admit some feeling of gratitude toward Robert as my avenger.

Eight bullocks in stampede couldn't have trampled Robert's youthful insolence, but Vincent saw fit to give it a try nonetheless.

"You ought to knock, child," he observed, in a tone that

would have made most self-respecting adolescents long to *knock* the door off its hinges. It was a worthy thrust, well-delivered, but the ordinance was much too light to pierce Robert's case-hardened armor. Without troubling himself to shut the door behind him, Robert strolled over to perch on my chair arm and smiled down at me seraphically.

"When I was sixteen, I would have made an elaborate show of leaving the room, tapping on the door and reentering the chamber with farcical propriety. I've grown out of the game years ago, but Vincent still wants to play." He glanced at Vincent. "All this severity, Vince, and I've come to do you a good turn. I thought you'd like to be warned of Aunt Gwen's imminent arrival so you'd have time to straighten your neckcloth."

There was a swift change in Vincent's expression. "What are you talking about?"

"Didn't Alex have time to tell you then, my dear?" asked Robert. "Our redoubtable great aunt has arrived to countenance little Liza."

Vincent's gaze flashed to Brockhaven.

"Checkmate!" observed Robert and there was a crisp rap on the open door.

"Lady Gwendolyn Cleaver," announced the footman.

The woman who entered was small and trim, and carried herself with the dignity of fifty-seven years. Her nose was sharp and bony, her eyes prettily shaped and long-lashed, and her mouth as dainty as a pansy. A starched lace cap held tidy her soft brown hair, and she wore old-fashioned turquoise earbobs that precisely matched her charmingly designed gown. In all, she was a spruce lady with a soothing air of well-bred calm about her. She stopped a few feet beyond the door and subjected the occupants of the room to a frank examination that indeed *did* cause Vincent's hand to stray instinctively to his neckcloth.

Then she came right to me, taking my hands and drawing me to my feet.

"Liza! Have I said your name right?" she said. "Imagine, after all these years we are blessed to discover you.

It's like having a piece of your father with us all over again. We were good friends, you know, your father and I. Our families were quite close. How proud he must have been of you! You're his image, my dear, his very image! Such glossy hair! Such speaking eyes! Brockhaven said in his note that your father's passed away—how sorry I am. We'll sit together and talk, shall we? I'll tell you about his life as a gentleman and you must tell me of his life as a gentleman gypsy. What a joy it is to have you with us."

"It's not a joy to me," muttered Isabella, sorely tried.

Lady Gwendolyn gave my hand a meaningful squeeze and released me to stand on tiptoes to touch cheeks with the lovely blond girl.

"There, there, Bella," murmured Aunt Gwen comfortingly. "This hasn't been welcome news to you, but you must forbear."

"There is nothing I loathe more in this world," Isabella pointed out, with absolute sincerity, "than forbearance."

"I understand, dear," replied Gwendolyn. "You know, though, how the world loves to gossip about you. If you don't mind yourself, we'll be having them say that you're a shrew and a trial to Vincent and why must you always conduct yourself like a Billingsgate fishmum. You *know* what people can be! When anyone asks you about Liza, you must muster a sad little smile and say that your new cousin is a very sweet girl and you're sure you wish her well."

"I don't wish her well! I wish she was in a pit, a dark pit, with adders and spiders and rats and—"

"Quite," interrupted Gwen hastily. "That is what you *really* wish, that is *not* what you must say you wish. If you are charming and cheerful, though of course a bit downcast, then it will be said you are brave and *such* a lady! Do remember, my dear. I'll make a visit to you tomorrow and we'll talk of it more, shall we? You must excuse me if I take a moment to kiss your handsome husband."

Vincent stepped forward quickly to kiss his great aunt's offered cheek, and said to her, "I'm happy to see you,

Aunt, though I confess, I'm surprised. I had thought you were to be another month staying with the duchess."

"*Your* surprise at finding me here in no way rivals *mine* at being here, I assure you. I was dragged from my guest bed yester eve at midnight by Brockhaven's whippity-snippet of a footman."

"Banbury tales, Aunt," retorted Robert. "I've just come from talking with Will the footman. He said he found you in the midst of a card game with your hostess and her lady's maid."

"Perhaps!" she allowed tranquilly, "but we *were* in my boudoir."

"Fully clothed. In your dinner gowns," teased Robert.

"Impertinent boy! It was as you say but"—she held up a triumphant finger—"we had on our nightcaps." She fondly patted her nephew's dark curls. "Lud, boy, you're surely growing prettier every time I see you. You may catch up to your brother yet. Well! Let me see, where was I? Ah, yes. The long and short of it is, Alex fired off a message for me to come and chaperon his ward. And as soon as I read who she was, why, I couldn't wait to rush back and see her. What a time there'll be, and what a to-do!" She smiled ruefully. "I confess that I was beginning to pine a bit for home, despite the duchess's hospitality, and I had begun to miss Ellen dreadfully, so on every score I'm happy to be home. Make yourself easy, Vincent. Alex is *not* taking mean advantage of me, whatever you may be thinking."

A faint flush appeared under the tight skin across Vincent's cheeks. "I beg your pardon, Aunt Gwen, I intended no criticism. Only I cannot help but feel that it's the outside of enough for Alex to drag you away from a visit with your dearest friend to chaperon a young girl with no conceivable claim on you. I've been trying to let Alex give Liza into my care, if only he would listen to an appeal to that most underused of his organs—"

"My word! What organ is that?" inquired Gwen with some alarm.

"Don't be coy, Aunt. Obviously Vincent is referring to

72

my brother's heart," said Robert with a grin.

"Well, I wish he wouldn't," replied Gwendolyn. "Brock-haven's anatomy is much too stimulating a topic for the sunroom. I'm sorry, but I shall have to make you all go. Yes, yes, you and Isabella, too, Vincent. I know it's been a great shock to you both, but really, we must give ourselves time to reflect so we won't start behaving in ways that don't become us. Isn't that so, my little Bella?" She ignored the needle-sharp glance she received from Isabella and continued. "Liza's had quite enough excitement, and the kindest thing we could do for her would be to provide a few very dull days."

Chapter Four

We gypsies have a saying: In fog, the wildcat walks with wakeful paws. In our language, of course, it sounds a bit different, but I think my translation gives you the sense. The gorgios have a proverb that's much the same if more efficient than ours. They say: Watch your step! I've been told, since the first time I heard that proverb, that I tend to read more than is there in gorgio admonitions and "watch your step" is nothing more meaningful than a friendly warning to anyone going for a walk in a meadow where cows have been grazing. Nevertheless, my first days at Edgehill were days in which I watched my step. Ellen, I might add, was a great help.

After Vincent and Isabella took their leave, Lady Gwendolyn dispensed a carriage straightway to the Perscough home, where Ellen had been staying, and had her brought back to Edgehill. Ellen's arrival considerably brightened that day and the days ahead. It's not that Lady Gwen was not everything to me that was kind, for she was that, truly, but I was altogether conscious of the differences in our customs and, if I were to inadvertently do a thing that to the gorgios is an act of hopeless barbarity, I would rather learn about it from Ellen, who would *never* consider me a barbarian.

In Ellen, there beats one of the most romantic hearts in

the west of England. She loves gypsies, and pirates, and good fairies, and tales about princesses turned into cats. Her heroines were Lady Godiva and St. Dymphna, who was beheaded by her mad father for refusing to become his wife. Ellen can talk by the hour about legends that the robin's breast became red when it was singed as she carried water to the poor sinners in hell, and that honeysuckle will give you erotic dreams should you sleep with it by your bedside.

I was happy to know gypsy lore enough to set Ellen marveling to her heart's content, and for her part Ellen began to help me unravel the mysteries of my new environment. Take the aprons, for instance. I had noticed that wealthy gorgio women never wore aprons to cover their gowns. Where was it that they wiped the grease of cooking and eating from their hands? From Ellen I learned that they (and the menfolk, as well!) used square, tieless aprons of linen which were set out for them at mealtimes and either laid on their laps, or, if they were prone to sloppiness, knotted by the corners around their necks like a scarf. They are called napkins, a full set of which are stored in special cupboards and known as "the napery." That the gorgios would have so elaborate and ceremonial a procedure for dealing with the grease rubbed from their hands and faces was an amazement to me, and I was to discover stranger customs yet! On my second day at Edgehill, Lady Gwendolyn took a slight chill, and as I sat with her and Ellen in the drawing room, I saw Lady Gwen take a piece of material from her day bag, blow her nose on it and return it to her bag! I was so embarrassed that I could barely bring myself to ask Ellen about it later. When I did mention it, Ellen treated it as though it was the most commonplace occurrence in the world.

"Oh that?" she said. "That was a handkerchief. Just a handkerchief. Haven't you any? Never mind, you can have some of mine. My Great Aunt Anne is forever giving them to me as gifts."

I puzzled for a long time that evening on why the gorgios would want to preserve the blowings from their noses.

As for the gypsy men, I could imagine what they would say if their womenfolk tried to make them do anything so effete as to set a linen napkin on their laps!

In the main, I tried to live each moment as it came. Thoughts of what future would be for me here, I put from me. Grief for my grandmother was fresh and undimmed, despite the things that had happened to me here, and I suffered still from malaise and a feeling that if I couldn't be with her, then I might as well be here, or anywhere. Flashes of fear came to me at times, some so strong that I would feel as though I should hitch my team and wagon and run far away. Then, before there was time to translate my thoughts to purpose, and that purpose to action, the fear would fade to dullness, and I would be again like the wildcat walking in the fog.

Everything changed when the household heard of my new identity. The servants fairly glowed with kindness toward me, and Betty, who had been nothing so much as my gaoler the night before, went so far as to say that she would never have allowed me to help her polish the silver had she known that I was a lady, and in all her born days, never had she seen the like. A poor gypsy might be an object of scorn and suspicion, but a rich one was the pure embodiment of romance.

I was reassigned from the attic to a bedchamber beside Ellen. It was a pretty room with the walls hung in printed damask with yellow, stencillike camellias. The curtains were real lace, and Ellen found a series of pictures of a family picnic in one of the wardrobes on the third floor and nailed them onto my walls. She brought porcelain pots with forced tulips and crocus from the hothouse and with her paints she colored on my windowsill, "Light and shade by turn, but love always." From my wagon, she helped me carry my books and feather quilt. When all was arranged, things looked very snug, and while it was not like the home I was used to, I'll confess it was a good deal warmer than our wagon had ever been.

I spent more time than was good for me worrying about Lord Brockhaven and his cousin, Vincent, about Isabella and Brockhaven, about Isabella and Vincent. My isolated childhood had given me few instances to observe the married state. Be my experience ever so limited, I was sure that the relationship shared by Vincent and Isabella was a trap and a heartache to both parties. Underneath her wheedling, her dramatics, and her artificiality, one could sense that Isabella was deeply in love with Lord Brockhaven. It might be a selfish love, and a possessive one, but it was nonetheless strong enough to have torn to tatters the fabric of her marriage. Though she had not been kind to me, I pitied her. Only misery could come of giving one's love in keeping to Lord Brockhaven, for surely few men were more alienated from their own emotions. I knew what drew her to him, though, and held her with so tight a bond. Even if he were not stunningly attractive, even if he had only a tenth of his self-assurance, Brockhaven still would have been able to draw people to him with as little effort as a falcon gliding toward heaven on the wind. It was too fascinating, that hint of gentleness in him, long-drowned in the shadows of his life. Everyone around him wanted to touch it, I could see that. Everyone wanted to be the one to come close to that lost sweetness where none was allowed. Robert came the closest. They might never have said much to express the bond between them—certainly they never did so in public—but it was there, nonetheless.

Lord Brockhaven's relationship with Lady Gwendolyn was simple, superficial, and direct, which seemed to suit both parties very well.

"What it really is," Ellen explained to me one afternoon, "is a standoff."

We had been sitting together in the stable, in the boxstall that Brockhaven's groom had allocated to my stallion, Kory. It was a lovely place with shiny brass tackle and fresh paint and sunny windows. The stall itself could have housed, in comfort, an elephant and her young.

Kory was lying on a pile of clean, dry straw, with my head against his withers. Once in a while, he would take my forearm between his teeth with a great show of fire and nibble gently for a joke, and I would dig into the bag I had brought with me from the kitchen and pull out another carrot for the old moocher. At first, our antics terrified the grooms, but as I had been here more than a week now, and Kory hadn't killed me yet, the grooms only shook their heads, grinned, and said that I had *something* on that stallion, all right.

Ellen was sitting on the blacksmith's pull around and munching, with an endearing lack of elegance, on one of the raw carrots from Kory's sack.

"The thing about Mama and Brockhaven," she said, chatting energetically, "is that they've got nothing in common. Nothing! Politics: Mama's as staunch as a sitting cat and Brockhaven's a liberal. Society: Mama loves people and Brockhaven hates them. Economic development: She likes the way things used to be and Brockhaven's a progressive. She's a moralist and Brockhaven's . . . well, the opposite. I'll tell you, Liza, the secret to harmony between a lady like Mama and a rakehell like Brockhaven is for them both to shut their mouths around each other. 'Sides, if he wasn't so austere, I suppose she'd try to coddle him. Can you imagine Brockhaven putting up with that? We'd both be out on our ear in the time it takes to say— Liza! Here comes Robert!"

I hadn't been at Edgehill above three nights before I discovered that Ellen was more than fond of Robert, a fact known and treated with charming delicacy by everyone from the lowest to the most elevated of the domestic staff. It was quite a humble devotion: Ellen never did more than dream, in a remote way, that Robert would ever take any special notice of her. I think she admired him because he was the closest thing to a pirate that she had ever met.

For his part, Robert remained mercifully in ignorance of Ellen's feelings, partly, I'm sure, because she was rather shy around him and Brockhaven. Ellen was in the unique position of being treated by them with some kindness, which Ellen said Robert did because she stuttered like a bullfrog around him and it touched him with a casual pity for such a majestic lack of self-confidence. She claimed

Lord Brockhaven did so from a natural disinclination to expose such a poorly defended individual to his acerbic tongue.

Kory put back his ears as Robert came up the boxstall.

"By God," said Robert, "your beast hates me."

"Oh, no," I said quickly. Kory had so frightened the stable boys on his first days there that Brockhaven had warned me that he'd get rid of that "wild nag" if he didn't calm down, and I still hadn't recovered from my fear that Brockhaven would make good his threat. "Kory's only making a warning. He'd never attack anyone unless I told him to. My grandmother trained him that way, because she worried that someone might try to molest me."

"Then I'll remember to molest you in places far removed from the stables." He gave me a wink. "Stand up. Lord, this is the first time I've seen you in . . . what's that word you have for us?"

"G-gorgio," Ellen supplied.

"In the guttural, yet, Ellie. Soon we'll have you hopping around with a hoop in your ear." He grinned. "Gorgio. This is the first time I've seen Liza dressed like one of us decadent gorgios. Where'd you get the toggery? I thought Lady G. said that your dressmaker outfits wouldn't be done until Thursday."

"They won't be," I said. "Isabella sent this riding habit for me with a note that said she thought I might like to ride."

His grin broadened. "And break your neck, with her compliments. Stand up."

With Robert, that's that. I was supposed to jump to my feet and stand heedless as a marble statue as he examined me at his leisure, unknowing or uncaring about the mortification it caused me. I'd learned by now that it was less than useless to say no to Robert. There's no man better at getting his way. If there was nothing else that I blessed Lord Brockhaven for, I blessed him for interrupting Robert and me that first day in the library, because the better I knew Robert, the more sure I was that he would have had what he wanted of me, by fair means or foul.

80

That had been before he learned that I was a "lady," and now he would no more ravish me than his own sister, so he had told me, to my embarrassment. The gorgios have a very bewildering code of honor.

At any rate, I stood up, and Ellen knelt beside me to brush the straw off my skirt, saying, "It is pretty, d-don't you think? R-red velvet! Mama felt it was a thought risqué for Liza, but the c-color is so b-becoming, is it not?"

"*Very* becoming," Robert agreed, his gaze sparing no part of me, until I thought to distract him.

"Would you like to see the bonnet?" I asked, grabbing up the matching hat and squashing it down on my head with the scarlet and black feathers every which way, to make Ellen laugh. I think she looks very pretty when she laughs. You couldn't tell if Robert thought so because he was laughing about the hat, too, and it's hard to tell what people are thinking of when they laugh.

"Marvelous. The Unattainable in Red, they'll call you," he said.

"Will they? Who are they?"

"Oh, the hoi polloi who hang around the Park in London to watch the gentry on their afternoon trot. I don't doubt the crowds will double to see the gypsy heiress on her half-tamed stallion," Robert said. "I suppose Vincent put Bella up to sending you the dress, as usual, sparing no pains . . ."

As lightly as I could, I said, "You don't like him, do you?"

"Vincent?" He put his hand through his dark hair, shrugging his shoulders in a loose, nervous motion as though my question were a cage that might trap him. "Old wounds, Liza. Bad associations. Alex and I lived with Vincent's family after my parents died, did Gwen tell you? An uplifting story! My mother was shot by one of her lovers in a jealous fit and . . . what's the matter, Ellie?"

"It's only th-that my mother said sh-she had died of influenza."

Robert's grin differed little from a grimace. "Wishful

thinking on the part of the relatives who felt disgraced. My father was dead before the year was out, another admirable mortality. That story even Ellen has heard."

"Yes. H-he had drunk to excess in a g-gin shop, in d-despair over the death of your mother . . ."

"In anger that her parents had stuck him with her funeral bill," corrected Robert, leaning forward with his elbows resting on the stall door. "On the walk home, he espied an elderly watchman and decided it might afford him a moment or two of amusement if he beat the old fellow to death with his cane. All was going just as dear Papa had planned when a good Samaritan passing by thought to object. My father was so enraged at the Samaritan's ungentlemanly attempt to interfere with his pleasure that my father challenged the man to a duel. Right won the day, as they say, and my father died with a bullet in his heart."

"L-like your mother!" said Ellen softly, struck by the irony of it.

Robert smiled, not pleasantly. "Not quite. My mother died with a bullet in the head. Alex told me. He ought to know. He saw it."

"Oh, no," Ellen cried.

I felt her arm come around my waist.

"Poor, poor little boy," I whispered.

Robert made a restless movement with his hand. I could tell that this was a memory on which his mind never lingered. He said, "It was a scandal, and a slur on the family, and a black mark on the honor of the name. So Alex and I heard for years from Vincent's mother."

"But surely," I said earnestly, "you couldn't be blamed for the things that your parents did!"

"But then you didn't know Vincent's father, the Right Honorable William T. Randolph," said Robert curtly. "On the day we arrived to live at his home, and every Sunday thereafter he took us to the big, dark vault of his family chapel and made us kneel on the flagstone floor from dusk until midnight. I was four then, just turned four. I remember how tall Randolph looked to me, blond with that exquisite, controlled face, the replica of Vincent. Like some wrathful archangel, telling us to pray that our souls wouldn't decay, as our parents' had done. Then he'd lock us in and it would be quiet, and black, and cold. Alex wrapped his jacket around me and set me on the pew. For hours, he'd tell jokes and stories, to keep me from being afraid . . .

"And Sunday chapel was only the beginning. I was spared the worst of it. Alex saw to that, though it made things harder for himself." He made an impatient gesture. "Why am I telling you little monkeys all this? Oh, yes. Vincent. Why don't I like Vincent? That's a hard question, isn't it? He's such an exemplary fellow, pious, devout, mannerly. All my youth, his parents held him up as the model after whom I should mold myself. It's a miracle, isn't it, that I don't like him?"

Chapter Five

I was not supposed to ride that afternoon, for underneath the heavy full skirts of the riding dress were the same bare feet I'd worn since my birthday. There had been no time for the shoemaker to finish the half boots Lady Gwen had ordered for my use. Inside I was glad of it, because the binding pressure of a shoe is intolerable to one who has known the freedom of unclad feet. No use to tell this to Lady Gwen. It would only grieve her terribly to think that I was uncomfortable. I had suggested—casually—that it wouldn't really be so bad, would it, if I didn't wear shoes. Lady Gwen had made a face that I'm ashamed to say reminded me of a thorned sheep and said that you might as well show a man your bosom as your naked feet.

The second reason I was not supposed to ride was that Lady Gwendolyn was afraid I might meet somebody, and it would make no good impression if I was jouncing around on the saddle like a hoyden on my first acquaintance with anyone of note. She would arrange a more dignified entrance into society for me.

This was why Ellen and I waited until Lady Gwen left to pay an afternoon visit to the parson's wife before we rode out and why we took only the loneliest backroads. Ellen has this funny way of grinning and saying, "We won't want to upset my mother," which means the same thing as, "Let's go, she'll never find out about it."

Ellen's mind was so lively that she managed to inject the trappings of an adventure to any outing, and today was no exception. I discovered that it was thought befitting to the station of a young lady that she should ride accompanied at the very least by a trusted family retainer. To me it sounded like the height of splendor to be accompanied by a fatherly groom in dashing livery, but to Ellen it was dull, safe, and confining. She got rid of the well-meaning accompaniment by repeated assurances that we would go no farther than the lime avenue that bordered the south lawn. You might have guessed, though, that when we reached the last of the limes, she turned her mare to the east, smiled at me, and laughed, calling over her back, "This way, Liza. We're off to hunt for missing treasure."

Off we set; our only claim to chaperonage was Caesar, Lord Brockhaven's lion-sized mastiff. Lord Brockhaven had left home early that day, much to the dog's disgust, so he had been happy to attach himself to us as a diversion from moping around the stables waiting for his beloved master's return. Caesar was the most intelligent dog of any species I'd ever met, and the most well-trained. Immediately, Brockhaven made it clear to Caesar that I was a friend and since that moment, Caesar had treated me with a dogged devotion. It was Ellen's opinion that since mastiffs were among the first dogs, probably Caesar's ancestors had been the prized hunting dogs of Assyrian emperors. Brockhaven only laughed and said that more likely Caesar came from the line of mongrels that hung around the streets of ancient Jerusalem, eating carrion and spreading rabies.

As we hitched past an old slate barn, Ellen pulled her mare into a trot beside Kory.

"We're off on a mission of mercy," she said.

"I'm all for mercy! What's toward, O Noble Companion?"

"You recall, don't you, about the littlest Perscough boys?"

"Measles," I said.

"Yes, indeed. The day before they were stricken they were playing pirates, and guess what was the booty? An old Chinese lacquer box of their mother's that had been a birthday present from one of her cousins, and that she had always declared she detested. Well, as it happened, the boys forgot it in the woods. It was a couple of weeks before Mrs. Perscough discovered it missing and, instead of being indifferent to its loss, as the boys thought she would be, with typical motherly perversity she had the house turned topsy-tipsy to look for it and went on and on about how it was a gift from her dearest cousin and how valuable it was and so on. You can see that it's imperative that the box be found, returned to the house, and planted ingeniously under a tumbled cushion in an antechamber before it's been discovered that the boys ever had it out of the house! Since they're not well enough yet to travel out of doors, I'm to find the box. They've even provided us with a treasure map."

The lane had narrowed to a wide, uneven cowtrack, bordered on two sides by a deep, quiet woods. Honeysuckle flowed across the track like tendrils of fog and wood pigeons cooed among the branches. We slowed to a walk and studied the crumpled scrap that Ellen had drawn from her reticule.

The map was a funny little diagram, with many scratchy lines and Xs and box-shaped buildings with chimneys giving forth a screw of smoke. Edgehill faces to the east, but the map had marked it facing west and there was an ink blot and lopsided star below that located the lacquer box by an area titled "Palace of the Dead Arches (ruin)."

Ellen chuckled at my expression. "Never fear, I know the place well. It's an old Roman villa on the hill crest. It was burned down more than a thousand years ago by the Saxons, or the Jutes, or whoever. All that's left is rubble, but you can see one of the mosaic floors and the line of a wall. People used to go up there for picnics. That's all stopped now, though, since Isabella's older brother died there. Come to think of it, he would be your cousin!"

"How did he die?"

"In a word—he was eaten."

"That was three words," I pointed out in an unsteady voice. We passed Caesar, digging in a foxhole beside the track. "What ate him?"

"A large—thing. They never found out for sure and as I understand it, th-the er—body was so mangled that they wouldn't have known it *was* Frederick except that there were the remains of the red coat he was last seen wearing."

The air changed as we entered the deep woods, the fresh smell of spring giving way to the dank, fertile odor of the deep forest.

"We're going right to the spot, are we?" I made my voice tremble as if in terror and was rewarded with a laugh.

"Oh, Liza, you're a p-peach. Whatever did I do before you came to Edgehill? Have no fear. The creature hasn't been heard from since, aside from a few farmers saying they've heard howls late at night. You know how country people are!"

We rode without talking. The spongy forest floor cushioned the hoofbeats of our horses and above us came the eerie whistle of the breeze and creak of sawing branches. Many trees were still bare of new yearly growth, and the limbs speared the sky above the path at sharp, jutting angles.

Ellen's face was deadly serious when she spoke again. "To be perfectly honest—no, I shouldn't tell you this, probably. I don't know. But then you might hear it from someone else sometime and . . . the truth is, Liza, there was a rumor at the time that Frederick's murder was done by Lord Brockhaven."

My hands clamped on the reins so forcefully that Kory jumped and lifted his forelegs from the ground in protest. When he had grown calm, I said, "That doesn't surprise me a bit. I've always suspected that Brockhaven could eat someone alive."

Ellen giggled. "I meant that there were some who thought he ordered Caesar to do it. Brockhaven had not only dog, but motive, you see. Today must be your day to see the family linen aired! Would you like the story?"

"I have the feeling that I'd better. The more I know . . ."

"Quite! The whole story centered around Isabella, or at least, it might have. Before she married Vincent, she was the belle of the county. No, more than that. She took the season in London and was an enormous success there too. Men were mad after her! Duels were fought over who would lead her out to dance. Poems were written about her hair. She was courted and sought out and admired—you can't imagine what it was like. She was the *rage*. She could have had her pick from half the eligible bachelors in the kingdom, and who do you think she wanted? Brockhaven! It's not to wonder, really, when one considers. He's wild and a little crazy and cruel and tender and handsomer than . . . well, you know how handsome he is. Isabella's parents were horrified! This was before Brockhaven came into the title and his income was minimal—not near enough to support Bella, who's renowned for her extravagance. Besides, Brockhaven's reputation was enough to set your hair on end. Isabella's family wanted her to take Vincent, who was just about your model suitor. Elegant, attractive, very upstanding, and most of all—*rich*."

The lane met a slow stream bordered with a ribbon of green algae, and we crossed single file over an arched bridge carved with stone elves spewing fruit from grotesquely open mouths. About us were an ancient stand of oaks, gnarled and massive, their trunks circled with shelflike growths of toadstools.

"Whatever her parents might have thought," Ellen continued, "Isabella did everything *but* have a ring put through her nose and command Brockhaven to lead her around like a tame sow. Then, that September, the parson caught Isabella and Brockhaven together in the muniment room, of all places, at Chad, and they were doing a lot more than kissing, let me tell you, because the parson had a *fit*! The servants all heard him yelling, so the story was well spread by nightfall and everyone expected to hear their engagement announced the next morning. But the next morning, Frederick was found eaten."

"If it was Lord Brockhaven that did it, then why Frederick? Why not—the parson?"

"Exactly! It would have been more in character! Yet rumor said that Brockhaven ordered Frederick's death to be rid of the fellow so that Isabella could claim her brother's property. Let me tell you, Liza, that if ever there was a man that Brockhaven would have been happy to murder, it was Isabella's brother, Frederick. If you think that Alex and Vincent don't cheery well together, then you should have seen Alex and Frederick! Freddy was that loathsome type of man who whips his horses bloody, and slaps the laundry wenches if his collars don't come out snowy white, and pulls the whiskers out of poor old marmots he catches in the woods."

"He sounds terrible," I said, looking down as Caesar shot past at a gallop.

"Oh, the veriest blackguard. Even so, Isabella was very fond of him for some reason that no one can ever fathom. She wasn't a bit happy about his being eaten, and it might have been that she suspected Brockhaven for plotting it that caused her to accept Vincent's suit. No one really knows what happened between Alex and Bella, but regardless, one year later, Isabella was wed to Vincent. They'd only been married a matter of months when the previous Lord Brockhaven and his three sons were killed in that dreadful boating accident and Brockhaven got the title *and* money. That was the last rumor about Alex as murderer you ever heard! Society couldn't wait to fawn and toady and cringe at his feet like an overpampered dog pack. I'm not saying that Alex didn't cast a cynical eye at human nature before that, but after . . ." Ellen snapped her hand expressively to show it was futile to describe in words the depths of Lord Brockhaven's contempt for his fellow creatures.

With sudden drama, the path emptied into a sun-flooded meadow, and sleeping under Apollo's fiery ball was the roofless remains of an ancient villa. Heaps of masonry rubble dotted the ground and broken colonnades jutted upward from a snarl of vine and weeds. A pair of wood pigeons had been feeding near one of the low chipped walls, and they exploded into the air with a roar of feathers as we slid off our horses.

Ellen pulled away the brush to show me the designs inlaid on the remaining patches of a mosaic floor, and I saw a pheasant, one gangly foot lifted to scratch his head, and ten yards away, Pan's face bearded in drooping leaves.

It was a wonderful place to explore, the stuff of legend and dreams. In spite of the painful secrets I had learned that day about my guardian, I was able to rest my mind in this peaceful haven. Here, it was easy to look once more through the awed eyes of a child.

As it happened, the lacquer box was easy to find. The boys had hidden it inside an arched dent in the pockmarked wall and there it had remained, undisturbed save for a light speckling of mud, splashed up, no doubt, from last week's rain.

I could see that Ellen was anxious to take it to the Perscough boys and put their fears to rest, so I told her to go on, since I hadn't intended to accompany her there anyway. I would stay and enjoy the quiet of the glen.

Ellen rode off with a comic flutter of her handkerchief as farewell, and I settled into the feathery shade of a walnut, taking off my bonnet to rest against the tree's gray-ribbed bark. The Romans had introduced these trees to Britain, so my father said, planting them for the nuts as well as beauty, and it was pleasant to sit under this one and wonder if it had grown from the direct line planted two thousand years ago to grace the villa's garden. Absently, I crushed the leaves from a fallen twig and rubbed the juice over my skin, as Grandmother had taught me as protection against the sun. I closed my eyes, deep breathing the thick, nutty bouquet of walnut. It had been a long time, so it seemed, since I had lain out of doors in the heart of a forest, and I fell to sleep at once, as though cradled in my mother's arms.

I awoke suddenly, but not quickly enough to catch the memory of the sound that had disturbed me. A glance around the glen told me that nothing had changed here. Kory was nibbling idly at the new growth of a goat willow about twenty yards from where I lay, and Caesar had settled companionably near, his chin resting on his great paws. They looked peaceful, and yet, as the sleep ebbed from my eyes, I realized that the ears of the animals were erect and intent.

I stumbled gracelessly to my feet and faced the dark, tangled wall of the forest.

"Hello!" I said. "Is anyone there?"

My only answer was the humid breath of the wind.

There was the small scrape of a misplaced pebble behind me. I turned and saw Caesar coming toward me at a slow, stiff-legged pace, the cords on his shoulders taut and his ruff lifted like a porcupine's quills. Beside me he stopped and stared with me into the green shield of leaves. He had taken a scent. Together we waited.

Suddenly the peaceful glen was ripped by an inhuman, piercing shriek, ragged and hoarse and hungry, that ended on a death-rattle purr. Never had I heard such a bitter, unworldly wail. It came again and went on until the very air seemed to vibrate with torment.

In a flash of muscle and bone, Caesar tore into the underbrush, cutting a path like a low-flying cannonball. When I could no longer see him, I could still hear the crash of his progress and the echo of his angry howls.

Without being able to see, I knew the moment Caesar met the nightmare beast. The wild, raging snarls sliced through the muting foliage, and there was a roar that sounded like a battle of demons. My spine turned to ice as gust after gust of savage, demented growls split the meadow until at last there was a clear, triumphant yodel that sank into a steady rumble that I knew belonged to

Caesar, and the sound of another, heavier body making its stumbling way off into the forest's depths.

I had barely stopped trembling more than an hour later when Caesar and I reached the orchard's edge. I set Kory to a canter down one of the smooth, grassy concourses that split the orchard like spreading seams. All I could think of was getting home—funny that I would think of Edgehill as home—when Caesar was off with a joyful puppylike yip down one of the narrow alleys that divide the fruit trees into ordered rows. There was a note of exasperation in my voice as I called Caesar back. I might as well have saved the effort, for the dog dove out of sight with the quick wag of a tail. He could have got home very well on his own, I knew, but a sense of obligation for his gallantry in the wood caused me to swing Kory around with the pressure of one knee and set out after the mastiff.

The moment I reached the planting of naturalized bulbs that bordered the last row of fruit trees, I realized that I had made a mistake. There was Caesar dancing on his thick hind legs, looking for all the world like a trained bear, his sloppy tongue flowing out sideways from his wide, black gums. The object of this ecstatic performance was Lord Brockhaven.

You could see that he had been out inspecting the fields, for he was dressed in stone-colored buckskins with his shirt most improperly laid open at the neck. It was the kind of casualness and disregard for social amenities that Lady Gwen deplored, but with saintly resolve never mentioned—to his face. The wind had disordered his hair with a lover's touch and had teased a flush of color over his cheekbones. Naked daylight did nothing to burn away the haunting attractions that candlelight gave Brockhaven. If anything, he looked better.

Behind him, there was his big roan stallion, cross bags crammed with rolled planting diagrams and pale green specimens from the spring growth. When the roan saw Kory, it laid back its thin ears and nickered with calculated malice. The grooms had told me that Brockhaven's stallion hadn't welcomed Kory's admittance to the stables.

Lord Brockhaven heard the roan and looked up.

It was his first sight of me in the garment conventional to women of his station and culture and, while I must admit that he looked his fill, there was nothing in his expression to suggest that his opinion of me was warmer. By gypsy standards, I was untidy; by gorgio's, a mess. His gaze raked me, missing, I was sure, not a single detail of my disheveled appearance. My skirts were dotted with crumbles of gray bark, my gloves so soiled that no doubt they'd forgotten how it had felt to be white. My hair was loose and down my back, and my hat—what had happened to my hat? Oh, yes, I had left it under the walnut tree. I was convinced his look of disgust was occasioned by my slovenliness. I was wrong.

He made a gesture that I had seen gorgios do when they mean you'd better get over here right now. When I reached him, he said coldly, "Where's your accompaniment?"

I was grieved that I had made him angry with me, and more than a little frightened of him, but his tone, on top of the terror I had suffered at the Roman villa, was too much.

"I didn't know that I needed an accompaniment, my lord," I said, trying to equal the frigidity of his voice. "I intended riding, not singing in a chamber concert."

As soon as the words were out, I wished them unsaid. A slattern, a hoyden, and now, unbecomingly pert was the way I must appear to him. I thought he would make a caustic remark to show me that when it came to dueling with the tongue, I was a pale amateur when compared to him. He did not, though. Lord Brockhaven was as proficient at staying to the point as he was at avoiding it when he felt the need. He stuck with the subject, but altered his strategy.

"Which one of my grooms is so unhappy in my employ that he takes the liberty of sending you out unaccompanied?"

My remorse was instant and genuine. Brockhaven's servants were extraordinarily fortunate in their circumstances and they knew it. Not only were their hours of duty meted at a reasonable schedule—a rarity, in our age—but they were very comfortably housed and generously paid. I had not encountered a single man or woman who was not happy in his lot, and extraordinarily loyal to Brockhaven. They bore him an affection which was hard to understand on the surface of it, especially when you considered the way he barked out orders at everyone. It might have confused me if Ellen hadn't told me about his sending the gardener's bright, eldest son to the university, or paying the way to the mountains for his old tutor's daughter, when she was taken with consumption. There was security at Edgehill, and hope, and I wanted no one to lose that for my error.

"It wasn't their fault," I said. "Ellen and I snuck out."

"Where is she?"

"We split up. She went on to visit the little Perscough boys. I . . . I am sorry that I've made you angry."

Brockhaven's lips curved into a sort of smile. "I suppose you are, but I'll lay blame where blame's due. Ellen's up to her old tricks. I wondered how long it would be before she began corrupting you. Just don't do it again."

"As you wish, my lord," I said in a stilted tone.

"Liza . . . Get down."

I stared at him blankly. "Now? Do you mean get off my horse?"

"Of course that's what I mean." His voice had a trace of impatience. "What other possible construct could you have put on what I said? Dismount. I want to talk to you, and it might as well be here as anywhere else."

I wasn't so sure I agreed with him, but I slid from Kory's back and gave him a pat that meant he was free to wander nearby. It was more than I could manage, to stand there staring up at him. I began to walk forward through the soft grass, through thousands of crocuses that stained the meadow in shades of pink, purple, and white like puddles of spilled watercolors. Brockhaven fell into step beside me.

"How's your hand?" he said.

"My—?"

"Where you were cut on the trap. Is it healing well?"

I stopped and looked down at my palm, and then turned it up to show him. He took my palm in his hands, studied the wound's fading impression, and curled and uncurled my fingers several times.

"Looks good. Does it hurt when I do this? Make a fist. Does that hurt? Can you use it now?"

"Yes, thank you. It's fine." I tried to smile and sound light. "I guess Grandmother was wrong. Gorgio medicine won't kill you after all."

He made a short noise in his throat, as he does sometimes when things amuse him. "Depending upon the physician. Do you hate the food still?"

"No. I'm growing accustomed. I don't eat the slimes, of course."

"Slimes?"

"The slippery things. The eggs. The milk. I don't understand how it is that English *adults* can drink that as though they were babes at their mother's—" I blushed, took back my hand, and went back to walking. "Never mind." I swallowed. "Lady Gwen says that I shall go to church with her on next Sunday."

"Good Lord. I never thought of that. Are you a pagan?"

"Grandmother followed the Old Religion. Father believed in the Bible and taught me to read it, though Grandmother made rude comments about it. She said that it was too full of violence and that gorgios like it for that because they are fierce people, always having a war. What's so funny?"

"My civilization, through your eyes. Tell me about the old religion."

I thought a moment, then said in a serious voice, "There's not a practice to it, like going to church or prayers at certain times of the day. It's more like a set of beliefs. In the beginning, you see, there was a great . . . how do you say it—an absence of anything?"

"Vacuum?"

"Yes! A vacuum. And inside this great vacuum there was a second emptiness—a smaller void—although size had no meaning at that time, you understand. The smaller void was the slumbering mind of God. The sleeping brain began to dream. Each dream became a spark. Each spark was drawn deep into the center of the nothingness, and the center grew and grew until it was an immense fiery ball that exploded outwards, with every flaming ember cooling as it traveled. The gods of good and evil were born and the emptiness was filled, yet all exists only in the dreams of the sleeping God."

A low, flat-topped stone wall threaded between the crocus meadow and a field planted in barley. The wall was thick, gray, and lichen-encrusted—the perfect sort for wall-walking. I set my hands on the top ledge, swinging my feet after me, and stood up with one arm outstretched for balance as I walked. With the other I held up the heavy, dragging skirts of my riding dress. I glanced down at Brockhaven and was relieved to see that he was smiling.

"There's no end to your accomplishments," he said. "Were men born from the explosion of the fireball also?"

"No, Moshto, O puro devel—that's the god of life—was the maker of Man. Shall I tell you?"

"Please."

A smile began to bloom on my lips. "Moshto made First Man from clay, and laid him in the sun-kiln to bake, but you see Moshto was so excited about Man that he couldn't wait until the baking time was done, so he pulled First Man from the kiln too early, while he was still all white and doughy. Moshto said, 'Ugh!' and was very disappointed. Moshto was too kindhearted to destroy First Man, though, so he put him down to live in Europe."

Brockhaven and I exchanged amiably wicked grins.

"For Second Man," I went on, "Moshto tried to be more patient, so he left Man in and left Man in. This time he waited too long, being overcautious after the first bad attempt, so that when Second Man came out of the kiln, he was a bit overdone. Still, he looked awfully nice, and

Moshto was very pleased. Second Man he set down in Africa, and Moshto almost stopped there. There was one tiny piece of life clay left though, and Moshto couldn't bear to let it go to waste, so he finally decided, 'Oh, well, why not?' and put Third Man into the sun-kiln. By this time, Moshto was quite an expert. He pulled Third Man out when he was baked *just* right and was wonderfully handsome, and Moshto was so pleased that he made rainbows all over the world and put Third Man down everywhere there was a rainbow. And that was the first of the gypsies."

Brockhaven looked so good when he laughed. You could only wish that he would do it more often. He had an attractive way of laughing, open, unself-conscious, and effortless.

Staring admiringly at a man is no help when you're wall-walking; I stumbled over a loose stone and had to jerk my hips back to keep from toppling over. My father's medallion banged against my chest, and reminded me of something I had been wanting to ask him.

"If you would be so good as to tell *me* something, my lord . . . ? I wondered if you might explain the significance of the Saracen on my medallion, if you know it."

"Ah, the Saracen. Do you always wear the medal? I see. It was cast in Asia Minor during the Crusades, and the Saracen represents the hundreds of Arabs slain by an ancestor, one Sir Oswin, in battles to liberate the Holy Land. Sir Oswin never made it back to England. His page boy returned with the medallion in a party connected with King Richard and no doubt there's an ancestor of the Saracen tramping the streets of Constantinople with a medallion cast in Sir Oswin's image. There. You've reached the end of your wall, my dear. Let me help you down."

I had indeed reached the end, but somehow the idea of being lifted down by him was beyond bearing because it would mean he would put his hands on me and when he put his hands on me, I always felt like my stomach was floating to my throat, and the sensation was so intense that I always felt sure that he could sense it and so it was too embarrassing. Before he could offer again, I said, "No, thank you. I'll jump!"

So I jumped, meaning to land on the grass beside a little leafy bush on the opposite side of the wall, but because I was nervous, I missed my mark and landed smack in the bush. My usual luck was with me. The bush was a thorn-bush.

"Ya-a-ow!" I screamed. Brockhaven vaulted gracefully over the wall and pulled me out of the bush with me screaming, "Ow! Ow! Ow!" all the while.

"Of all the stupid things!" he said. "Quit wiggling. You're only making it worse for yourself. I'm going to carry you over there to that clump of trees behind the field. We have a well there. The thorns will come out more easily if you soften them with water."

In less than a minute, Brockhaven was setting me down under the drooping curtain of a weeping willow in rich, silky grass high enough to hide a cat. He drew a full pail fresh from the well and, tossing my skirts up past my knees with remarkable nonchalance, he doused my legs with an icy splash of well water. I gasped like a trout and fell back on the grass with a groan.

"It got your mind off the thorns, didn't it?" he asked, starting to pull them from my legs.

"Ya-ouch! Ouch!" was all the answer he got from me. He kept pulling and, in a moment or two, sent another frigid shower of water over my thorny legs.

"Cold water's analgetic," he informed me cheerfully.

"Well, it's not—ow!—very effective."

"Close your eyes," he suggested, with a grin. "Let your imagination run unfettered. Try this: You're at a gypsy encampment, and over the hot blue flames of an open fire hangs an iron kettle filled with your favorite gypsy food. You can smell the aroma. Let me see. There's black beans, and white beans marinated in vinegar, and sharp peppers, and black olives, swimming in seasame oil and onions, oh, and goose blood . . . What did you say?"

"I said, how many more of them are there?"

"Thorns? Fifteen, maybe twenty. Would you like my handkerchief to bite on?"

I unclenched my teeth enough to say, "I wonder if you'd be this witty if it were you with the thorns in your legs."

"Tut, tut, sweetheart. Let it be a lesson to you to wear boots next time you leave the house. Here, try this. Close your eyes and count to a hundred. Concentrate very hard! I promise I'll be finished before you reach the one hundred and first."

"I had reached fifty-three when he said, "That's all I can find. Have I missed anything?"

I sat up slowly. "Yes," I said, "you have. If you would be kind enough to turn your back to me for a couple of seconds, I will endeavor to rid myself of them."

"Oh, it's like that, is it?" Giving me a last satirical grin, he stood, scooped up the bucket and, turning his back to me, carried the bucket back to the well.

Pushing my skirts up a little higher, I gingerly plucked three remaining thorns from the inside of my thigh and one from my rump.

"That's the last of them," I choked out. Eager and clumsy, I threw my skirt to cover my scratched limbs and rolled forward to my knees. I was pushing up with my palms, taking the weight on my shoulders, and had almost achieved an upright posture when a jackrabbit came whipping through the grass in front of me like a bolt of lightning. I started, stepped backward onto the side of my foot, and fell back hard into the spongy grass.

"I had thought," said Brockhaven, coming back toward me, "that gypsies were particularly renowned for their sureness of foot. Any bones broken?" He stretched out a hand to help me up.

I was about to assure him that my fall had borne me no ill consequences when Caesar, hot on the rabbit's trail, came lunging through the grass. I had forgotten about him, and it was obvious that he had forgotten about us as well. Oblivious to everything but the jackrabbit, the mastiff brushed past his master, hitting him just below the knees.

Caught off guard, Brockhaven was pitched forward beside me in a nest of grass and butter-colored marsh marigolds.

His fall had so little in common with my conception of an earl's dignity that I stared and then felt the tickle of laughter begin to rise in my throat. My voice was thick with suppressed mirth as I said, "I was about to tell you, my lord, that in falling I suffered no hurt."

Brockhaven raised himself on his elbows with some deliberation. "I'm so relieved."

I was pleased to see that a smile had touched his lips. It was not his usual sort of smile, either, for it was without its faint, ever-present edge of mockery. Instead it was warm and amused as any boy tumbled by his puppy. Small bits of dried leaves and tiny light stems had webbed themselves into his hair and . . .

"A flower."

"I beg your pardon?" he said.

"One of the flowers has been caught in your hair, my lord." My voice quivered with laughter.

He began to brush wordlessly through his dark hair with his fingers, which served to further entangle the golden petals in their glossy bonds.

Perhaps it was the brightness and heat of the spring sun, perhaps some magic drug carried airborne in the glittering pollen, but I began to laugh like a child, made silly and young by the sudden shared ignominy of being hurled earthward by the chase of a bounding mastiff. What unthinking strain it had been to be every moment on guard, and what blessed rest it was to be fleetingly joined in unembarrassed intimacy with this powerful man, this near stranger. Later I wasn't sure what made me so bold, but truly my intention was only to do him a service. Reaching up my hand to his hair, I plucked the fragile blossom from its inky net. Laughter made me clumsy, and my fingers brushed by accident against his hard cheek, and I felt his skin, smooth and warm beneath my fingertips.

The contact appeared to startle him as much as it did me. His expression became intent and so unfathomable that if I could have captured his image and studied it at length, I would not have been able to guess at his thoughts. He said my name carefully, as though it was an easily misunderstood word in a complex foreign tongue. My laughter fled, and in its place came a fragile calm that hovered like golden ribbons of sunlight streaming through the quiet center of a gale. I was aware of the tongues of warm color that lit his black, tumbling curls, of his eyelashes, thick and dark against the crystal blueness of his eyes, and his lips, well-drawn and firm with their elusive hint of gentleness.

Shame burned in my heart that I could lie and stare so closely at him, and I felt the need to look away. He stopped me with the touch of his hand, his fingers resting lightly on one side of my face, his thumb resting on the other. His hand made no attempt to imprison me, though I felt a bondage as forceful as an iron vise. It would have embarrassed me to pull away like a flirting barmaid. Grasping at indecision, I shut my eyes, hoping that he would stand and walk away.

"Well, that's something." There was a quizzical note in his voice. "And I'm not even pulling thorns out. I suppose you know about those giant birds in Africa. The ones with the very long necks . . ."

"I know. The giraffe."

"Giraffe isn't a bird," he pointed out amicably. "You weren't listening."

It was hard to listen and hard to pay attention with him so close to me, with his fingers caressing my skin.

"I was referring," he said, "to the flightless birds, taller than men, that stick their heads in the sand when they are frightened."

"Ostriches," I whispered through dry lips, my eyes beginning to ache behind the squeezed-shut lids. "They don't really hide their heads. My father had a book by an Italian diarist who said they did not."

"Lord. Italian diaries," he said. I felt his thumb trace the outside line of my lips, and the fingers he had rested on my cheek spread out over my face, his fingertips gently touching my closed eyelids. "When I look at you, I won-

102

der . . ." He stopped, as though he had been thinking aloud and his thoughts were nothing he would have liked to offer me.

I shivered, an involuntary shudder which shook me under his hands; I wished above all else for control, but it did not seem possible.

"Are you cold, little one?" he said. I could tell from his eyes that he knew the trembling came not from an external chill, but from the fire within me that made the air under the willow seem cool by contrast. But to spare me, he lied. "We'd better get up from the ground. Let me help you."

My body seemed stiff and clumsy as he took me by the arms, bending over me, and the strong upward pull of his grip became the physical manifestation of the heady flow of an attraction. Harmony met motion; I managed to get to my knees, and he was on his knees with me.

His lips took mine tenderly, moving slowly and with langor across my swollen skin, soothing and burning where they touched, tender, yet with brutal effect, for I was ripped from my innocence and thrust, shivering and unprotected, into a new plane of existence. With my senses focusing first on the insistent pressure of his questing kisses, then spreading to encompass his hands at my back, our bodies pressed into each other, the hot brilliant light of the sun, the breeze stirring the grass around us, the birdsong gliding through the trees. And then we were kissing, and I responded as if my life depended on it, as if my body, my mouth, could not get close enough to his.

His arm grew tight around me and held me hard. Sharp, dizzy seconds came and fled, looping together like gold links on a bracelet chain. I couldn't seem to hold onto who I was, or where I was, or what this meant. I knew only the prickling texture of the air, the drooping green canopy of the willow above me, and the blinding need to be touched and quenched by the man holding me.

My past life seemed like a dream of happy but unknowing solitude, and my blood coursed to the tune of ancient rhythms piped by the Mother of All Things. There was no room in this burning heaven opened to me at his touch for such mundane processes as thought and common sense.

He lifted his lips from me and drew back. Fear began to grow in me as a cool breeze touched my lips, so recently warm beneath his. A cloud passing across the sun dimmed the light, and his face fell into shadow. Slowly my blood cooled, and my brain filled with the underroar of a grotesque, babbling hindsight. Had I gone mad, to kiss with him like that?

It couldn't have been love that had drawn him to me. Lord Brockhaven was not the man to fall abruptly in love. There had been so many other women before me that he had held and kissed and loved with his body, without his heart; his caresses had not been those of an inexperienced boy.

I bent down my head, afraid of what I might see in his face. Scorn? Indifference? Or that unsettling, unreadable, but intensely powerful expression that I had seen as his lips had raised from mine? The soft whistle of the spring breeze filled in the silence, and the high-pitched call of a green woodpecker came from the woods behind us. And then even the breeze stopped.

Brockhaven made a slight motion, and I tensed, afraid that he was going to force me to look at him. But that wasn't his intention; he was standing up from the ground and walking a few steps away. I felt cold, ridiculous, and alone, like a lone bookend, and the spring wind dried the moistness from my lips, leaving them parched and sore.

I found my feet somehow, raising from the ground like a jerky wooden puppet.

My voice was a muted whisper. "I shall get Kory . . ." Any action was better than to stand in his painful scrutiny. On shaky knees I began to walk toward the orchard. I was brought up sharp by the hard grasp of his hand on my arm.

"Don't panic, child—it won't happen again," he said in a strained voice.

"No," I said hollowly. I had been allowed to visit

104

Heaven, then exiled with the gates permanently locked to me.

"It was my mistake," he said, on a note of repressed anger. He stood close—too close to me. "A stupid mistake. Put it out of your mind."

A fierce pebbling of hurt raced through my body at his words. I know it must have shown in my face. How could it not have? But my vision was so paled by tears that I could not see his expression. His hand left my arm and gently brushed my shoulder as if to hold me. Swinging away from him, I ran toward the orchard with Caesar reappearing from nowhere to run after me, yapping playfully at my heels.

Chapter Six

As I cantered into the yellow stone courtyard that fronted the stables, I saw Ellen in the corner by the mounting block, handing the reins from her mare to a stable boy. I had hardly time to say, "Ellen, please, I must talk with you," when a smartly trimmed coach nipped around the drive and passed to where it would stop in front of the columned carriage port.

"My mother!" cried Ellen.

"Do you think she saw us?" I asked.

"No doubt of it," she returned. "Brace for Trouble."

Trouble there was, though nothing nearly as bad as I supposed. Lady Gwen called us to her dressing room, poured us both a cup of tea, and favored us with a gentle lecture on why a lady must always take a groom with her when she goes riding. It discourages gentlemen acquaintances from taking liberties, provides protection against wandering vagabonds, aid if she should be thrown from the saddle and—heaven forbid!—take an injury. Our penance would be to dust Lady Gwen's collection of marble fruit for a month, which was no small chore, since there were one hundred and fifty-seven pieces of it, sixty-two of which were grapes.

When we had achieved the privacy of my bedroom, Ellen confessed to me that she thought we had brushed through it pretty well, considering, and added, "What were you going to talk to me about? I hope that nothing's happened!"

"That's just it," I said, "something has."

Before I could get out a single word more, there was a knock at my door and Goudette, who is Lady Gwendolyn's lady's maid, came into my room, bearing a huge, flower-painted wooden tray that was filled to overflowing with what Goudette identified rather alarmingly as the articles with which she would make my toilet. Ellen kindly explained that Goudette meant that she'd come to furbish me up for tonight. Had I forgotten? This was the first night since I had come to stay that we would dine formally, with Brockhaven and Robert, instead of ladies only in the morning room.

I believe I answered, "Oh."

Ellen asked if she should leave, and I said no, not knowing what the formidable Goudette had in mind.

With quick, artistic fingers, Goudette pinned my hair on my head and ordered me to strip off my clothing, which was the bare beginning to the painful and embarrassing procedure of having the sun-browned and walnut-stained skin bleached off my body. I had to stand on a thick square of linen holding slabs of cucumber over my eyes while Goudette rubbed caustic creams on my skin and then scraped them off with handfuls of sand. To remove the sand, she scrubbed me with sea sponges and lavender soap in a tub of cold water. It was an unpleasant business, and not one that gave me any kind of atmosphere to tell Ellen about the things that had passed between me and Lord Brockhaven. Instead I told her about the animal that Caesar had chased away from me in the woods. Ellen was lively and fascinated and funny in her remarks, and I slowly began to lose some of the utterly desolate feeling that had preyed on me during the ride back to Edgehill.

As Ellen and I speculated on what animal it might have been, Goudette produced more creams, alcohol-based softeners that stung my rubbed, raw skin. When she was done, I was white and pink, tingling and soft. Goudette

108

was ecstatic at the result, but for myself, I couldn't see the reason for her eulogies. Really, who cares about having light-colored skin? We gypsies say, "The darker the berry, the sweeter the juice."

Goudette was not done. With a flourish, she unveiled a selection of shining, silver instruments that looked as though they would have felt quite at home in a medieval torture chamber, and informed me that these were to "do" my nails. Probably that's what the inquisitioners told their victims when they came to rip out their nails by the root. It took the better part of ten minutes for Ellen and Goudette to convince me that nail trimming, and filing, and buffing weren't painful. I discovered that they were right; it wasn't painful, only time-consuming. I could have bitten off the lot in the time it took Goudette to fix one nail. It was not easy to get used to, the habit gorgios have of turning the simplest activity into a ceremony.

Goudette's final deed was to pluck my eyebrows, which was surely an act of unparalleled savagery. By the time the final piece of excess hair had been torn from my flinching brow, it was clear to me that whatever luxuries the ladies of the gorgio aristocracy may possess are heavily counteracted by miseries that they must endure in the name of fashion. Perhaps it was Moshto's way of making all things equal.

I was most relieved when it came near to dinnertime, and Goudette was forced to stop her dreadful acts of beautification. I never thought I would be so happy to at last don the strange, revealing gown Lady Gwendolyn's dressmaker had designed for me. Other than the full-skirted riding habit, it was the first time I was to wear one of the gorgio's dresses. It was not for me to question the taste of Lady Gwendolyn, but to me it was a poor thing of a dress, not only pale in color, but immodest as well. Gypsy colors are vivid and rich, blues caught from the early dawn sky, green like spring grass after a rain, reds that matched the skin of an apple. The color of the dress I would wear to dinner was a blue as weak and cold as a low moon. The cut of the neckline displayed far more of my breasts than was seemly, and the exquisite drape of the material clung as though someone had damped it, revealing curves I hadn't known I possessed, and countering the notion that clothing was supposed to cover the body and not expose it. What good is a dress that would show the soil after carrying one load of firewood, or be torn to pieces if worn while helping to push the wheel of a cart out of a rut? As I gazed critically into the mirror at my own reflection, I wasn't sure why Goudette should stare at me so, and "ohhh" and sigh; or why when Lady Gwendolyn entered the dressing room, she should stop at the door and exclaim, "My dear girl, how proud your father would be of you!" My discomfiture was completed in the hallway when Ellen whispered to me "Liza, you're a . . . a . . . you're far prettier than Isabella!"

The dining hall was an immense cube of a room, with four pairs of massive crystal chandeliers and wheat-colored walls. The color was picked up again in the upholstery, and the luxurious made-to-order Turkish carpets that spanned the room's sixty-foot length. Great golden bowls of daffodils added periodic bursts of sunny color throughout, complementing the fires which burned in two of the four fireplaces, driving the chill of rain that had begun to fall outside.

Even without my shocking encounter with Lord Brockhaven this afternoon, I could hardly have felt at my ease in this exquisite chamber.

The lightly carved double doors were so wide that I could enter the room, flanked on either side by Ellen and Lady Gwen, like a pair of gentle sheepdogs herding a bashful lamb. Stepping inside, the first thing I saw, really *saw*, was Lord Brockhaven. An urge swept me to bolt from the room, hide in the stables with Kory, and cover myself with dry straw. Two years would have been too soon to see Lord Brockhaven, after our kiss under the willow, and thinking that made me remember his lips, his hands, the way he had looked at me, and then through me. For the space of a heartbeat, I had the terrible fear that I might begin to cry like an idiot. I tried desperately to suppress the tears, and the hurt, and the agonizing wish to find myself in Lord Brockhaven's arms again, and regretted that I had not made time to be alone during the afternoon, so that I might have spent my tears and been rid, at least, of those.

Near Lord Brockhaven stood Robert, dressed in a blue coat for evening and holding a delicately etched glass filled with some expensive, hard spirit that I supposed must be brandy. Ellen had told me he had a taste for it.

I focused on Robert, to avoid looking at Lord Brockhaven. To my dismay, I discovered that Robert was studying my face strangely, in the fashion of one who senses a distress and is wondering what could have caused it. It worried me that he might soon be making guesses, so I forced my lips into what I hoped was the semblance of a brisk and cheerful smile.

With a quick, nervous gesture, Robert set his glass on a side table and came to take my hand, though when he spoke it was to Lady Gwen.

"Why is it that the girl looks more exotic now than she did dressed as a gypsy?" he said. "The contrast between her hair and skin . . . and those enormous brown eyes. We'll see a lot of hearts breaking over this one."

"I hope we shall," said Gwen with a smile. "I think it would do Liza a great deal of good to break a few hearts. Well, Alex, what do you think of your ward?"

It was not my will to look at Brockhaven, yet somehow, my eyes were drawn to him. My heart thumped uncomfortably as his gaze joined mine. For the smallest fraction of a second, I had the odd sensation that it cost him something to meet my gaze, and yet, before that impression had registered in my brain, his blue eyes were calm and unwavering, as much a mystery as always. He ran me over with a disinterested assessment that showed not a flicker of uncertainty, as though he were cataloguing my parts for a ledger sheet as addeds and debits. Finally he gave a rueful, lopsided grin.

"She improves with bathing," he said, "like the rest of us."

"An appropriately fatherly accolade," Robert said, releasing my hand slowly. "Things will be so much calmer now that Alex has reached twenty-five—the age of the elderly immune. Gwen, may I escort you to the table? I've had notice from the kitchen that the chef's trout flambéed faster than thought, and if we don't sit down and eat it forthwith, we'll have cold fish and a hot chef."

Among other things, formal dining for the gorgios means many courses and a great superfluity of table hardware. Lady Gwendolyn had coached me so carefully on its use that if the monster from the forest had leapt into the room, I believe I would have known which fork to use to fend it off, and from which glass I might appropriately take my last sip. I was glad to have the intricacies of etiquette to concentrate on, and surely, since it was my first meal in this room, no one would think it strange if I stared at the glittering reflection of the convex looking glass over the mantel, or the elaborate garland pattern of the plaster ceiling, or even the mirrorlike, hand-rubbed surface of the dining table. I wanted to look anywhere and everywhere, except at Lord Brockhaven.

A footman set a bowl before me of brown soup made with foie gras and swimming with mushrooms as Lady Gwen began to talk to Lord Brockhaven about dressing the third best guest chamber.

"We must have *new* paper on the walls, my dear," she said, taking a silent sip from her spoon, "though I know it's an expense. We shall be receiving company, you know, as soon as the season's out in London, and we cannot put anyone in a room with water-damaged paper! If only Lord Monck had not gone to sleep with the window open during his March visit! Though how he slept through that thunderstorm is more than I can imagine."

Ellen looked at her mother with innocent surprise. "Why, Mama, d-didn't you know? Robert and Lord Monck had gone out cocking and returned quite drunk, so Betty told me, and . . ."

"That will do, Ellen!" said Lady Gwen with unruffled fi-

112

nality. "I wish you will not continue to gossip so with the servants! We shall return to the subject of the paper. Alex, if you will come to the morning room after we finish the meal, I can show you the paper samples I've selected as most appropriate. We *could* use the blue mohair flock, which can be had at nine shillings a yard but if we plan to use the Norwich crimson damask, then we will have to pay twelve shillings. Either color will do with the carpet, though I own a slight preference for the crimson. You, of course, must have the final say."

It was clear from Brockhaven's face that he little relished the prospect of having to spend time poring over sheets of wallpaper samples.

"Use the red, Gwen," he said.

"But you haven't seen it, my dear," she pointed out, "and the blue *is* more of an economy. For all I know, you may prefer it to the crimson, and if so . . ."

With a grin, Robert said, "Gwen, Alex wouldn't care if you'd paper the walls in raw cowhide, as you very well know. You can go ahead and deck the bedroom's walls in crimson with a clear conscience. If I know you, you've ordered it already!"

Lady Gwen denied it with just enough guilt in her voice to lend credence to Robert's claim.

The footman brought in the fish in Madeira sauce with green peas, artichoke soup, two quail, a custard, miniature potato soufflés, and cucumbers in white sauce, the last of which had the misfortune to remind me of Goudette's bleaching applications of the afternoon. I stared with melancholy down at my plate while Robert and Brockhaven began to talk about how the plowing was going on the forty acres in the marsh.

There was a sudden shift in the wind and big drops of water began to splash noisily against the dining room window, so the conversation turned to the weather and when that subject had been summarily exhausted, Ellen said to her mother, "Do you know, Mama, that this afternoon on her r-ride, Liza had an experience that was *too* exciting!"

I knew, of course, that she was talking about the animal

by the ruin, but Brockhaven, of course, did not. He had
been affording the dinner table conversation an interest
that even the generous would have been forced to label as
tepid, but which changed like quicksilver at Ellen's words.
Seeing his expression made me take in a breath rather
quickly and, since my mouth also contained a swallow of
lemonade, I began to cough and choke. The room erupted
into a flurry of concern, while Ellen tried to make me take
a sip of water, Robert and one of the footmen patting me
energetically on the back, and Gwen standing by to cluck
sympathetically.

Brockhaven's voice cut through the chatter of my res-
cuers, telling them to leave the girl alone, for God's sake,
and when I emerged watery eyed from behind the handkerchief Ellen had thrust into my hand, Brockhaven said
tartly that in all probability I had been more afflicted by
Robert's vigorous backpounding than by the choking.

When everyone had returned to their seats, Lady Gwen
said, "Liza, my dear, tell us, please, what happened?"

"I fell asleep by the ruin on the hill," I ventured, "and
when I awoke, there was some kind of animal hiding in
the underbrush."

"Badger, probably," said Robert from behind his bowl
of artichoke soup.

"I don't think so," I said. "Caesar attacked it, and as it
ran off, I could hear it crashing through the brush. The
sound of its progress was loud, as loud as Caesar's."

I had half-expected Brockhaven to treat my whole story
as the nervous exaggerations of a hysterical girl. Instead,
he set down his wineglass with a snap that must have
placed a severe strain on its fragile stem and looked at me
with hard, angry eyes.

"Why didn't you tell me this at once?" he snapped.
Without giving me time to answer, he asked, "You've
grown up sleeping in wagons in the forest. What do *you*
think it was?"

"I saw tracks," I said softly, "as big as a breadplate."

"Where?" asked Brockhaven sharply.

"Inside the woods, where I fol—"

Brockhaven's expression was black enough to frighten the words from my lips. But he merely said tersely, "Pray, continue."

". . . followed it," I continued. How queer it sounded in the telling. "I came to a shelf of rock and the beast's feet seemed to—to become those of a man."

Not unnaturally, my announcement caused something of a sensation. Lady Gwendolyn dropped her spoon, which speared into the soup dish and ricocheted into the middle of the table with a clatter. Robert gave a sharp whoop of laughter, and the footman standing behind him very nearly let slide to the floor an entire platter of baked minced beef.

"My dear child, what precisely are you suggesting?" said Lady Gwen.

I thought a moment before I made my answer. Then I told her seriously. "My grandmother would have said it was one of the Demon People, a man doomed by the evils of his life to rise from the grave and walk the land as a wolf."

Robert put up an eyebrow. "Liza, child, surely you don't believe in werewolves."

"N-no, of course she doesn't," managed Ellen. "B-b-but what w-was it then?"

"Lord knows. Maybe it was Caesar's tracks, several days old," said Robert.

"I don't think so," Brockhaven said. "I've been keeping Caesar close to home since the big rain last month. You remember, Robert, when David Cooper claimed a large animal attacked his sheep and carried off three of them." He stared moodily into space. "There hasn't been a wolf sighted in England for more than half a century."

"That's true," said Robert. "But what else has tracks that size? Unless . . . My God—do you think this could have any connection with whatever tore Freddy to pieces?" He grinned. "Hungry again after three years!"

There was an edge of alarm in Gwen's voice. "Robert!" The rosy patches over her cheekbones grew pale. "When

I think that Liza might have been exposed to such danger . . ."

Brockhaven directed a quelling frown at his younger brother, and turned back to Lady Gwen. "I doubt there's a connection. The hillside near the old villa is sandy, which probably exaggerated the size of the tracks. And don't forget—two weeks before Frederick was killed, there was the report of a circus in Epping having lost an African hyena; knowing Freddy, he probably came upon it in the woods and teased it until the thing turned on him. If it was the hyena, there isn't much chance that an animal that had been raised in captivity could survive this long in the wild—and without anyone catching a glimpse of it. What Caesar more than likely fought was only a big fox or a stray dog."

Though she looked much reassured, Lady Gwendolyn said, "Will you ride out tomorrow morning and look at the spot?"

"Of course," he assured her. "I'll have a patrol put on the area for a month. As for tomorrow, though, the tracks will likely be obliterated by the rain, and I doubt that we'll find anything."

"I doubt you will either," I said, irritated by his skepticism. "It's difficult to milk a running cow."

Brockhaven gave me a cold look, but said nothing, and the subject was dropped.

During dessert, over the orange Isinglass jelly, Lady Gwendolyn announced that she was sending out cards for a small soirée on Saturday next if it suited Lord Brockhaven.

"No date is suitable for a soirée as far as I'm concerned," said Brockhaven, his expression in keeping with the sentiment he expressed. "Cards to whom?"

"The Perscoughs, of course; the Aldgates . . ."

Robert interrupted, looking no more enthusiastic than his brother. "Specify on that invitation that they leave their widgeon of a daughter home."

"Certainly not!" said Lady Gwen. "We'll want to invite all the young people so Liza can begin to make friends.

The sooner she is introduced, the sooner the gossip and speculation about her will die down. I know you won't care for this, Alex, but I've invited Vincent and Isabella also. It's for Liza's sake, my dear."

Brockhaven pushed back his chair and stood up. I realized then with an inward tremble that he was looking into my eyes. I was powerless to avert my own. At length, he shrugged and said, "Why not? For Liza's sake."

Chapter Seven

Saturday was to be an emotional day for me. In the morning there was the meeting with Lord Brockhaven and a man who I learned to my apprehension was my lawyer, Mr. Cadal.

He was a younger man than I would have thought, no older than thirty-two, with small, clever eyes, a wide mouth with grayish-pink lips that were cut up-slant toward the corners, and an old white wig that he kept pushing the end of his pen under to scratch at his scalp. Wide-shouldered, short, and hard-muscled in build, he resembled a mule driver, but his manner was firm, businesslike, and not without humor. For an hour he talked to me about the land which was legally mine, until my head was aswim with words like grazing rights, and leaseholder, and subordinate clauses, and reciprocal arrangements. He showed me papers concerning a quarry he claimed was mine, full of statistics about stones moved per annum, and wound up with a complex report about two mills in my hapless possession. The Upper was a cornmill and the Lower mill made paper, and the income and operation was divided between Isabella and me in a manner of which Mr. Cadal heartily disapproved. The mill statistics proved worse than those of the quarry; how many shillings duty per cwt on scaleboard, price per bushel of tar ropes and coarse rags for making pasteboard. When at last he finished, I felt as though I had aged ten years.

"Well," said Mr. Cadal, with undimmed vigor, "I'm sure there are a thousand things that you'd like to ask me. Never hesitate to barrage me until your curiosity is completely satisfied! Please, ask your questions!"

I hadn't a single one, which I felt very guilty about. In an attempt to comply with his expectant look, I said, "Do you think I might have some tea, sir?"

Mr. Cadal stared at me as if I'd just been sick on the carpet.

"I told you, Mark," said Lord Brockhaven in a voice filled with lazy humor. "She doesn't understand. No matter what you say to her, she doesn't comprehend the idea of herself owning property. Liza, tell Mark what you said to me this morning when I tried to outline for you the purpose of Mark's visit."

Nervously, I said, "I only said that—that man never *owns* anything, he only borrows from God." I could see that Mr. Cadal was still looking at me dazedly, so I tried again. "Why do we need to own?"

"Why do we need to—? My dear young woman!"

"Does the caterpillar own the leaf on which it nibbles? Does the jay own the bush it nests in?" I asked earnestly.

"There you have it," said Brockhaven. "The concept is philosophically alien. But I'm sure you'll be able to make it clear for her, Mark."

Mr. Cadal certainly did his best. For two endless hours he did his best, though to his credit it must be put that he was kind enough to see that I had tea first.

Afterward, as I reached my bedroom, drained and weary, Goudette appeared with scissors in hand and announced her intention of cutting my hair. I wish I could say to you that I behaved with a pride that would have pleased my grandmother, and a tolerance that would have pleased my father, but instead I flew into Lady Gwendolyn's room, fluttering wildly as an overwrought sparrow, and told her that on no account was Goudette going to

120

take an inch off my hair. The fight that followed was long and vigorous. I did my best to explain to her that a gypsy maid would never willingly submit to having her hair cut, while she did her best to explain to me that the society in which I was to be introduced would view such unfashionably long hair as an uncomfortable reminder of our differences. It seems incredible, as well as a great pity, that two people who were both trying so hard to respectfully communicate their sincere beliefs could fail so miserably in making inroads in the other's resolutions. The argument ended with us both in tears.

It made matters worse that Ellen wasn't there to mediate the clash of cultures. She had ridden out to the cottage of Madame Nefare, an emigrée from France who gave Ellen her weekly language lesson. There was no one to whom I could turn. I crept miserably off to the reading room and curled up in the hard wingchair that faced into the fire, and then cried until my eyes were empty.

When I had finished, I felt warm and wet and a little drowsy. Idly I picked out a two-month-old copy of the *Lady's Monthly Museum* and thumbed through a list of paintings to be seen at the National Gallery, read "Anecdotes of Distinguished Females No. 162," and glanced through "On Domesticity." A paragraph caught my eye. It read: "The blessed bond of matrimony lifts the fair hand of affection and wipes away the tear of sensibility, exalts the mind, and solaces sorrow by a heavenly mingle of congenial souls. Oh happy state! Avaunt ye scoffers!"

The door opened and Isabella's voice came floating over the back of my chair like a hovering wasp.

"Vincent," she was saying, "I've listened to you counseling patience until I could scream!"

"Isabella, my beloved." There was an edge in Vincent's voice. "He's within his rights. If you scream, it will only succeed in making us both look foolish."

The door closed behind them. The last thing I wanted to do was stand up and make my presence known.

"We already look foolish!" she snapped. "By heaven, if you were half the man Alex is, you wouldn't be sitting there telling me to lower my voice and mind my needle! If only I'd married Brockhaven, he'd know how to protect what was rightfully his. He'd know what to do about that gypsy brat. If I had followed my heart . . ."

The fire waved into a sheet of blue flame as the opening door sent a cool draft swirling around the room. Someone else had entered my sanctuary, and I hadn't long to wait before I learned who it was.

"I could hear your dulcet tones in the hallway, Isabella, though I confess at first I thought one of the peacocks had flown in the window," said Lord Brockhaven. "How fast you are! Cadal's barely left to call on you, and here you are already. I suppose he's told you about the mill?"

"Yes, he has," ground out Isabella. "You plan to deliberately and unconscionably destroy the mill as a profitable business venture. How dare you! Grandfather's will specifies that the mill's profit is to go to me!"

"Specifically," quoted Brockhaven, " 'Be there profit from the mill, it should go to my granddaughter, Isabella.' Since your grandfather placed the management of the mill in the hands of Liza's guardian, we can assume that your grandfather had the impression that you were better at spending money than making it. What the will doesn't say is that the mill must be run at a profit. Furthermore, I'm not destroying the mill—I'm modernizing. Eventually the improvements will pay for themselves."

"No one is arguing against your improvements, Alex," said Vincent in a quietly angry voice. "It just needn't be done in one lump. Enlarging the pond, replacing the stone wheel with iron, leveling the road—these are all things that could be done gradually."

"That would be neither safe nor efficient," retorted Brockhaven with succinct finality.

At last I began to understand some of the things Mr. Cadal had been trying to tell me about the paper mill. He had been describing to me the changes that Lord Brockhaven had undertaken in its management.

Vincent's voice cut into my thoughts. "And what are the

mill workers going to do for a livelihood while the mill is closed?" he said. "They live hand to mouth as it is!"

"They live hand to mouth, do they? How iniquitous!" said Brockhaven with acid amusement. "And who was it that authorized their miserable wage? Yourself, Vincent. But as you're so concerned about the mill workers, you'll be pleased to know that I've tripled their pay."

"You can't *triple* pay!" bleated Isabella, as though she was sure that such a thing must be prohibited by law. "How can you do it?"

"Easily, if the original begins low enough," Brockhaven informed her.

"You—you revolutionary! That's how the French Revolution began, with indulgences like this! Give the rabble a finger and soon they'll want the whole hand!" Isabella's voice began to rise and the warm hardwood floor echoed with the stamp of her soft-soled shoes. "It's sacrilegious too. Yes, it is! The poor are wretched because they're sinful and lazy, and God punishes them with ill fortune."

"That's it, rave like a maniac," endorsed Brockhaven affably.

There was an indignant rustle of skirts, and when Isabella spoke again, her voice shook as though she were trying to bring it under control.

"I know what you think. That I am horrid and mean and bad-tempered! But I can't help it, Alex. It's not in my nature to be good and quiet! When I want something, I must have it! No one ever understands! Truly, Alex, this time I am not being willful. I must have the mill's profit now! You know how you always say I am too extravagant? Well, I'm trying very hard to be more frugal and that's why I must have the mill money. If I don't have it, all the money I've spent last August on my summer house will go to waste. That wouldn't be good, would it?"

"No doubt I'll regret asking—but why will the money you've spent on the summer house be wasted?" Alex asked.

"Because I can't bear to use it. You know how I planned to have teas there on warm days so I could enjoy the view from the hillock. But I hadn't properly considered. King Road runs right below, and how can one enjoy one's tea while looking at farmer boys herding their filthy, sloppy cows not thirty yards away? I've talked to our architect in London, and he says it would be perfectly feasible to cut a fifty foot tunnel through the hill underneath the present lay of the road and with a few clever plantings of trees we need never be troubled with the traffic again. It's terribly expensive to do such a thing —hundreds of guineas per foot—and without the mill profits . . ."

There was a pregnant silence, and then Brockhaven began to laugh. You could tell from the way he laughed that he was genuinely amused. As a matter of fact, I found it rather funny myself. She had said it just as if she had not a suspicion in the world of the frivolity of her idea. I was so caught up in what I was hearing that I made an inattentive move in my chair which accidentally sent *The Lady's Monthly Museum* sliding to the floor with a papery crash.

I stood immediately. Better to come forward myself than to be dragged in ignominity from my hiding.

Brockhaven was standing beside Isabella, his eyes still bright with laughter and his lips tilted up at the edges. His long fingers had been cupped on Isabella's chin, as though in a caress. She turned to face me as he took away his hand, her soft white gown floating around her like spun sugar. White ribbons wound angelically through her golden curls, but the expression on her lovely face was far other than heavenly. Vincent was exactly as I remembered him—tall, gray-eyed, and graceful, with regular, well-schooled features.

"Good afternoon," I said, despising myself for sounding so timid. "I was in the room before you entered—I couldn't seem to find a moment to announce my presence."

"I'll bet you couldn't, you little sneak," sniffed Isabella. "So you've heard it all! Well, then. I hope you intend to tell Brockhaven that he hasn't your consent for his ridiculous scheme to *ruin* a perfectly well-managed business."

"According to what I understand from Mr. Cadal," I said seriously, "Lord Brockhaven doesn't have to get my consent for any of his actions. I do think, though, that renovating the mill will be a good thing. The incoming road, Mr. Cadal told me, is quite steep, and when there is rain the horses slip dreadfully as they pull heavy wagons in and out. If a gentler grade is put in . . ."

Isabella's furious look killed my words. She strode toward me, raising her hand. I feared that she was going to strike me, but she only snapped her fingers angrily in my face.

"I care *that* for your opinion," she hammered out. "Ignorant chippy! So Alex has made you his puppet already, has he? The least he could have done for you is seen that someone gave you a haircut. You've got more wool on your scalp than a yak."

Of course it was the worse thing she could have said to me, after the argument I'd just had with Lady Gwen.

"And yet, I wouldn't trade what I have for yours," I said, with a voice contemptuous as any my grandmother had ever used. "Beauty without a heart is like an empty gourd, worth a glance in passing, but a bane to the stew."

It didn't help matters that I set Brockhaven off to laughing again. In the scene that followed, I think I might have hid my head under a seat pillow, if the wing chair had possessed a detachable one. Clearly, Isabella was not a believer in tit for tat, particularly from an upstart like myself. It was amazing how pretty she looked, even yelling at me at the top of her lungs.

I began to feel sorry I had made her so angry. She was my cousin. I had never known any other, and it would have been so comfortable, if only we could get along. And I remember how she cared for Brockhaven, and it stirred my pity because I understood what a sad fate it was to be barred from his arms.

Gathering my courage, I walked to her, put my arms around her, and said, "I'm sorry, cousin," which shocked everyone into silence long enough to allow Brockhaven to whisk me from the room and down the corridor.

When we were out of earshot, Lord Brockhaven said, "Good thing you took her by surprise or you'd have left the room with Bella's fingernails imbedded in your cheeks."

I stopped and looked up at him. "Does that mean you don't think she'll want to be friends with me?"

Brockhaven studied my face before he spoke. After lunch I had braided my hair in two thick plaits, and my guardian lifted one that had fallen forward and hefted it gently over to my back. At last, he said, "That's what I mean. Why have you been crying?"

"You can tell?"

"Your eyes show it. Did Cadal's visit distress you so much?"

I shook my head, and then explained despondently about my argument with Lady Gwen, and how ashamed I was of causing her to be upset. He listened in silence until I was finished, and said, "I'll talk to her."

"Oh, no, no! She'll think I've been complaining to you. Imagine how mortified she would be!"

"No she won't. I'll handle it. Go to your room and wait for her there. No, don't argue. Go now. And don't worry."

A half hour later to the minute, my bedroom door opened and Lady Gwen entered, flew to my side, and smothered me in a hug.

"My poor little Liza, why did you not tell me that you didn't want to have your hair cut because it is the tribal punishment for adultery? Alex has explained it to me, and I understand completely why it would be so repugnant to you. Society will just have to get used to you with knee-length hair!"

Lady Gwen's statement was all the more amazing, because I hadn't told Brockhaven about the gypsy law. I would have been too embarrassed to even think of telling him such a thing. It was evident that Lord Brockhaven knew more about my people than he had allowed me to believe.

And, as soon as I was given permission to keep my hair, my perverse spirit felt less need to clutch tight every inch of hair. Goudette came in and the three of us talked like three generals planning a military advance, until it was finally decided that if I could bear to have my hair trimmed to waist length (which I discovered I could), and snip some short ends near my face, Goudette could cause it all to curl and Lady Gwen could tell her friends that she couldn't stand to have me cut it because it was really such lovely hair and perhaps it would set a new fashion, as Goudette called it, à la gypsy!

In the course of the last week, it came to pass that the soireé Lady Gwendolyn had planned to hold at Edgehill became the soireé that Mrs. Perscough planned to hold at Lambelle Manor. The switch had been the product of a Wednesday afternoon visit from Mrs. Perscough, who recommended that it might seem more natural if I was introduced to the local gentry at another house than Edgehill, and besides, it would show right off that Mrs. Perscough considered me an "invitable" in case any doubt of it lingered in the minds of the more socially insecure. It was her opinion that it was best to define me immediately as a sought-after rather than a seeker. Though I might not understand the delicacies of their social world, I got the point and was grateful, not only for the invitation and support, but also because I had found another person to chalk up as a friend in this strange new world.

I could see why Ellen considered Mrs. Perscough a second mother, for she was a warm and maternal lady, generous and acute. At our first meeting she told me how my father had led her out to dance at the ball her parents had given on her eighteenth birthday, and how all the young ladies had sighed over him, he was so handsome and dark and poetic. How impatient he had been with convention! How bored he had been with the ponderous formalities in his father's home, and his father's endless interference in his life! "Mark my words," Mrs. Perscough's mother had

127

said. "One of these days the lad will run off, see if he won't!" And, of course, one day he had.

That Saturday evening I was finished getting ready for the soireé before anyone else, and went to stand in the entrance hall underneath a red silk banner painted with three animate lions that had belonged to one of Brockhaven's ancestors, a man who had sailed against Spain for Queen Elizabeth, and who had astonished his attendants by crawling from his deathbed to don armor so that he "could meet death like a gentleman."

The hall floor was a pattern of pieced Italian marble in white and black that alternated like the squares of a chessboard. Ellen had told me that it was a thing she liked to do, when she was younger, to hop from side to side in the hall, trying to avoid touching the black squares and pretending that she was Princess of the Saxons and if she could so perform, the cruel Danish pirates had agreed to spare a helpless Saxon village. It was a very childish game, and I can't think what made me try it, but I was just saving my fifth Saxon village when Lord Brockhaven came down the grand staircase.

"Good evening," said Lord Brockhaven in a voice that was, for him, cordial. "Oh, no, don't stop hopping for my sake. I've yet to see a child that can resist jumping on those squares. That's why Gwen won't have them waxed."

I gathered myself up with dignity and dropped him an icy curtsy which in no way camouflaged my chagrin. I longed for the courage to ask him if he had thought of me as a child when he kissed me under the willow.

"Very pretty," he said, crossing the floor to join me, and I wasn't sure if he was referring to my curtsy, the new cut of my hair, or the dress I wore.

My gown was a soft white, trimmed at the bodice in gold Brussels lace and at the hem with braiding, with an overskirt embroidered in glittering golden threads. Lady Gwen had spent twenty minutes last night at dinner discussing what jewelry would be fetching and appropriate for me to wear to the soireé, and she had ended by choosing a small pearl hairpin that Ellen had received as a confirmation present. Lady Gwen herself had affixed it to a thick curl above my ear. After she had left, I had looked in the mirror, and thought how Ellen's pin matched my dress well, both artfully demure, soft and subtle, and revealing instead of colorful and concealing like the clothes I had been raised in. I had pulled the pin from my hair and replaced it with one of my own: a crescent moon of hammered gold and uncut topaz gems that had belonged to my mother.

I should have known that Lord Brockhaven would notice it at once. Reaching up his hand, he touched the golden ornament and said, "That you didn't borrow from Ellen."

"No, I didn't. I suppose you don't approve of such things."

"That depends whether it's on my ward," he said, viewing me with mocking eyes, "or on my mistress." He lifted one of the curls that Goudette had labored so lovingly over and said, "It's beautiful. Like the woman who wears it."

A graceful compliment was the last thing I expected from him, and it threw me completely off stride. In a feeble way, I replied, "It's kind of you to say so," though I suppose my eyes said much more. It was extraordinary, the power he had to send my emotions into fierce confusion, and produce in me happiness and pain and languor by turns as though he had poured down my throat dose after changing dose of potions that captured and usurped my will. The fancy frightened me, as did the feelings that came with it, and to compensate, I told myself to stop being foolish, and reminded myself that I was unused to young men and gorgio manners, and that I must stop letting myself be overset by Brockhaven's smallest twist of whim. Suddenly I wished I had confided to Ellen about the kiss.

"Then you aren't going to ask me to change it?" I said with a forced smile, to make some remark, any remark.

"Did I say that? I'm afraid, my girl, that you look more

129

like you're about to appear as chief goddess and love idol at a pagan fertility rite, than an unassuming young female endeavoring to attend an evening with the cream of the local squirearchy."

My smile was more natural as I said, "From what I've learned from Ellen, the aforementioned unassuming young females not only assume a lot more than their parents credit, they also know a lot more as well!"

"Or," suggested Brockhaven sardonically, "so they assume."

Lambelle Hall was a red-brick manor house built early in the last century and much refurbished in the last ten years by Mrs. Perscough for the comfort of her large family. The entrance hall was filled with baskets of flowers, and the wainscotted hallways were redolent of beeswax and lemon polish, and lined with large oil paintings in the style of Stubbes that portrayed the ponies ridden and loved by the young Perscoughs. It was a lovely, homey place, and yet my stomach knit into knots as we reached the long drawingroom door, and our party was announced by a footman, whose stentorian tones had probably qualified him for the post. My fingers curled involuntarily, and Robert, who was escorting me, said, "Brace up, my girl! Where's that brave gypsy spirit?"

"At Edgehill, I think. Let's go back and look for it."

"Now, now, none of that," commanded Robert, leaning toward me and speaking in a low tone. "I'm going to look after you, and there's Gwen and Ellen to hover around too. There are only two things you need to remember. One's when you meet the squire, tell him immediately that you admire his scholarship excessively."

"But, Robert, I've never heard of his scholarsh—"

"Hush and listen, will you? The second thing is: give Peregrine Absalm the sharpest setdown you can manage as soon as he makes you his first indecent proposal."

"His first *what*?"

"You heard me. Be quiet. We've about reached the reception line."

I reflected with nervous irritability that it was just like Robert to say something to wrack my nerves to bits, and decided to put both very odd bits of advice from my head.

But when I was introduced to Squire Perscough, I stood trembling as he twitched his two black caterpillar eyebrows, looked down his very long nose, and said, "What do you have to say for yourself, young lady?" I grabbed at Robert's words like a body sinking in quicksand reaches for a clump of swamp grass, and vowed meekly that I had heard of his scholarship. For a moment, I thought I had made a terrible mistake, for he waggled those awful eyebrows furiously and turned beet red.

"You have, have you?" he trumpeted. Silence fell on the room, all ears tuned to his voice, all eyes turned to us. Then he clapped me on the back, set me on the window seat, demanded two glasses of champagne from a hovering footman, and said, "Young lady, I take my recognition where I can find it."

The squire, so I learned, had spent the better part of the last twenty years developing a one thousand page document in support of his assertion that William Shakespeare was married in the parish church a mile from Lambelle, a theory that was based in its entirety upon the squire's discovery of an entry in the Episcopal register in 1582 which alleged the issue of a marriage license to one W. Chas. Pierre, which the squire said any idiot could see was the phonetic spelling of an underlettered church clerk for William Shakespeare. Pierre wasn't an English name, was it? No, it was French, and what would a Frenchman be doing getting married in a British church in the year of 1582? He'd be married in France, wouldn't he? Unless I'd be wanting to be damned unpatriotic and attribute Shakespeare's plays to some misplaced Frenchman! I said that I did not, and the squire looked extremely pleased with me, said I was a likely lass with more in my head than most silly things my age, offered to lend me a copy of his treatise and handed me to his wife with the admonition that he bet I'd like to be spending my time with the young people.

He was wrong; there was nothing I wanted less. Still, Ellen came to my one side, and Robert took the other as he had promised, and I soon discovered they were as invincible an armor as any. Ellen might be shy in a group, but she was very well-liked by both sexes, and I could see that Robert was easily the most popular blood of the young set, as well as the chief arbiter of taste. It was very clear that anyone who was unkind to me would be so at their social peril.

Robert guided the talk into such unalarming topics as the upcoming festivities to celebrate May Day and who was going to London for the finish of the season. While Robert and Ellen directed their remarks frequently to me and encouraged others to do the same, they left no chance for the conversation to become more personal, or for anyone to ask me questions that might be awkward. I was to be given the generous opportunity to wait and catch my breath and to sit and observe without fearing that I would need to defend myself.

As I began to separate out the faces, Peregrine Absalm was one of the first to which I put a name. I would have noticed him even if Robert had not mentioned his name to me as we came in because to be noticed was a thing into which Mr. Absalm put a great deal of effort. He was a tall young man and good-looking in a heavy, hard-jowled sort of way. I guessed his age to be about two years under Robert's and everything he did seemed to be centered around proving that he was a young man who had *seen it all.* He held a wineglass that he let dangle from his fingers with such artistic negligence that you'd think he'd spent a month practicing it. He threw back his head like a rearing stallion when he laughed. When he talked, he made a habit of letting fall a few carefully chosen profane words and then apologizing profusely to the ladies present, to bring home the point that he was accustomed to the company of females of a far more risqué order. His companions received each peculiarity with the tolerance of old friends, though Peregrine's sister, a prim girl in pink, did

132

sometimes say, "Peregrine, will you *stop*? Or I shall tell Mama!" which crimped some of his better efforts.

Then there was John Lennox, a tall, rakish blond with a long neck and tumbling blond curls, who had a quick, secretive grin, made some of the funniest puns I had ever heard, and was a third cousin to Robert and Lord Brockhaven. Julie Aldgate had a habit of tossing her head to and fro while she talked to make her curls bounce, and I wondered why her mother didn't tell her to stop, until I met her mother and discovered that she had the same habit. Ellen's closest friend was a girl named Claire, who was pretty and lively and made much over by the men; Claire's younger sister was Roberta, though everyone called her Bobby, which she seemed to like. There were the Nettel twins, good-natured young men who both affected the use of a quizzing glass, which made it quite startling to be beheld by the two of them at once.

Before dinner was announced, I had been introduced to more than forty people and acquired a miserable headache.

There is a custom of the gorgio aristocracy that is called "leading the ladies in to dinner," which reminded me of "leading the cows to the pasture" as if we couldn't be trusted to find our way there on our own. During this process I was left unattended for long enough to give Peregrine Absalm the opportunity to rub his omnipresent dangling wineglass against my arm suggestively and leer at me with the lecherous precision of a randy goat.

"You glorious creature! They say that gypsy women can take whatever men they choose as lovers. Is that so, sweet dream?"

His words and manner afflicted me with a variety of emotions, the most prominent being amazement that anyone had garnered such a fallacious notion about the privileges accorded gypsy women.

"It's hardly likely," I said, headache and embarrassment adding an unintended edge to my voice. "Our tribal justice decrees that promiscuous women should have their nostrils slit."

133

I saw right away that I had horrified Mr. Absalm, for he blanched and swallowed loudly and said that he begged my pardon. It occurred to me that I had just received the predicted indecent proposal and, to my shame, I realized that John Lennox was standing only a few paces away and that he must have heard everything. I looked at him, blushing, only to find that he was regarding me with voluptuous approval and, as our gazes met, he lifted his hands and made a gesture to me of mute applause. As for Peregrine Absalm, for the rest of the evening he treated me with a respect that bordered upon awe.

Dinner went off very well, "considering," as Ellen would say. Lady Gwen had impressed upon me the importance of dividing one's attention equally between the partner on the right and the partner on the left. This was easy enough to do, because on my right was an elderly baronet who needed little encouragement to talk about the disastrous drop in the prices for farm produce since the end of the war, and on my left was the rotund and red-faced parson who announced straightaway that while he was sure I would know much that interested him about the ways of the gypsy, we would have to discuss it at some later date, for it was death on his digestion to talk during dinner.

Mrs. Perscough deplored the modern trend toward allowing one's guests to speak across the table on formal occasions, as it allowed uncongenial people access to their various foes, rendering null and void a hostess's careful efforts to separate the incompatible, and inevitably making the meal a less than peaceful occasion. To discourage this practice, she had placed huge silver bowls at frequent intervals down the table and had the gardener fill them with arrangements of tall white hothouse lilies surrounded by an impenetrable array of green foliage. Ellen, seated toward the end of the table, I could only see if both of us happened to crane our necks at the same instant; Lady Gwen caught us at it and frowned me down.

My cousin, Isabella, and her husband had arrived late, delayed by a strained spavin on one of their coach horses, and they were seated when they came in halfway through dinner, though not before Isabella had made a great show of being happy to see me, followed by a more restrained greeting from Vincent. I smiled back at them with as much animation as my throbbing head would allow, feeling relieved that whether at Vincent's advice, or at Lady Gwen's, Isabella had not carried her ill feeling toward me into the public eye.

Isabella and Brockhaven were seated side by side. Through the foliage I could see them talking to each other in a steady, intent way I found painful to watch, no matter how much I chided myself for it. They had been lovers once, and she still cared for him. And she was so pretty, like a vision. For all Brockhaven's apparent hostility, was any man ever proof against a beauty like Isabella's?

I kept my smile in place and continued to mind my manners, but my headache continued to grow, and with it my loneliness and my sense of being an outsider.

After the meal the gorgios segregate by sex, with the ladies retiring to another chamber to "leave the gentlemen to their port," which is a practice that occurs only by accident at Edgehill. Lord Brockhaven leaves the table immediately after dinner to shut himself in his study with piles of estate business, and Robert rides off to gambling or cockfighting with his cronies.

Gypsies do the same, my grandmother had told me. The men sit together, looking very pleased with themselves, as though they have cleverly and by stealth shed their petticoat government so they can swear and smoke and argue about business, politics, and horses. The women form a group of their own, looking equally pleased with themselves so they can discuss the men; who has put on weight and who has lost it, how best to cure your husband of snoring, and the clever thing their youngest child said when he had seen his father cut himself during shaving.

As I walked to the white drawing room with the other ladies, the throbbing in my temples was so intense that when Ellen asked me how I had liked dinner, she had to repeat her remark three times before I could make sense of it. I apologized and told her about my headache, and soon I was surrounded by ladies speaking in solicitous whispers of headache powders and warm compresses and having our carriage brought round to convey Gwen and Ellen and me back to Edgehill. I demurred quickly, and raised my eyes to Mrs. Perscough, and in a voice that I distantly recognized as pleading, asked if I might lie down alone for a few minutes in the dark. No, thank you so much, I didn't need Lady Gwen or Ellen to come with me.

I hardly recall being led to a guest chamber, being tucked under a soft blanket, or Mrs. Perscough's whispered message that she would return to see how I did in one hour, and that I should ring the call bell and send a servant for her at once, if I should need something before then.

My eyes closed in blessed relief, my mind faded restlessly into sleep, and I dreamed that I was a Saxon princess held captive by Danish pirates. Lord Brockhaven fluctuated with bewildering speed between the identity of a Saxon hero who was come to rescue me, and the leader of the pirates.

It was more than an hour later when I woke up, so said the small bracket clock that sat beside a single lit candle on the mantelpiece. A note propped beside it from Lady Gwen said that she had come with Mrs. Perscough on the hour and when they had found me sleeping, decided it would be better not to disturb me. The note ended by saying that I should ring for her to come to me as soon as I woke up, and that she knew how sensitive I was, and I mustn't allow myself to feel awkward about lying down—*everyone* understands a headache—and she loved me.

I smiled mistily at the note, tucked it into my reticule, made what reparations I could to my hair, and determined to find my own way back to the white drawing room.

The corridor was dark and quiet, with small, glass-globed tapers that burned many yards apart, shedding pale, flickering light in silver haloes along the blue walls. I passed door after anonymous door, stopping at intervals to listen in vain for the sounds of conversation. The corridor reached an abrupt end, so I had to retrace my steps, which built in me a feeling of failure that began to nibble away at the well-being that Lady Gwendolyn's note had given me. At length I found a well-lit staircase hung with a chandelier, and remembered I had climbed it on Mrs. Perscough's arm. Almost running down it in my relief, and not looking anywhere except the steps ahead of me, I reached the bottom and barreled full speed into the tall figure of a man.

"What's this?" he said, above my head. "Why, Liza! Hello, little Liza."

"Vincent!" I gasped, then corrected myself hastily, "I mean Mr.—Mr. . . ." Elves had fuddled my tongue, for I couldn't remember his last name.

"Randolph," he supplied, with some amusement. "But I liked hearing Vincent better from your lips. Please continue with that. I hope you're feeling better now. Mrs. Perscough told us that you had a headache. We were very concerned about you."

I wondered who he meant by we, and why he was so kind to me when his wife hated me so, and why he always looked at me in that particular, discreetly analyzing way. My words were as disjointed as my thoughts, as I said, "Oh, no! There was no cause! I had the merest trace of a . . . that is, I'm ashamed to have been such a baby about—" I broke off, realizing that I was doing exactly what Lady Gwen had cautioned me not to do in her note.

He put up his hand, as if in one gesture to reassure and show me that he understood.

"I don't think you're a baby," he said, his gray eyes searching my face from under heavy, long-lashed lids. "What would have put such a thing into your mind?"

My thoughts flashed back to Lord Brockhaven and what he had said to me in the front hall at Edgehill this evening. I found myself beginning to blush.

"Nothing. I babble sometimes."

"Nonsense!" he retorted, with a cool, direct grin that reminded me in a small way of Brockhaven's. "You handle yourself magnificently. I can't imagine a more self-possessed young woman, or one with greater courage. Surely, you must realize that the sweetness of your charm holds center stage, whatever company you find yourself in and whatever situation—and I have seen you in the most difficult."

I stared at him blankly, and he laughed.

"And modest in the bargain," he said. "Never mind. How has it been, settling in at Edgehill? Gwen is quite a lady, isn't she? She must be a great support for you."

"Yes, she is, and Ellen also. I don't know how I could have gone on without them."

"Nor do I," he said, a little too dryly. "I've wanted to come to see you but . . ." There was an odd, almost wistful quality to his voice that I found disturbing, and as though he sensed my unease, he lifted his long graceful arms and rested his hands over the bare curve of my shoulder, his thumbs brushing gently the flesh that covered my collarbone. "You've noticed, haven't you, that Alex and I don't get along."

"Yes," I said through a tightening throat.

"That makes it a trifle difficult for us to become friends. And that's all I've wanted, Liza, from the first moment I spoke to you. I don't mean you any harm. How could I? Do you believe that?"

There was a silence that I somehow found frightening, and I nodded, because he seemed to expect it and because it had never occurred to me to think that he might want to harm me. I heard a door open behind him, but his shoulder blocked my view and by the time he turned to look, the door had closed again.

As he turned back, he gave me the smile of a sympathetic advocate. "So. A pledge to our mutual trust. Your hand on it?"

I lifted my hand right away, hoping it would make him take his from my shoulders, but he only raised one hand and curled it around my fingers, bringing it to his lips.

"Here's to friendship," he said in a low tone. When he spoke again, his voice had changed. "I'll tell you what! Why don't we talk to Gwen, and ask if we can't get you over to visit us at Chad next week? I was looking through the old schoolroom in the west wing yesterday, and do you know that I found a copybook that belonged to your father? He must have been around seven or eight years old when he made it, and it's full of diagrams for mechanical banks and spinning jennies, and poems like an 'Ode to the Land Under a Tree Stump.' We have a miniature toy coach and four that belonged to him too, and a pull-duck from when he was an infant. I know he would have wanted you to have them. If we can arrange a visit, then I can show you his old rooms, and where he played, and give you his toys. Would you like that?"

"Oh, yes! So much! How kind of you to think of it. Several times I've thought of how I'd like to see Chad, because it was my father's home, but I haven't wanted to impose."

There was a sharp crack as the door behind Vincent was pushed open with some force, and Brockhaven strode into the corridor. Vincent removed his hands from me, though not before Brockhaven had seen.

"Touch her again," said Brockhaven in a soft invitation, "and I'll flay open your hide with a horse whip."

Clamping a bruising iron grip on my upper arm, he pulled me with him into the drawing room. I barely noticed the cheerful groups of chatting guests that surrounded us as I stared in mute amazement at Brockhaven.

"Enjoy your latest conquest, my dearest love?" he said in a quiet tone that felt as though I was being flayed with the same horse whip with which he'd threatened Vincent.

"What do you mean?" I said, fighting for control over my voice. "What have I done to make you so angry? I met Vincent in the hallway. What would you want me to do? Walk by him, ignoring him when he spoke to me?"

"Of course not," he said in a suddenly indifferent tone that reminded me that Lord Brockhaven was much better at playing this game than I. "Would I expect you to say no to a man? And stand still to let him run his hands over your body, so we can be certain you won't hurt his feelings? The next time Vincent makes love to you, don't do a damn thing to discourage him, so I can have the pleasure of killing him afterward."

"Makes *love*—?" I repeated in a voice that sounded pathetically like a squawk to my own ears. "Kill him? How dare you say that? How dare *you* say that?" My heart began to race, and I could feel the color flame into my cheeks. Shame that I had not had the confidence to take Vincent's hands off my shoulders did nothing to lessen my discomfort, and the vaguely guilty feeling that there was a small measure of justice in Brockhaven's accusations made me angrier and more defensive than ever. "There was nothing indecent in the way Vincent treated me! In fact, he was kind, and respectful, which are two things that—"

". . . I am not." He finished my sentence with a sardonically raised eyebrow. "Spare me your comparisons, valid as they may be. It's so delightfully opportune for the male sex that you're so easy to seduce."

Blood surged through my heart in scalding bursts. "To which seduction do you refer—Vincent's or yours?"

I knew immediately from the coldly suppressed fury on his face that I had said too much, but for once I was too hurt to care. "Oh, I beg your pardon," I said with a heavy-handed flippancy. "We're not supposed to talk about that, are we, my lord?"

His fingers tightened on my arm until I was half-afraid that I might whimper. "My sweet little girl," he said in a calm, hard voice, "that's one rein that you had better not pull. Do I have to explain to you why?"

"No," I gasped, wishing I was of a loftier frame of mind than to be curious about what he would have said. Brockhaven released my arm, and I might have collapsed with relief if I had not been mesmerized by bright blue flames that burned deep in his eyes. After a moment, the fire seemed to bank and fold into itself, and he said, "Don't stay alone with Vincent, Liza. Never."

It was more than a minute before I could answer him, so harsh was my battle to keep tears from invading my voice. "In the name of heaven, what's made you so angry? I *know* that in your world it's acceptable for me to be acquainted with your cousin. Lady Gwen told me so. How can you tell me I cannot? Why would you want to?"

"I've told you as much about it as I intend to tell you."

"You can't expect me to obey you without giving me a reason."

"By all means, let's have the classic childish garbage. It behooves you to remember you're a minor, my pretty one, and under the laws of this nation, I can do what I please to see that you adhere to my wishes, without having to convince you by rational persuasion that I'm right."

My jaw was so taut with emotion that I could scarcely cause it to speak. "Whatever are you going to do, beat me?"

"With the greatest pleasure," he assured me without so much as a skipped beat, and with blistering sincerity.

"What in the hell has gotten into you, Alex?" said Robert, appearing at his brother's side to bring me back to earth with a shattering jolt. "This is no time to heat the chit into hysterics. Half the room is staring at you."

Brockhaven turned to his younger brother, his harsh, set lips stretching into a narrow smile. "Are they? Well, well. I'm sure it will do Liza a great deal of good for society to see her as the oppressed victim of my tyranny."

"Doubtless," said Robert sarcastically. "But since her eyes are full of tears, and her angelic bosom is quivering magnificently with restrained sobs, I think we could both agree that you've done enough now to create sympathetic interest. Mrs. Perscough is gathering the unfledged chicks together to mother-hen a candlelight walk in the gardens. Ellen and most of the other girls are already below. Would you mind if I took Liza?"

"By all means. Take her," agreed Brockhaven with unflattering readiness. "The garden should suit her to perfection. She needs cooling."

Oh, what I would have said if Robert had not removed me from the drawingroom, posthaste. In silence, he took me to the ladies' cloakroom to fetch my shawl, but as the maid handed it to me the only thought that crossed my mind was the joy it would have given me to strangle

141

Brockhaven with it. Robert had apparently spent the measure of our walk to the cloakroom in an inner debate about whether or not to mention my fight with Brockhaven, because suddenly I heard him take a breath and lead me off the main corridor into the hushed stillness of a twilight hall.

"All right," he said, "what happened?"

"Lord Brockhaven says I am not to talk to Vincent," I said, pulling my shawl tightly around my shoulders.

"Oh."

"Oh? What does 'oh' mean?" I demanded, turning on him. " 'Oh' is not an answer."

With an asperity that I sensed was contrived, he said, "I wasn't aware that you'd asked me a question."

"I beg your pardon. Why is your brother angry at me for talking with Vincent? He's been kind to me and . . . and he promised to show me my father's schoolroom at Chad. There was nothing more than that in our conversation, and yet—" I looked up at Robert. "He dislikes me, doesn't he?"

"Of course Vincent likes you," Robert replied. "He's made that clear."

"I meant Brockhaven."

A guttering wall candle above us sent a warm, yellow wash of light over Robert's dark hair, accenting the masculine features, the hollows beneath the high cheekbones, the smoothly cut jawline. I watched him, trying to guess his thoughts.

"Damn," he said, to my surprise. His voice sounded loud in the empty hall. "Has something happened between you and Alex?"

I stared hard at the floor. He swore again, under his breath this time, and repeated his question.

I slowly nodded.

There was a return to a very loud silence before he said, "Oh Lord," and then, reluctantly, "You'd better tell me about it."

"I don't know if I'm able," I whispered, torn between the need to unburden my desperate secret and the strain of

142

making such an admission. I looked up at him with an expression that I realized unhappily must be beseeching.

I was so prepared for a curt reproach that I was surprised when it didn't come. Instead, Robert ran a hand distractedly through his hair, took a step backward as though to bring me into better focus, and said incredulously. "Is it that bad?"

My face must have told him yes. He enfolded me in his arms with a tenderness I hadn't imagined he possessed, and took me to sit on the deep violet folds of a cushioned window seat that ended the hall.

"Liza, could you talk about this to Gwen? It might be the best thing."

"I had thought of that," I said in an aching voice. "But—but think how she would feel! What good would it do to give her such distress? There's nothing she can do about it, and I haven't told Ellen either, because I just can't seem to bear for anyone so dear to me to learn . . . Robert, my emotions, my very being has been in such disorder!"

Robert looked grim, though his voice strove for gentleness. "Have you and Alex been intimate?"

I hope I can say without appearing to boast that my English is very good, but there are subtleties of the language that only broad experience can give. Nor would I have suspected that Robert might try to put a thing delicately.

"Worse than that," I said.

"Good Lord," he started. "I didn't know Alex *did* any worse than that! Liza, tell me immediately what you're talking about, because I have a very ribald imagination. Out with it!"

And so that was how I came to tell Robert, surely the strangest of confidants I could have chosen. I told him simply because he was the one who asked me, and I had wanted to tell someone but was too much of a coward to introduce the topic on my own.

As it was, I hesitated and hesitated, not knowing the words that could label the sweet, burning passions that I had learned at my guardian's experienced hands. I finally

143

settled on the hopelessly inadequate phrase, "We kissed under a willow tree."

"Kissed under a willow," he repeated. "My dear girl, I think we had better be blunt so we don't misunderstand each other. Has Alex taken you to bed?"

"No! Was that what you meant by intimate? I know this is a terrible thing to say, but if he had, in some ways it would have been . . . not *better*, certainly, but more clear. As it is— Oh, I don't know what I'm saying."

"On the contrary. You're doing very well. Were you forced?"

"To—to kiss Lord Brockhaven, do you mean? No. No, I wasn't. In fact, I—you might say that I—Robert, I think you should know that when we kissed, we weren't standing up."

"Oh. That was unfortunate."

"I can't seem to stop thinking about it."

"I don't suppose you can."

"Then you don't think it's so bad?"

"I didn't say that," he responded in a measured tone. "*Your* part in it wasn't bad. With Alex, it's a different matter."

"But I told you, he didn't force me!"

"If he had, that would have put him beyond the pale."

I stared out through the thick window glass at a lone star that winked forlornly above the black line of the horizon. "When I met you, you had John Stewart take me to the library in Edgehill. Have you forgotten?"

"That was before I knew you were a lady."

"Of course. That changed everything."

"*You* may not think so, but believe me, society would. If it became known that Alex kissed you, there's a chance the courts would yank you straight out of Edgehill and stick you in Chad under Vincent's care."

Leaning slightly forward, I rested my cheek against the cool window glass, feeling its mist damp against my skin. "I don't think Lord Brockhaven would let that happen. He likes too much to have me as a tool against Vincent and Isabella."

144

"A strong motivation for Alex not to touch you again."

I nodded, my head making a small, dripping smear on the wet pane. "After he kissed me he said that it wouldn't happen again."

He reached up to cup my wet cheek consolingly. "It seems cruel, I know. But it's best, Liza."

"Is it so awful for me to wish that he cared for me?"

"He cares for you. Do you think it was easy for him to stop, after one kiss?"

"You don't understand, Robert. I want him to care far more than that. I want him to care so much that he wouldn't have to stop. But you don't have to tell me. It's not likely."

I had no anticipation that Robert would contradict me, and he did not. He knew as I did that Lord Brockhaven was hardly an impulsive romantic who might fall headlong in love with an untried girl in her teens.

Later when I looked back on that conversation with Robert, it amazed me that I hadn't known shock, or even any sense of discovery, as I admitted for the first time aloud, as well as to myself, how much I felt for Lord Brockhaven. To concede my love seemed as natural and guileless as the new leaf uncurling from its stem. It was a soft emotion, linked forever in the past with the dripping sands of time, as though it had been there from my earliest beginning, even before I had met him in the library. My love had been like a bud that was born with me, always there, always waiting for the sunshine of this man's smile to fall upon it and press it open with gentle, unseen strokes.

Only the hand of a heartless destiny would have chosen Brockhaven for my love. We were as different as the falcon is from the butterfly, he the subtle, soaring hunter, and I vulnerable and full of fears. We were unalike in custom, in temperament, and in the way we looked at and touched the things around us. How could I cross the vast canyons of indifference he had made around him, raised as he was in a way that would have been the ruin of most

145

men? It would be my destruction, more brutal than any other, if I tried to reach him.

We walked for more than a quarter hour in the garden, with a bright candlelit group whose happy conceited chatter rose in the night while I stared into the shadows wishing that I could fly away into the blackness and lay alone on the damp, sweet-scented earth and know myself held in the palm of the Mother of Peace.

I was sad when Mrs. Perscough began to speak of chills and too much exposure to night air. Turning aside laughing protests, she began to shepherd us inside. I did not relish a return to the battle to discover who I must become in this new environment, for I had the added burden of keeping my heart safe from its yearning for my guardian. But I tried to smile with the others and show cheer. Grandmother said if you moan over a missing toe, the devil will come and take the foot. And I wished to conceal my smarting heart from Lord Brockhaven.

Both gorgios and gypsies have a custom that after the dinner, and after the talking, comes a time for the music to be made. For gypsies it's a way to make merry or to sorrow; the gorgios have made of it an excuse to sleep on the sly. Ellen had warned me that the mothers with daughters of marriageable age would use this occasion to showcase the talent, or lack of it, of their offspring. In vain would a young lady protest to her mother that she hated to play in public and that she could barely stumble through a scale, much less a sonata. What matchmaking mama could acknowledge that she had for years been wasting money on expensive music masters! Happily for Ellen, Lady Gwen thought it intolerable that girls of no ability should be allowed to assault the eardrums of invited guests, but that didn't stop people from saying, in the course of an evening such as this one, what a pity it was that poor Ellen had no affinity for music. Accomplishments and force-fed doses of European culture were linked inseparably with gentility, and I had claim to none.

The footmen had set out chairs in the music room in precisely straight lines that were immediately rearranged

146

by the company, moving here and there between songs to talk with friends.

I enjoyed the performances more than I had expected to, given Ellen's grim description. I was no judge of the music, since I had never heard enough gorgio songs to know how things were supposed to sound, and, in all honesty, one piece of gorgio music sounds to me pretty much like another. The worst of the pianists I enjoyed the most, and the best I liked least. Julie Aldgate was the worst, and I'm sure I could have watched her all night. She played a lively tune with many, many verses that she punctuated by hopping on her seat in time to the music until it looked as though her piano stool was connected to the floor by a wire spring, and she pumped the foot pedals with legs that hurled up and down like a thumping jackrabbit. Adding to that were such atrocities as stopping in mid-bar for as long as twenty seconds (I counted) to glare with avid concentration at the music sheet, as though she suspected it of switching around the notes on purpose to baffle her. She reminded me of a pretty, mechanical toy that one delights in paying a penny to see at the fair, and I'm sure my applause was quite the heartiest when she was done.

Isabella's talent was so far at the other end of the scale that I wasn't even sure it should be judged in the same spectrum. In my ignorance, I could still see that she was an outstanding pianist. Her first selection was long, tedious, and melancholy, written by a dead composer in whom the gorgios put much store, though I have forgotten his name. The composition was one that for a time travels a slow, redundant, and quiet pace and then, when one least expects, it goes *bang, bang, bang,* and almost puts you out of your chair. About Isabella's playing there was not an ounce of silliness. She looked beautiful, stately, rich, intelligent, and utterly feminine, and somehow I could not keep myself from drawing comparisons between us that made me feel like a shabby kitten that sits meowing in a gutter.

No sooner had she finished playing but she was urged

on to give the company the pleasure of a second piece. She agreed merrily, but only, she said, if *dear* Alex would come sit at the piano with her and play a duet. Lord Brockhaven was instantly besieged by witticisms and mock commands that he join the fair Isabella at once. He went, though I can't say that he did it with any eagerness. It appeared likely that he only agreed in order to escape what he plainly regarded as the persecution of the many well-wishers who were encouraging him to play.

Lord Brockhaven played as well as Isabella, perhaps better, for he had a greater natural affinity. I learned later that they had been trained by the same music master. It showed in the fluid blend of their styles, a ballet of sweet, blurring notes that met and melded with the pure sensuality of experienced lovers. His dark head against her light one, she, small and fragile by his shoulder, was as articulate and perfect a thing of beauty as the music they played. Isabella sat so close to Brockhaven that they were touching, but he seemed indifferent to their contact, as though intimacy had bred in him an endless acceptance for their closeness, though I had seen him reject her physical overtures at other times. They were a beautiful and stirring couple, and when the last strain of their melody had died away there was a thunderous applause, even though everyone in the room, save myself, had seen them play together many times before.

I was forced to hear much eulogistic commentary about the charm of their duet before the evening could continue. No sooner had Peregrine's sister Miss Absalm sat down to play at the harp, but one of the strings snapped under her fingers, and all turned back to conversation while the repair was made.

Across the room, Julie Aldgate had succeeded in cornering Robert and was talking to him animatedly, her expressive hands fluttering through the air like fairy wings, and her curls flying. I saw him put up his hand to catch her chin, no doubt to hold steady her poor little wagging head, but Julie saw fit to interpret it as a caress. She gave Robert a meltingly adoring smile. The squire walked past my view, speaking in a jolly way with Vincent and with his neighbor, Sir Maxwell Whitely, and I tried to apply my mind to what Mrs. Littledean had to say about the acquisition of new altar hangings for the church.

"To be sure," she was assuring Mrs. Aldgate and Lady Absalm, who were both sitting to my right, "the Norwich cloth is quite pretty, but ladies—tradition! Since seventeen hundred and three the altar scarves for this parish have been made by the ranking lady at Chad Hall, and if we can only prevail upon dear Isabella . . ." Her voice lifted tactfully and succeeded in catching the attention of Isabella, who had taken a chair in front of me.

Isabella swiveled around, her lips smiling like half a Christmas wreath. "My dear Mrs. Littledean, you know, of course, that I am not really of any importance at Chad anymore," she said, her tone implying that she had been beggared by my advent in the parish, which Brockhaven and Mr. Cadal had both assured me was far from the truth. "Why don't you ask my *new* cousin, Liza?"

Looking nonplussed, Mrs. Littledean said to me, "My word! I had never thought of that! *Do* you embroider, Liza?"

Feeling low and clutching my hands one in the other on my lap, I replied, "I'm afraid that I don't, ma'am. I can mend, of course, and make window curtains, and horse-blankets . . ."

"Horseblankets!" exclaimed Isabella. "Really, how handy! If one's grooms and stable boys should all come ill at one time, we can send for Liza to keep things tiptop in the stables."

Tall, dignified, and blue-veined, and with the posture of a broomstick, Mrs. Absalm inclined her head graciously in my direction. "A perfectly appropriate and practical skill for Liza to have, bred as she was. I have always held the maxim that a lady can do as she must, if only she conducts herself with nobility. It's obvious to me that Liza has nothing to learn about the true womanly graces!"

Abandoned by Robert, Julie Aldgate came to slide into the seat beside Isabella and said gaily, "Well, I, for one, am in envy of you *completely*, Liza. I'd liefer sew at a horseblanket than take piano lessons any day of the week."

Everyone laughed at that while Mrs. Aldgate said indulgently, "Oh, Julie, '*liefer*.' What *will* you say next!"

I felt a warm and gentle hand rest for a moment on the curve of my bare shoulder and looked back to find Brockhaven watching me. He moved his hand to the chair rail, and his gaze fastened, suavely benign, on Julie.

"Very cogent, Miss Aldgate. Liza would tell you—if she weren't so meticulously courteous—that it's only the materialistic gorgios, imprisoned in their false notions of status and possessions who would commit themselves to owning cumbersome instruments like the piano or the harp."

"Who are the gorgios, my lord?" asked Julie, wide-eyed, fascinated, obviously thrilled to have attracted Brockhaven's notoriously elusive attention.

With a rather wicked smile in his blue eyes, Brockhaven said, "That's the Romany word for any non-gypsy. Liza tactfully translates its meaning as 'outsider,' but it really means 'peasant.' "

I was learning rapidly that Lord Brockhaven knew the most unexpected things! For a moment I was afraid that someone might be offended to learn this, but I need not have worried since everyone clearly thought the gypsies among the most wretched of God's creatures. It didn't occur to them to believe that the gypsies consider *themselves* to be superior, a philosophy strongly encouraged in me by my grandmother and just as forcefully opposed by my father, who said that good and evil are found in equal amounts in every race. But then, my father was not gypsy.

Brockhaven looked down at me. "Those questions aside," he added with a lazy grin, "Liza plays the violin."

I hadn't touched it since my grandmother's death, being in mourning, but he had seen it, probably when he had searched my wagon. Mrs. Aldgate thought that Brockhaven was still teasing.

"That we *know* is a whisker," she said, waggling her finger flirtatiously. "The violin is much too difficult an instrument for a woman to play."

"Oh, but no, ma'am," said Ellen, who had just left off helping to bring the new harp string into tune. "The very first violin was p-played by a gypsy girl, so legend has it. Liza, you m-must tell the story, p-please."

The room had grown quieter as more and more people had begun to focus their attention on me. It dismayed me greatly to have to talk with so many listening.

"I have no wish to bore . . ." I began, only to be interrupted by the squire, three rows away from me, who boomed, "Humdudgeon, lass. It ain't every night that we get to hear gypsy folk tales, let me say! What about this violin?"

There was nothing for it. I must speak, or appear churlish. "Many years ago," I began, trying to rid my voice of nervousness, "when lion and boar still roamed abroad in the Forests of Dean, there lived a gypsy maid whose heart was lost to a handsome Lord of the gorg—that is, the English. To him, she was dirty, dark and repellent; no matter what things she did, she was unable to win his love." An image of Lord Brockhaven appeared in my mind, flustering me, and I could only hope that people assumed the tremor in my voice had come from shyness. I was glad that Brockhaven stood to my rear, so that I did not have to awkwardly avoid his eyes. I continued.

"Each day increased the maiden's despair, and at last her need became past bearing, and she promised the souls of her own family to Satan, if he would help win the man she loved.

"Satan grabbed up her family in his fiery hand, and from her father, the devil made the body of a violin. The gypsy's mother became the bow, and each of her four brothers formed a string.

"Cradling the violin sorrowfully in her arms, the maiden began to stroke the bow over the strings and the violin sent forth music so irresistibly compelling that the young lord fell under its spell and came to love the gypsy maiden."

There was a short silence, into which Mrs. Absalm exclaimed, "I can't believe such a tale could come to a happy end."

"Alas, it does not," I said. "Satan came to bear the gypsy maid and her lover away to Hades in a chariot of fire. The violin slipped from the maiden's fingers, and was caught up by people of her tribe, who gave it to their children, and then their children's children, and thus it went until this day, when we play it still, a perpetual reverence for the eight souls tragically lost in its making."

"By Jove, that's the most intriguing lore I've heard in a twelvemonth," proclaimed the squire enthusiastically. "Stab me if I don't record that in my journal as soon as I'm up tomorrow morning. Tell you what, young lady. I've got a fiddle that belonged to my Uncle Ned—not that he was much of a hand with the thing. Keep the old fiddle locked up in the morning room cupboard, don't you, Mrs. Perscough? Well, then, Liza! Why don't you and I trot next door and see if it's in shape to play, eh? Make the night something above the common run if you'd throw us a tune or two."

"I don't know!" said the vicar's wife with a deep frown, "I'm sure that I don't! Gypsy music is said to be—that is to say, I cannot think that Lord Brockhaven would approve at all of his young ward playing such music as is reputed to—to inflame the *animal* passions."

Although my acquaintance with Lord Brockhaven was not of any significant length, I knew him well enough to recognize that this was precisely the kind of remark he most detests, and sure enough, he smiled in that way he has of smiling when he's out for blood, and said in a sensual drawl, "Liza, fetch your violin and play—for me."

I was happy to be out of the room before I saw the reaction *that* statement brought from the vicar's wife.

Chapter Eight

The morning after the soirée brought in the kind of day you expect to find in late April. A gray rain poured down on Edgehill, splattering the window glass with noisy abandon and filling the air with the sound of water rushing from the downspouts.

Betty was to wake me at half past seven to ride with Ellen and her friend Claire, but our plans were pending rain, so Betty didn't come in until after nine o'clock. She helped me dress, gave me a tray of breakfast, and with it a note from Ellen that said:

"My dear Liza, Rotten luck to have our riding rained out, but what's to be done? Don't get up, if you've still the headache, which I shouldn't wonder at after all the 'to-do' last night! Mama is still going on, as she did in the carriage coming home, about what a success you were! I'm to be found in the blue room, the one next to Brockhaven's study. And I've got something to show you, if you're in the mood. Your affectionate E."

Considerably intrigued, I entered that room a half hour late to find my friend bending over her portable sewing table and staring anxiously at the feather picture to which she had been giving sporadic and unenthusiastic attention for the last three weeks. Ellen had been gathering feathers for six months and she had collected a basketful—from wild birds in the woods, goosedown stolen from feather bedding, tail feathers from the peacocks at Chad Hall, owl feathers, pheasant feathers, chicken feathers. The object was to arrange the feathers in an appropriate design on a sheet of textured canvas. Ellen had chosen to create a forest scene, with rabbit, and was intending it as a gift for her Great Aunt Anne's birthday.

As I came in the door, Ellen cried, "Carefully, Liza, carefully—th-these aren't glued yet, and the s-slightest b-breeze from the door will . . . Oh, *no*!" Then after a moment, a resigned, "Ah, well."

"I'm very sorry, Ellen. Oh, dear, there must be a hundred feathers in your hair!"

"I don't mind that so m-much, Liza," said Ellen, pounding her chest with a fist and giving a delicate cough. "It's the ones that went into m-my throat that I p-particularly object to. No, don't come over and help me, the movement makes them fly around more. I'll h-have it right in a moment or two." She began picking the feathers from her hair. "So—you were the belle of the hour last n-night! I've never heard *anything* like the way you play the violin. And that one s-song, what is it called . . . colo . . ."

"Kaulochirilo. It means 'blackbird,' " I said.

"It was the l-loveliest thing I ever heard. I swear you'd n-need a heart of stone to remain unmoved during it. And himself, the squire, admired it p-profusely. Mama told me at breakfast that he's showing an alarming d-disposition toward changing his alliance from Shakespeare's marriage to the study of gypsy customs and legends."

I laughed a little and said, "He was most kind to me and I was honored by his interest. Would it disturb the feathers if I sat down?"

"N-Not if you do so with care. Sit in the blue chair by the revolving bookstand, if you please. Yes, that one."

I sat down gingerly and watched as Ellen dipped a bit of feathery fluff into the little pot of glue and carefully set it in place. As she dipped, she said, "I p-particularly wanted to talk with you this morning, of course, more about the s-soirée last night. But I have something I wanted to show you first." I waited patiently while she waved her fingers in the air and tried to remove sticky feathers from one hand with the sticky fingers of her other hand, transferring the small bright bits of fluff rather than ridding herself of them.

"Something to show me from here?" I said curiously, indicating the bookcase.

"Yes!" she said. "Generally I n-never use this room since it's rather considered Robert's domain. The corner desk there is where he writes his letters, keeps his accounts, etcetera. Before Brockhaven inherited his t-title, the room belonged to the sons, who you will remember, d-died with their father, the man who was earl before Brockhaven. As for the bookcase, I always th-thought '*boy's* books' and never considered them of interest— books about fishing, hunting, horses, and fighting. Well, l-last night at the dinner, I took too much champagne and had the m-most profound indigestion! I couldn't get to sleep, and I couldn't take a book from the library to help put me to sleep because Brockhaven and Robert were still in there talking, and I didn't want to come bursting in upon them in my nightdress. So I c-came in here, and found—well, I want you to read it for yourself. You see the thin book on the lower shelf with the green binding?"

"Just a moment," I said, searching. "Oh, yes, here it is." I pulled out the volume.

"Open to page fifty-six and read from the top," she said, not turning.

I opened to the page as directed and read aloud. " 'As I opened my languishing eyes and delivered up my lips, he continued unbuttoning that part of his garments, and with the same calmness, he displayed what is not fit for me to mention . . .' "

Ellen dropped the picture, clapped her gluey hands over her ears in astonishment and rushed over to join me in a large-eyed study of the amazing passage.

"That's not the book I was reading last night!" she said finally.

"No, I don't suppose it would be just the thing for a person with indigestion."

"What d-does it say after that?" she said, her surprise turning to curiosity. She looked at the page and read, her lips moving, and when she was finished, said in a shocked voice, "I didn't know they put things like that in books. Well!"

"Do you know what I think?" I ventured hesitantly. "I think that if someone came into the room and found us reading this book—your mother, perhaps, or Lord Brockhaven—they might not like it."

Ellen clapped the book shut and slipped it back into the bookcase. "Not like it! Liza, if my mother c-caught us with this book, she'd have us in our bedrooms for a week on bread and water. Young ladies are not supposed to know about things that are not fit to mention. That's why if you ever have occasion t-to talk about a man's trousers, which is a th-thing you're not supposed to have an occasion to d-do, but if you should ever have to, it's the *thing* to call them inexpressibles."

After pondering this, I replied, "I will if that's the correct way. But it's not very logical since we don't refer to our skirts as inexpressible, but our skirts cover the parts of us which . . ."

Ellen interrupted me with a burst of laughter. "D-don't ever expect logic and propriety to coincide. When they do, it's the v-veriest accident. Now let me show you my *real* discovery." She spun the bookcase slowly, studying the titles, and with a little cry of triumph pulled out a volume called *The Hows and Whys of Cotswold Monsters, or Tested Triumphs O'er Evil.* She opened it to page fifty-six and read from it after unsticking her fingers from the page.

"It says here '. . . that dreaded spectre the Werewolf. Is it man-beast or beast-man? Only the wandering gypsy knows the full sum of it, and he t-tells his tale to none.' "

"That wandering gypsy isn't me, because I don't know a

156

thing about werewolves. Vampires perhaps, and goblins, and demons, of course . . ."

"Liza, you're giving me c-crawling skin," said Ellen with a shudder and a laugh.

"Crawling skin! That's more frightening than anything I've said!" I protested.

She giggled. "D-don't keep changing the subject. Of course the author wasn't referring to you—it was j-just a figure of speech, romantic speculation. It's what comes later that caught my attention. See? Read here." She pointed at a paragraph; I took the book from her and read aloud:

" 'It is not mere superstition that I describe here, but scientific methods that have been used around the world, from the impenetrable forests of the Rhineland to the wild swamps of the Orinooko. To actually render the werewolf harmless, no, not frighten away, not kill, but to tame, for if in it be the spirit of a loved one, taming is ever the choice of humanity and benevolence. Prepare a fresh joint of raw beef stamped and steeped with opium. Herein the Scientific Method!' "

"What do you think?" said Ellen. "That's logical, d-don't you agree?"

"I don't know," I said mildly. "And since we'll never have an opportunity to experiment with it . . ." Suddenly I began to dislike the look on Ellen's face. "*Will* we?"

"That's th-the b-best part! Listen to this. Now where w-was that? A pox on these pages for sticking to my fingers. Oh, h-here it is. 'The m-most propitious of all evenings for thus disarming the C-Creature is on the ancient festival of May. Wear h-heavy dark robes, scent your hair with f-flowers, carry the prepared meat in a wine-soaked leather satchel and leave it thence in a clearing notorious for the creature's presence.' " She looked at me with a beatific glow. "Liza! This Th-Thursday is May Day."

"May Day is also the day that witches meet," I said, controlling a shiver. "My grandmother used to make rowan talismans without using a knife, and tie them to the tails of our oxen on May Day to ward off the evil eye."

"That's the dark side of the holiday, Liza. B-but here we have the loveliest celebration, with more zest than Midsummer Night's Eve! The parson doesn't approve, of course. He says May Days are an excuse for debauchery, and that what we are really celebrating is a dreadful pagan fertility rite. But every year the celebration goes on, since the Saxons or Romans or D-Druids or whoever, began it. The custom the parson deprecates m-most is the tradition of everyone spending the n-night in the woods—well, n-not everyone, of course—the young people, mostly. Young ladies of our station are l-left out, of course. Can you imagine L-Lady Gwen or any of the m-mothers you met last night allowing such a th-thing? Our reputation would be in shreds forever if we were ever f-found in such a scrape. B-but that is neither here nor there. The p-point is, it will be the perfect c-cover for us. There will be so many people about we won't seem in the least suspicious. What could be b-better?"

"Almost anything!" I said. "I thought you just said our reputations would be destroyed forever if we went into the woods on May Day."

"We won't have to worry about that b-because we aren't going to tell anybody. I go about incognito all the t-time. Don't you remember when I came to visit you in m-my old gray cloak? Not that I've ever d-done anything this ambitious, of course."

I laughed out loud. Underneath her shy and retiring exterior, my friend Ellen had an adventurer's soul, and I wondered what she would be like in a few years when she no longer had her mother to stand over her and tell her to make feather pictures. Looking at her animated face, I asked curiously, "Ellen, do you really think there's a werewolf?"

Ellen was thoughtfully transferring a feather from one forefinger to the other until the glue was dry and tacky, and she lifted her finger to her lips to blow loose the feather into the air.

"Well, n-no, but I like to pretend there might be one. I know this. There is some kind of a large animal; you saw

158

its tracks and Caesar fought it. M-meat soaked in sedative will work as well for a beast as for a half-beast. M-maybe there will b-be too many people out, and it would be frightened to show itself, but Liza, what if w-we should capture it?"

I shook my head, unable to share my friend's excitement. "I'm not fond of the hunt, Ellen. I never seem to be able to shed a feeling of sympathy for the animal."

"Oh, Liza, I understand, I really d-do," Ellen said warmly. Then she stopped, and a troubled look came to her face; she turned and walked to the fireplace, stooping to pick up a feather which had drifted to the floor.

"Ellen, whatever is the matter?" I asked.

She rolled the feather between her hands and said in a low voice, after glancing around the room, "Liza, I know this may seem like quite an unusual observation, but has it occurred to you that th-this animal seems to have a propensity for attacking people who stand in th-the way of Isabella's ownership of Chad Hall?" She clenched her hands in distress. "It's a t-terrible thing to insinuate, I know, and I d-don't mean that Isabella herself would ever . . ."

I fairly leapt from my chair and the heavy old book went banging to the floor from my lap. "Do you mean to say that my life was in danger in the woods?"

"I d-don't know, Liza. But I think Brockhaven does! D'you remember the night at dinner when you told about the strange animal? Brockhaven had John Stewart and a group of armed men out the next morning beating the woods. And he's m-made rules saying you c-can never go anywhere unaccompanied by a groom. He w-was n-never that way before; he n-never insisted that my mother keep such a close watch on *me*, for instance; rather he w-was quite lenient. I think he knows something about it th-that he isn't saying."

Perhaps she was right about Brockhaven. I could see what she meant. There had been a certain watchfulness, too, from certain of Lord Brockhaven's servants here, as if it was important to make sure frequently of where I was.

159

Did they think someone might try to do me harm? And if so, then who? Like Ellen, I could never imagine lovely, passionate Isabella at the center of some dark plot for my murder and no one else had a reason to wish me ill, surely. Useless, less than useless, to ask Brockhaven, who would have told me by now if he wished me to know. It was as though Ellen had pulled away a dark veil and revealed a mute enigma wrapped in a second shroud of mystery. Or perhaps it was all fancy, and the animal in the woods had been a badger, as Robert thought, and Brockhaven had sent men to the woods only as a precaution, and to comfort the maternal fears of Lady Gwendolyn. And, of course, the servants stared at me. I was new and different and therefore of interest.

I said thoughtfully, "Ellen, it seems so—so farfetched to me. If there was the faintest grain of truth to it, though, we couldn't possibly go into the forest that night, for not only would my life be risked, but yours as well."

"That's just it," cried Ellen triumphantly. "Liza, May Day is the s-safest night of the year for us to be abroad, because that's the l-last night anyone would suspect we'd be out."

I couldn't help laughing. "You feel that anyone would assume we'd have the sense to stay snug in our beds . . .?"

"Instead of wandering a w-woods filled with rakish sorts participating in things which it is n-not fit to mention!" she finished with a grin. She appeared to be applying herself further to the pros and cons of her idea while she spun the bookstand idly with one finger. "I wonder, Liza," she said finally. "Do you think that Robert's read *that* b-book?"

I didn't make the error of supposing she meant the book on supernatural phenomena. "I don't know. Why don't we ask him?"

"I wouldn't doubt he'd turn us s-straightway into my mother. Mostly he thinks I'm a b-baby . . . I wonder, Liza. D-did you remark the name of that volume?"

"*The Adventures of Countess T.*," I responded helpfully. "It's there; no, you're passing it. You put it back on the first shelf."

"D-did I?" she said with careful disinterest. She went back to her feather picture, poured some water into a basin, and worked at her sticky fingers with a tiny chip of soap. "Really," she said as she scrubbed, "I don't know why m-men would want to have a b-book like that around. It's d-disgusting, isn't it?"

"Very," I agreed cheerfully, coming over to inspect her picture. The rabbit in her picture looked rather like an irritated mole. Aloud, I said, "You know, Ellen, rather than calling this a forest scene, I think you should tell your aunt that this is a picture of the Eygptian pyramids. See the shape of the trees?"

Ellen, drying her hands on her apron, looked over my shoulder to view her handiwork. "You're right, it d-does. But what's the rabbit, then?"

"The Sphinx," I said. "You see, if you add a turkey feather here, like so, and a bit of crow down . . ."

"That's wonderful! Much m-more original than a fforest, don't you think?" Ellen glanced back at the bookcase. "Liza, don't you think women should t-take some kind of action about men reading b-books like that?"

"Destroy them, you mean?"

"Oh, no. We couldn't d-do that. My father would turn over in his g-grave at the thought of a book being destroyed! I d-don't think we should do anything so drastic."

"Oh. Well, I suppose we could just"—I waved my hand and lifted my eyebrows—"carry it away. To the sunroom, for instance. There's never anyone in there at this hour."

Ellen was quick to enter into the spirit of the idea. "I'll bet it would fit behind a copy of *Young Ladies' Household Companion*. I d-do think we should read it so w-we can learn what we are struggling against."

With this praiseworthy object in mind, we proceeded to the sunroom to follow up on the adventures of the Countess T., the slim green volume concealed under a stack of commendable books for young ladies whose excellent authoresses would have been much surprised if they had known they were being used for such a shady purpose.

We had just broached the third chapter, which concerned the Countess's encounter with the ninety-two-year-old Caliph of Baghdad, when Lord Brockhaven came in upon us. He was carrying a blue ledger, his purpose evidently to check some correspondence filed in the bound volumes of household records which filled the better part of a long cabinet in the room.

His inky curls were a bit more disarrayed than usual, which meant that he had been up working since early this morning, and I remember Mr. Cadal's repeated assurance to me that I could never have found a more able or intelligent guardian to have the charge of my land. I wonder if it wearied him, to have that charge on top of his own property, but there was no trace of tiredness in his taut, healthy skin and athletic strides. He hadn't been in to breakfast with Lady Gwen, because he had no jacket covering his thin lawn shirt, and the collar lay open without the respectability of a neckcloth. Gwen had forbidden him to appear at breakfast in that condition, saying it was *too* hard on her nervous sensibilities, particularly at an early hour. He had laughed at her, of course. Secretly I agreed that she was quite right.

He gave Ellen the faint, uncritical smile he reserved for her, and looked at me with all the affection one would reserve for the doorknob. Ellen, who says that nothing makes her more nervous than awkward silences, straightway piped up, "Good m-morning, my lord."

It's not hard to irritate Lord Brockhaven. "How many times do I have to tell you that I wish you would call me Alex? I've only been an earl for two years! Someday I'm going to be standing in the path of a falling boulder and *you're* going to call 'Jump, my lord,' and I won't know who you mean. Did you know you have two goose feathers sticking to your hair?"

"Yes, sir. Liza's tried to g-get them out; they s-seem to be stuck fast. We are going to t-try soaking them out this afternoon."

"Well, I'm glad to hear it. If that doesn't work, you should paste more on because two look ridiculous. I hope this isn't some new fashion in female ornament."

"N-no. It's from my feather picture, the one you b-brought the eagle feathers for when you w-went to the lakes last fall."

"Oh, yes," he said, opening the sliding cabinet door and scanning the volumes. "The feather picture. I remember last year when you made the colored sand arrangement and spilled a cup of rosined sand on the piano keyboard. When you had your lesson that afternoon, it took us an hour to pry your Italian piano master from the keys." With deliberate civility he said to me, "How did you like your first taste of our polite society?"

"I thought some members were more polite than others," I said, trying to match his casual tone.

"Very subtle," he said, pulling a bound volume of correspondence from the pile, one marked 1806–1807 in gilt letters. "Gwen must be teaching you about the gentle reproach. I expect you didn't like me threatening to beat you."

"It's not so much that I minded you threatening to beat me," I said sweetly, "but when you specified that it would be with pleasure . . ."

Brockhaven gave me one of his smiles that makes my heart feel like it's going to collapse. "Do you think it was because I felt my authority was being questioned?"

It seemed to me that his anger of the previous night had more to do with the fact that I was talking to Vincent than the fact that I was questioning his authority. It also seemed politic not to say so, because if he wasn't going to explain his behavior last night, he certainly wasn't going to do so this morning. My conversation with Robert popped into my mind like a worm suddenly appearing in a half-eaten apple. Could it be that in his talk with Brockhaven last night in the library Robert had taxed Brockhaven about the precise nature of his intentions toward me? Could that account for Brockhaven's tautly constrained amiability? He was an amazing man in many ways, able

163

to push one away as deftly with his good humor as with his bad, and all for a secret motive that you may not see until much later. Reasoned judgment looked back on our argument last night over Vincent and I began to wonder if even that had been a smokescreen for something else. What would he think if he knew what Ellen was planning for May Day? What would he think if he knew I had fallen in love with him?

I had to answer his question. "I think that may have been a part of it . . ." Hesitantly I added, "Does this mean we are less angry with each other now than we were?"

He gave me a lopsided grin. "Oh, certainly, my pet. Let's be moderate. I'll make you a peace offering. My brother mentioned that you'd like to visit Chad."

"Yes!" I said, surprised that he would bring it up with such complaisance.

"Gwen will arrange with Vince and Isabella for you to visit one day next week."

"Oh, thank you!" I cried, feeling my skin pink up with pleasure. I had been so certain that he would say no to Vincent's idea, that I could scarcely believe his words, especially after his patent hostility to my encounter with Vincent. "I should so much enjoy seeing where my father spent his childhood! It's very good of you to consent! Lord Brockhaven, about last night . . ."

Brockhaven glanced again at the volume in his hands before snapping it shut with one hand and sliding it back into sequence. He came across the room to lean easily on a chair arm near me and said, "Liza, about last night. You realize, I'm sure, that your cousin Isabella has what Gwen likes to call a hasty temper and a strong instinct toward possession? If she had come upon you in the corridor last night, alone with her husband, there would have been a scene that would have kept the county in gossip for weeks."

Ellen was frowning at me with some concern. "Mother did tell me that you and Lord Brockhaven had argued, Liza, but I didn't feel right about bringing it up unless you did first. *Were* you alone with Vincent in the hall? Oh, dear. Alex is right! Isabella g-gets so jealous, which is a smart bit of hypocrisy when it is s-she—ahem! What I mean to say is, Vincent knows what Bella is. Why w-would he have kept Liza talking with him, knowing there'd be a scene if Isabella saw it? It's not at all like him! He's usually so careful about that kind of thing."

"He has his reasons, I imagine," Brockhaven said dryly.

More than that, Lord Brockhaven could not be prevailed upon to say, and I felt gauche and ashamed of my angry response to his intervention. Ellen was no prude, and if she thought I shouldn't have been in the hall with Vincent, then I must have been in the wrong. Later, in my bed that night, I would remember this conversation with disquiet. Brockhaven's explanation didn't quite fit with things he had said during our argument at the Perscoughs and the discrepancies would disturb me; but that morning I felt only sheepish and annoyed with myself.

As usual, my thoughts were an open door to Brockhaven. He gave the bridge of my nose a careless brush with his fingertip, saying, "Don't look so distressed, child. It wasn't so bad, as it happened. I was just keeping an eye on you, which is my responsibility after all."

He looked at the pile of books that Ellen and I had scattered on the side table. "Come to think of it, the housekeeper did tell me that you two were on your way up here with a stack of improving literature." He leaned forward to read the titles, *"Tatting for the Beginner; On the Appreciation of Floral Beauty; Sermons for the Bedridden;* and last, though I'm sure by no means least, we have *Mrs. Hobbs' Educatorium."*

Brockhaven's unwelcome interest in our reading matter caused Ellen to quickly snap shut the *Ladies' Household Companion* on her lap, trying to conceal the book which had *really* been occupying our time. It was an unfortunate gesture. The hidden volume made a starkly obvious lump and Ellen's expression of alarm was a dead giveaway.

Lord Brockhaven was not born yesterday, and he also happens to know Ellen rather well. He directed one sardonic glance at her, lifted the *Ladies' Household Companion* from where it reposed in her lap and gently shook out the pages. *The Adventures of Countess T.* fell out with a plop, and Ellen put it into his commandingly outstretched palm with a stiff, scared look.

Brockhaven's eyebrows shot up when he saw the title. "Oh, Lord. You have been into mischief, haven't you?" He flipped it open and read the first page. "Do you know, it sounds vaguely familiar. I seem to recall reading it with Dain Bredon when we were thirteen. Is this the one with the Prussian officer?"

Ellen hesitated, took her bottom lip between her teeth, and nodded.

"And who else? The French foot juggler? I see. When it comes to improving literature, I don't think that the two of you are improving the same areas that Gwen thinks you're improving."

"Are you g-going to tell her?" asked Ellen, gazing up in hopeful solicitation.

"God forbid," said Brockhaven. "I can't imagine myself finding the tact to describe to Gwen just what it is that happens in the plot."

Chapter Nine

No government spy, no ruthless conspirator had ever connived an escape with more verve and imagination than Ellen had in her May Day arrangements.

First there had been the horses. Ellen was sure that her pretty mare, Wendy, would be recognized anywhere, and Kory had already gained a local reputation. How many stallions stood as high as a cottage, and had a coat the color of pitch? Four shillings had bought the silence of a local farmer and the loan of two of his most disreputable dobbins. From the ready exchange of communcation between Ellen and the farmer, I decided that she had done business there before.

The clothes we wore were Ellen's, from fancy dress parties and suitably altered. She was Noah's Ark without the ark headdress and its painted wooden giraffes. The gown was long and white, and we spent an afternoon cutting off pairs of animals and the dove of promise from the shoulder. For me, there was a costume Ellen had worn two Augusts ago to a fête in Bath, and even without changing it as much as a tuck, there wasn't anyone in the county who would know it. It was a pretty dress with a red and white striped skirt and red tunic, with a black velvet bodice trimmed with red, so I didn't mind a bit becoming the Goat Girl. For our faces, Ellen possessed two of some-

167

thing called "the loo mask" which were made of velvet and covered the top half of our faces except our eyes, and so when we were completely dressed in our costumes, masks, and two cloaks (bribed away from the serving maid), we looked comfortably absurd. I believe we would have stopped there but, since the book recommended the addition of flowers to the hair, nothing less would do than for Ellen to dig through her wardrobe and find two wreaths of artificial flowers, bluebells twisted with fern that she had worn playing one of the fairies in *A Midsummer Night's Dream* at a private revel. The bluebells seemed appropriate to her, since it was the fragrance I wore always, from a recipe made especially for me by my grandmother to celebrate my ninth birthday. It was particularly fortunate, said Ellen, that she had two wreaths, having lost one, bought another, and then found the original.

The meat was a little harder to get, and the opium a nightmare. As it turned out, Ellen was able to buy a joint of beef from the farmer with whom we had conducted our other underhanded dealings, but people who will sell two young women an amount of opium are few and far between. Even if both Ellen and I pretended headaches for a week, besides making Gwen suspicious, we wouldn't have been able to save enough, and we couldn't steal it from her locked cupboard for fear the blame should fall on one of the servants. Notice that I have said we wouldn't dare to steal it from *her.* I am very ashamed to admit that we did steal it. I know there is nothing more detestable than the criminal who protests he was pushed into his crime by a forceful partner, but the truth is that I never would have gone along with the idea if it hadn't been for Ellen. She refused to go into the woods without the meat, and there was no sense taking the meat unless it had been treated with the opium. I knew that if we didn't go out May Day Eve, Ellen would consider her entire spring a loss, and I think I've mentioned before that I'd rather do anything than disappoint Ellen. Besides, and I confess this in all cravenness, Ellen assured me that if we were caught in the theft, Brockhaven would bribe us out of jail, and I knew she was right.

We took the carriage into Chipping on the pretext of wishing to visit the subscription library, which Brockhaven thought a very good idea, considering, as he said, that the paucity of proper reading material in the house had driven us to more exotic kinds of literature in our commendable thirst for the printed word. I shudder to think what he would have said had he known our true purpose.

On the carriage ride to town, we laid our guilty plans. Ellen was taken aback to hear that I didn't know many ingenious ways to steal things because she had quite thought I would, being a gypsy. I will admit that there are gypsies who do steal things, and Grandma did once say that God had made a special rule that it was all right to steal from gorgios but only from gorgios and only if it was something you really needed, like a chicken or a blanket. But the only how-to story she had ever told me was about her cousin, Rupa, who would beg at the front door of the house while her sister, Lala, would go around to the back and whip the wash off the line. My grandmother said that for herself, she would never do such a thing because the gorgios punish you plenty if they catch you at it, and I'd better never do it or my father's ghost would groan in his grave. But knowing my father as I did, I somehow think he would have appreciated this venture.

Ellen made a wonderfully quick recovery from my utter unhelpfulness, and soon she had conjured up a plan. We would send the apothecary to look for a hopelessly obscure item that would surely entail a trip to the storeroom and, while he was looking, we would grab the opium, leaving payment, of course, in an envelope, and run for the carriage, which would be left three blocks away by the subscription library. We spent the rest of the trip devising a suitable concoction to confound the apothecary.

Now, you might think this is just the sort of plan that was doomed to failure, but the spirits that want one to hunt werewolves on May Day were on our side. Ellen had read recently in an old herbal about "the white lillie, the roote of which makes an excellent plaister which bringeth the haire againe upon places which have beene burned or scalded."

The apothecary was a cross-looking man with a dusty old wig and a red chin. He looked at us morosely when we asked for the white lillie and said we'd better not drink any of it because he thought it might be poisonous, and next time to have more sense than to go scaldin' ourselves anyway. I could hardly believe our luck when he said he *did* have some for us, but it would take awhile for him to find it, yes it would. With dreary satisfaction, he warned us that it would take *quite* a while. When his shuffling footsteps faded into the basement, Ellen fairly leapt across the counter like an athlete at the Greek games, grabbed a bottle clearly labeled "Laudanum," came back over the counter and left the envelope, bulging with money. It was Ellen's last-minute inspiration to write "from a tormented addict" on the envelope. I don't doubt that we were in the carriage and well on our way back to Edgehill before the apothecary discovered our crime. A most successful theft. Next to that, procuring a satchel and soaking it in wine was as easy as hopping on two feet.

We set out May Day morning two hours after the midnight church bells had rung in the summer and the May. The necessity to give any revelers who might be abroad the impression that we were girls from the village meant that we rode bareback, leaving our expensive saddles in the tack room. The night was warm and dry and the half-moon lent a silver cachet to the piles of clouds which floated between heaven and earth. Black shadows moved with the rustling leaves over our heads, and the smell of damp limestone rose from the ground. The night air tasted heavily sweet and intoxicating, like a strange potion. Twice as we wound our way uphill we heard revelers singing and laughing.

Their torches appeared first, flickering through the faraway branches like will-o'-the-wisps, and we took refuge in the shelter of the trees, and watched as they passed, their faces looking queerly distorted with hilarity and overindulgence. It was ghostly to have them come so close without seeing us, and I had the feeling that if I were to ride in their path, they would step right through me. Then the clatter would fade in the distance, the torches would dwindle into sparks, and wink out in darkness, and we would have the path once again to ourselves.

The higher on the hillside we climbed, the quieter and darker it seemed to become. I had lived too much of my life in the woods to have any fear of these soft shadows and moving branches, and yet, I began to have an eerie feeling of being curiously unprotected. If I could have had Kory with me, or dear old Caesar, the mastiff—but as I have said, they would be too easy a clue to our identity. Poor Caesar had been left sitting grumpily in the stables tonight, waiting for Brockhaven to return from dinner and cards with his friend Dain, who was Lord Bredon, a young, unmarried landowner of rakish reputation whose land joined Brockhaven's on the side opposite the boundaries shared with Isabella and Vincent.

I tried to ignore my uncertainty and felt for the hilt of the knife I had sheathed and attached to my sash. I knew how to throw it with some precision—it was an art Grandma and I used to practice on long summer evenings, those timeless times after the bottom rim of the sun has touched the horizon and before it dips below. Once in Ellen's room, I had exhibited my skill, to her ecstatic delight, and there was a slash in the center of a chalked circle on her wall to testify. To hide it from Gwen's doubtless disapproval, she had hung over it a sampler which read "I Come Not To Bring Peace, But A Sword."

To be cheerful, I sang softly to Ellen in Romany, which is the best language for me when I feel uneasy. I taught her the words and our voices blended in the night; singing:

> To the forest, go,
> Dance with the fairies!
> Hold the hand of time!
> Feel the caress of Mother Earth . . .

Our first suspicion that the Palace of the Dead Arches (ruin) was haunted tonight by more than a malingering werewolf came as we crossed the stonework bridge into the oaks. We saw far distant in the woods a tower of red smoke reaching into the sky, patterned with scarlet cinders. Drawing on, we heard laughing, shouting, singing, the music of out-of-tune fiddles, screaming fifes, and a drum. We left the horses by the bridge and crept slowly closer to the ruin, Ellen dragging the satchel in both hands. Peeking through the tangle of brush around the clearing, we saw that we had come upon the scene of the May Day bonfire, the destination of the straggling groups that had passed us in the woods.

Blankets were spread everywhere on the ground. Some of the revelers were sitting; some, girls and men both, were dancing with wild abandon, black impassioned silhouettes against the leaping flames of the bonfire. To the rear, the freshly cut elm Maypole lay surrounded by five or six young people stripping off its last branches and winding its fifty-foot length with ribbons, herbs, and flowers. The workers sung May carols as they went about their task, the voices making a strangely harmonious counterpoint to the instrumental music being played by the group of musicians standing near. There was wine everywhere, in skins and bottles; we saw a man on the far side of the fire lift a flagon and pour the wine into his mouth as if it had been water and he lost in the desert for a fortnight without it. As I grew used to the brightness and jumping shadows, I found myself beginning to recognize faces: girls from the village, farmer's sons, and here and there young men to whom I had been introduced at Lady Perscough's soirée, every one of them looking drunker than a cork. Peregrine Absalm was playing some wild, drawn-out tune on the guitar, and near him John Lennox was wrapping festoons of flowers around and around a young, dark-haired girl whose gown was slipping perilously lower over her rounded shoulders.

I felt the pressure of Ellen's hand against my arm. "Liza," she whispered, "cast your eyes at *that*." I looked in the direction she had discreetly indicated. Not thirty feet from where we were hidden was Robert, seated on a blanket with his arm around a sloe-eyed village beauty and his hands . . .

"I can't bear to l-look," murmured Ellen, holding her own hands over her eyes.

"Well," I said in a sympathetic whisper, "if you can't bear to look, then you had better close your fingers together, wouldn't you say?"

Ellen's fingers curled down into little fists on her cheeks. "I don't know how she c-can stand to have him use her like that!"

I agreed dutifully and added for good measure, "I'm sure she must be cheap."

"Oh, a slut!" Ellen agreed vehemently. We didn't say anything for a minute or two, and then from Ellen came the inevitable. "I wish it was m-me."

I tried to think of something encouraging. "He respects you too much to treat you so."

"I suppose that's it," she said miserably and heaved a sigh. "If he did treat me l-like that, then everyone would t-try to make him marry me, which does, I th-think, tend to be a big deterrent. Even if he could bring himself t-to seduce me, a thought which I am sure has never c-crossed his mind, he hasn't the least disposition t-to marry anyone, least of all me."

From the path behind us came a crash and an incredible blare of bugles. A half dozen wild young men on horseback came into view, galloping their uncontrolled horses into the clearing through the place where we had concealed ourselves! Ellen and I clambered to our knees and fled like a pair of flushing pheasants. I ran blindly in my haste, not stopping to look back until my toe caught on a root and brought me up sharply.

I had taken cover by a large outcrop of limestone. The bonfire and its tumult had receded into the distance and my surroundings seemed strangely silent.

"Ellen?" I said, not whispering. My voice sounded so loud and sharp that I jumped. My only answer was the plaintive whistle of an owl. I stood still and then called again. This time I knew I was alone.

Hoping Ellen would come to me, I stood where I was, time like a demented spider spinning its cloying web about me. I waited until my nerves were aching and still there was yet no sign of her, so, hoping she would do the same, I slowly began to make my way back to the horses, or at least, made my way back to where I thought the horses were. I had no light, and the trees seemed to cut out the moonlight like overlapping bat's wings. Bushes caught at my skirts and scraped my face. I knew I had gone too far and in the wrong direction when I came upon a horsetrack that I hadn't seen before. The revelers were so far away that their noise was almost indistinguishable from the dry voice of the wind.

Then, terrifyingly, came the inhuman, crackling yowl I had once heard near the ruins, the time when Caesar had dashed into the woods to protect me. But Caesar was at Edgehill, and it was impossible to tell whether the diffuse howl was coming from two miles away or twenty yards. I drew the knife from inside my cloak.

There was a tiny crack of a branch behind me and I turned. A gray shaft of moonlight was falling through the trees. A mesh of leaves parted and a tall, black, cloak-draped figure stepped soundlessly into it. I drew back my hand and sent the knife slicing through the air. There was a solid thwack as it landed uselessly in an unseen tree trunk. I would not get another chance.

"What the hell?" said a male voice.

There is no one else in the world who can swear with the same fluid efficiency. Horror mingled with sweeping relief as I realized that I had just tossed a knife at Lord Brockhaven. My first thought was to thank God it was him, and not a ghoulish thing from the underworld. My second was to turn and flee like a thousand devils were at my heels.

Strong hands caught me from behind, pulling me back against his hard muscled body.

"Oh, no, you don't," he said, shoving me against a tree

174

with such proficiency that you would think it was a move
he did every day. Holding my hands easily in one of his,
he thrust his other hand under the folds of my cloak.
"Let's see if you have any more weapons where that came
from." Roughly, his hand explored my waist in a quick,
searching motion and then moved higher. Suddenly it became a caress.

"I'll be damned," he said. "A woman." He began to
laugh.

I shrank back until the tree's rough bark dug into my
back. It took me that much time to remember that I was
masked, and please God, in the darkness there was nothing else about me that could tell him who I was. Hope
pulsed within me that I might still, miraculously, be able
to escape with my identity unknown.

"What's the matter, sweetheart?" he whispered huskily,
his hands curving around my waist. "Why, you're trembling. Were you afraid all alone in the woods? Is that why
you threw your knife at me?"

His hands were a burning distraction, but I knew I had
to answer, and, not trusting my voice, I nodded, hoping he
would find that a sufficient reply.

"Poor little doe." He lifted his hand across the slope of
my shoulder and spread his cool fingers on the side of my
neck, barely touching my skin. I shivered. "Are you waiting for your lover?" I nodded again, to avoid a lengthy explanation. At my answer, he let his finger stray over my
lips for a moment, and then released me. "Nay, darling,"
he said. "It's no place for you out here. I can't leave you
by yourself. Come with me—we'll find your sweetheart.
No doubt he's by the bonfire."

I hung back, unpleasantly surprised by this spate of unexpected philanthropy. All it needed tonight was for me to
be unmasked in front of the bonfire. He took a step, my
arm in his hand, but stopped when he felt my reluctance
to go with him. I thought fast, not wanting to give him
time to think up any more questions, and said the first
thing that came to my mind, trying to imitate the slur and
rhythm of country speech.

"He's—he's gone off with—another girl," I said. One doesn't often have the good luck to know immediately when one has made a terrible mistake, but fortune smiled wickedly down on me this time. I had forgotten for a moment Ellen's statement that no young lady of good repute would be abroad tonight. Brockhaven promptly placed the worst possible construction on my words, and my seeming desire to remain in the woods with him had only one logical possibility. If this were chess, I would have just put myself in check.

His tone was light and tender. "Well, then, what *can* I do for you, darling?"

I could have wept with frustration. Short of a long explanation, I couldn't seem to think of anything that would get rid of him, and a long explanation would surely reveal me to him.

"Go," I said, still trying to disguise my voice. "Please." Even to me it sounded unutterably coy. I heard him laugh softly again, and he pulled me hard against the length of his body. I could feel his breath on my cheek as he bent over me, and then suddenly he placed a deep, searching kiss on my lips. My cheeks were cupped in his hands, and his fingers played with my earlobes as his mouth was on mine, probing, seeking, brutal, and erotic, his lips moving over mine, stroking, taking, and laying waste like a comet skimming too close to the breast of the fertile earth. It was not a kiss he would have used on a virgin, because the question it asked was a demand no man would make on an innocent girl.

His lips left mine, and I took a shuddering gulp of air. He leaned my head back against a large, slanting branch and found my mouth again. My knees were beginning to shake beneath me, and I was strangely grateful for the tree at my back, and the solid strength of his grip. When we had kissed before, in the glen, it had seemed the essence of heavenly love. There can be no heaven without the inferno, and this is what I experienced now—a match, carelessly thrown by Lord Brockhaven, on the dry, parched kindling of my attraction for him exploding us both into

176

burning cinders. I hadn't known the human body was capable of such a feeling, such a stretching of the possibilities, such a release of one's soul in a thousand directions at once.

When his lips left mine this time, my own felt scarred, swollen, and the harsh panting of my breath seemed forced out of my lungs with each chest-wracking pump of my heart. His lips searched gently for the pulse in my throat, and I was sure that if he found it, he would cause it to stop.

"Sweet, darling, so sweet," he murmured. Among his many talents, I discovered in Brockhaven a gift for the understatement. His hand reached behind my head, roaming with searing tenderness through the swimming net of my hair. "Hush—don't let it frighten you. Do you know who I am?"

"Yes," I whispered the word, swallowing painfully.

"That's fine, my love." Through the material of my gown, I could feel his palm as he touched me intimately. "Don't be afraid—I'll be good to you." His kisses tasted me deeply, and I felt intoxicated, my blood flowing like wine, burning and heady through my veins. My earlobe tingled under the caress of his breath as if in anticipation of the nip that followed, and, like a warm blanket, his hand covered my breast. And there was the pressure of his body on mine . . . I looked up at him. His face wavered before me, and I could see his half-closed, heavy-lidded eyes in the moonlight.

I summoned my waning strength and tried to pull away. Prevented by his hand on my back, I gasped, feeling my heart skip as he brought me back to him, and suddenly I felt powerless, my head falling back, my hair streaming as I could no longer keep my mouth from his. Far away, like drowning echoes, I heard him speak.

"You're so charming, love," he murmured. "I need you tonight, need you to help me forget someone—a lady . . . You smell so sweet"—He kissed my throat—"like wild bluebells, like—"

He stiffened all at once, looking down at me in the

177

moonlight, and I could only gaze back. "Like Liza," he finished. His body was still now; the insistent pressure had stopped; and, to my horror, he reached up his hand and untied the mask. I heard it fall with the slightest of rustles to the grass at our feet. Still in his arms, I tried to control the shiver I could feel beginning to overtake me.

"How far would you have let it go before you stopped me—before you told me who you were?" he asked, his voice husky, strangely uneven.

The silence caused by my inability to answer him was broken only by the hooting of a faraway owl. Finally I summoned my voice, and said, though I could manage but a whisper, "I knew you'd be angry."

"I see. Complicated, isn't it?" Slowly, with an almost painful deliberation, he pushed me away. "Never fear, sweetheart. I won't disappoint you. In a moment I'm going to be madder than hell at you, but right now I'm only . . ." He didn't finish his sentence before pushing me to arm's length, holding me there, staring back at him dumbly. "I'm trying to function with only half a mind," he finished.

"Half?" I couldn't keep the fright from my voice.

"The other half wants to carry you to that bed of leaves and love you until sunrise," he said dryly. "Do you think you could help a little?"

"What should I do?" I asked, looking at him in helpless misery.

"Lace yourself up, for God's sake. With the moonlight on your skin, you look damnably irresistible."

I tried to do as he requested, but my hands were shaking so badly that he had to do it, though he swore and said I was an incompetent little fool. At his words, the tears that had been shimmering in my vision overflowed, and I felt them run down my cheeks.

"Don't, Liza." His voice was raw. "Don't start that. Don't make me take you in my arms again. I don't think I could rip myself from you a second time."

I took two steps back from him and rested my hand against the rough bark of the tree behind us.

"Who is the lady you need to forget?" I asked in a low voice, hating myself for asking. "Is it Isabella?"

"Isabella?" he said wearily. "Don't be ridiculous. It didn't mean anything; and I didn't know I was talking to you." A breeze ran through the branches over our heads, sending a few old leaves somersaulting to the ground. "Or maybe I did. Your body was so strangely familiar," he said softly.

I said, "Like an old shoe you thought misplaced."

"And would still like to slip into," he said. "Don't let's flirt, sweeting. This is Thursday, and on Thursdays I never seem to have much self-control."

Anger shot through my chest like an explosion of icy splinters. "No, I suppose not, accustomed as you are to taking your pleasure where you please."

"What do you want, my pet? An all-inclusive apology for the impure course of my life?" he said. "Or will it content your blushing vanity if I hold you like this"—his fingers seized my shoulders and pulled me against him with unthinking brutality—"and let you feel what it's like to have a man want you? And I do want you, Liza. Would it interest you to experiment with all the facets of that? Let's see, what was it that you wanted to know? Ah, yes, about Isabella. Would you like to learn how to play with the style—" His hands traveled over me with savage fluid strokes and his lips took mine with expertly erotic cruelty.

When at last he let me breathe, the air came from my lungs in a frightened whimper. He heard it, and I was released instantly. A minute passed as I stood listening to his breathing surrender back into the bands of his iron control. Finally, he said, "That was a damnable thing to do. Forgive me, Liza."

My blistered heart was too heavy with grief to listen to his apologies. I heard myself yelling, "Why ever, my lord? I'm flattered that you find my half-breed countenance acceptable to your cultured tastes, especially since I remember a time when you found it none too appetizing, so you said when you first found me in the library with Robert."

"Does that rankle still?" he asked tersely. "I suppose

you would rather I encouraged him. If only I'd known! I could have said, 'Yes, she's a beauty, and if I were you, I'd waste no time in having her. Fetch me when it's my turn.' "

"No! No!" I cried, letting the old, unburied pain of it spill from me like boiling water from cracked clay. "You would have left me with Robert, if you hadn't noticed my father's medallion and decided to use me against Vincent. You've had me scrubbed and shod and taught the difference between a fish fork and a fruit fork, and you've dressed me in gorgio clothes, and now I'll do for Thursdays."

Sorting through this in remarkably short order, he said, "I wouldn't have left you to Robert, even if I hadn't seen the medallion."

"Then you would have had me hung for poaching your foxes!" In spite of myself, I felt a tear splash, cold and wet on the curve of my cheek.

"The word is hanged. No, I wouldn't have. Do you think I believe in killing children for misdemeanors against my property? However little you seem to feel that I cared what happened to you, you know damned well that I care too much for Robert to let his excesses run to self-destructive acts like taking terrified peasant girls by violence. As for finding you unappetizing, we've already covered that subject more thoroughly than we should have, when one considers that I'm supposed to be acting in the capacity of your guardian. What else have you on your list? I'm fascinated!" Taking my hand, he brushed his lips softly across my palm. He said, "Hang it, Liza. Are you drunk?"

"No! Why do you ask?"

"Your hand reeks of spirits."

"It must have been the satchel. The book said it had to be soaked in wine, you see, and Ellen was adamant."

Like an actress answering a cue, her breathing short and sharp as if she had been running, my friend appeared at the edge of the clearing twenty yards away. With a cry that lay between a sob and a gasp, I heard her call, "Liza!"

Because she was so distraught, and because I was so relieved to see her, I ran toward her into the moonlight, crying, "Ellen! Ellen!" without thinking how Brockhaven must have looked to her, standing black and threatening under the dark roof of the trees.

"Liza! The werewolf!" Ellen screamed, her voice cutting through to a new plane of terror. "It's after you!" Before I could tell her it was Brockhaven, she said, "The meat! I'll throw it the meat!" She grabbed wildly in the satchel, pulled out the joint of beef, drew back her arm with the grace of a discus thrower, and sent the opium-soaked meat soaring across the clearing to land with a soggy crash two feet from the polished tips of Brockhaven's boots.

I'm not sure whether it was his encounter with me, being called a werewolf, or having a heavy object hurled at him in the dark, but the meat toss put the final nudge to Brockhaven's toppling temper. I had never seen anyone move so fast. In less space than it takes an acorn to hit earth, Brockhaven had us collared and dragged back to the hideously oozing pile of red meat.

"What in the name of heaven is *that*?" he rapped, pointing.

"Th-that? That is opium s-soaked b-beef to d-drug the werewolf," Ellen said, shakily but succinctly.

Brockhaven looked at her incredulously. "I'm crossing you off the very small list of people I know who aren't complete idiots."

I had to admire Ellen's spirit as she looked him full in the face and replied, "Well, you d-didn't catch it, d-did you?"

"What you are going to catch, Ellen, my dear," he said with silky sweetness, "is not a werewolf. In my life I have heard of some hare-brained escapades, but this one defies description. Are you two out of your minds?"

Chapter Ten

Let it not be supposed that one caustic sentence would be all that Lord Brockhaven had to say about finding us in the May Day forest. His remarks were lengthy, withering, and peppered with deprecations on our characters that I would not care to repeat. When finally he began to wind down, he said, as though the thought had just occurred to him, "Is it just the two of you, or are there another half dozen of your friends skipping around in the dark somewhere?"

"No, no," said Ellen, "only us two. I thought it w-would only be safe for Liza if we didn't tell anyone."

Brockhaven gave her an arrested look; his eyes narrowed. "Did you, by God? You and I are going to have a talk about this tomorrow, child. It seems to me you've been doing altogether too much thinking."

Ellen pulled her cloak tighter about her and stared at him with great pansy eyes. "I c-care what happens to Liza, that's all."

Far off in the underbrush we heard a crash and suddenly I recalled the discordant howl that had so recently rent the night's taut fabric. Meeting Lord Brockhaven had driven it completely from my mind.

"I heard it again tonight," I said.

Almost as though he didn't want to, Brockhaven admit-

183

ted, "So did I, just before you nearly skewered me, Liza. Oh, I see now. *You* thought I was the werewolf too. Do you know something? A werewolf would pose less the menace to the unsuspecting local population than the pair of you out here tossing assorted grotesqueries at anything that moves. What's this about a book telling you to soak meat in opium? Was it a book you found in Robert's study? By God, if I ever find you in there again searching through one more discreditable volume, Ellen, I swear I'll lay the whole before your mother, which is what I ought to do anyway."

"I am sorry about the meat, Alex," Ellen said, in an appropriately cowed voice. "But don't you think it shows that Liza and I weren't *bad* at defending ourselves?"

Lord Brockhaven's expression was sardonic indeed, but he forbore to comment, so Ellen went on, "I also heard the howl! It was hideous! Indescribable! Alex, *please*, couldn't we three go now and hunt for it?"

"What a wonderful idea," marveled Brockhaven. "We could start out at once, except that the howl didn't originate from anywhere near here. Sound echoes back from the bluff so the . . . whatever howled must have been up the cliffside, miles away. It would be useless to try a chase without dogs."

Then, from up the verge, we heard the discordant notes of the reveler's band coming in our direction. All pretense of a tune had been dropped in favor of a kind of squealing fervor in which duration and volume took precedence over meter and harmony. There was the snorting and stomping of excited horses and the slurred chorus of "Farmer Shortroot's Courtship."

"It needed only this," said Brockhaven. "Damn it all, they've seen us." Scooping up my mask from where it had fallen under the tree, he handed it to me, saying curtly, "Cover your face. Have you got one too, Ellen? Thank God for that much. Put it on, and if anyones tries to take it off you, scratch his eyes out. I mean it, do you hear?"

From the midst of the clamoring concatenation came a greeting, tossed up like a ragged bit of seaweed from a nasty surf: "Ho there! What's going toward? *Ménage à trois*: Is it a private affair or can anyone come?"

"Oh, please, Lord Brockhaven," I said in an agitated whisper. "Can't we hide in the woods until they're gone?"

"It's no use; they're drunk as brewers' cats," he answered. "Like as not, they'd make a game of chasing us through the trees. Just keep your mouth shut and leave the talking to me. Don't blame me if you each receive a score of bawdy propositions. I didn't ask you to come here."

They were upon us and we were mired in a flood of torch light and the scents of wood smoke, wine, and horses. It was the group from the ruins, with John Lennox on horseback in the lead. He reached down to ruffle Brockhaven's hair affectionately, and offered him the wine skin, which my guardian accepted cheerfully. Entreaties rang out through the ranks for Robert to come forward and guess who they had found here.

Robert edged through the crowd on his gelding. The girl he had been kissing by the fire was perched pillion behind him with her arms low around his waist, her cheek resting on his back, and a silly satisfied smile on her face. Her eyes were closed, and I don't think she could have opened them to look at us if she'd wanted to. As for Robert himself—his hat was askew, his hair down in his eyes, and he had a swag of spring flowers draped rakishly across his body like a bandolier.

"Alex, dear fellow," he said with a mellow smile. "Have you finished dining with Bredon? What a meal he must have served." He indicated us with a wave. "Were these two among the hors d'oeuvres or did you find them floating in the punch?"

I heard Brockhaven say something caustically under his breath about who'd been floating in the punch. In a louder voice, he said meaningfully to Robert, "Neither. They're pure spring lamb."

Peregrine Absalm looked to be in worse condition than even Robert. He stood halfway up in his stirrups, weaving dangerously, with his guitar hanging from a twisted strap at a horizontal angle on his back.

"Did you know, little lamb," he said to me with a hiccup, "that I'm quite a shepherd?"

"The big bad wolf, more like," said John Lennox with amusement.

"Never, Johnny, he's a shepherd all right," laughed the slim girl who had been walking beside Lennox, her long arms spread in a serpentine weave around his leg. "Though his staff's crooked, poor thing, and he falls asleep on the job."

There was a roar of laughter while a boy I recognized as an older brother to Ellen's friend Claire leaned from his saddle and plucked at me, barely managing to make the maneuver without toppling to the ground.

"Don't need a shepherd anyway," he said, "needs a ram!" He reached for me again, this time with such improved precision that I had to step back quickly to avoid capture.

Nestling me protectively under his arm, Brockhaven said, "Oh, no, I've already claimed the wench."

Laughing repartee labeled Brockhaven as a dog in the manger, and my guardian saw fit to prove himself guilty as charged by placing a lingering kiss on my lips, to general approval, and I had no choice but to submit. Under the cover of cheers and bawdy remarks, he got Robert's attention by firmly grabbing his arm and saying, "The other girl's for you." There was a wealth of meaning ladled into Brockhaven's tone, and one eyebrow was raised in faint suggestion, but Robert was too well-steeped to catch the nuances.

"Is she now?" said Robert. "Here's generosity!" Robert's eyes swept boldly over Ellen. "Come to me, darling—let's see what you're made of." He dismounted, landing usteadily, and slid his arms around Ellen's waist. "How do you do, angel? Show me how you do." He brought his lips hard down on Ellen's.

Ellen did her best. In a fair imitation of the memorable Countess T., she threw her arms around Robert's neck and wound her fingers in his thick hair, as well as "letting her lips fall open like a tulip parting for the dew, and pressed

186

herself to him with wanton pleasure." From where I was standing, it looked like a very good effort. But Robert knew better. He had too much experience not to recognize the kiss of a green girl.

"Good lord!" he exclaimed, releasing her abruptly. He looked at Brockhaven. "You brought *her* for *me?*"

"Let us say rather that she brought herself. And it would seem a very good idea to return her from whence she came in the same condition," said Brockhaven, not mincing matters.

"And from whence did she come?" asked Robert.

"They've both come from the edge of the hill, if you take my meaning," said Brockhaven, adding in an undertone, "For God's sake, will you sober up a little? I need your help."

Robert missed a beat and then, from the dramatic way his face changed, it was possible to see the instant he realized it was Ellen he had just kissed. In any other circumstances it would have been comical. He stared at Ellen and at me and said, very slowly, "Well, well."

"Precisely," said Lord Brockhaven in a biting tone.

"Don't say you know the girl!" exclaimed the would-be ram.

"I thought I knew her," answered Robert, taking Ellen's chin in the crook of a finger, "but I see I was wrong. I'm beginning to think I'd like to become better acquainted, however. Will you come a-Maying with me, angel?"

"Yes, oh yes," cried Ellen with indecent fervor.

Robert laughed, but threw a questioning look at Brockhaven and then a nod to me.

"Oh, yes," said Brockhaven. "Guess who? I'll watch her. Just you keep track of the—what did you call her?—oh, yes, the angel."

Looking intrigued and a little less tipsy, Robert threw me a speaking grin and gave Peregrine a convivial slap on the leg.

"Perry, my good man," he said. "I've lost my heart to a new interest. How'd you like to ride with Nan? No, no, don't try to pull her on the horse with you. Just get off and ride my gelding, and I'll take your horse." And so the thing was done—Peregrine dismounting with a huge grin to climb on Robert's horse in front of the sloe-eyed girl, who, to the delight of the gathering, nestled against him with exactly the same comfortable smile she had before. It was doubtful whether she even noticed the change.

Robert took it in very good part, mounting Peregrine's horse and pulling Ellen to the saddle in front of him. "That's Nan," he said. " 'Tis no one of us she likes in particular, but all of us in general."

Brockhaven took me by the hand and led me across the clearing to the thickly growing bushes where he had left his stallion. "It will attract attention if Robert were to leave suddenly, and I don't want to leave Ellen with that mob, so we'll simply have to go along. Up with you." He lifted me sidesaddle on the roan. "Do you want the front or the back?"

"The front or the back of what?" I asked.

"You wouldn't be so alarmed by my question if you hadn't spent your time reading smutty books. You know what they say about the wages of sin. I meant, do you want the front or the back of the horse. Never mind, I'll put you in front. You'll be less noticeable there."

I stiffened as I felt his gracefully muscled body slide into the saddle behind me. My blood went racing again, with him so close, and to distract myself I asked him, "If it isn't an indiscreet question, my lord, what was it that you were doing walking in the forest?"

"I saw what I thought was someone lost in the woods, and rushed chivalrously to the rescue—after leaving the roan tied in the bushes. I didn't want to risk him putting his foot down a rabbit hole in the dark."

The stallion shifted beneath us as Brockhaven touched it into a walk, back toward the group in the clearing.

I gave a nervous chuckle. "Don't you think it would be funny, my lord, if all the girls here were young ladies from the great houses, celebrating incognito?"

"Fortunately, it can't be so," he said, "since you and Ellen are the only two masked." The stallion stumbled a bit, and he steadied me quickly with an arm at my waist. His fingers stretched lightly over the flat of my stomach.

"Lord, you're taut," he said. "Try to relax your legs, Liza. The stallion isn't used to you. Being straddled by a woman so tense is—"

"I'm not straddling him, and I can't help it if I'm tense."

"Acute, aren't you?" he replied. "It's as difficult for me as it is for you. More difficult."

As we rejoined the group, I waved to Ellen, who waved back, giving every appearance of having the time of her life. In fact, she was saying to Robert, "Do you th-think I could have a little of your wine?"

"Very well," Robert said, giving her the nearly flaccid skin. "But only a little. I don't want to take you home drunk."

Ellen took the skin and tipped back her head as she had seen others do, letting the wine pour into her throat. Robert roared with laugher at her bawdy appearance.

"That girl," said Brockhaven under his breath, "is bidding fair to becoming a rare handful."

"Robert's been doing it!" I said indignantly. "Why is it when Ellen does the same thing, *she's* a rare handful?"

"Have you ever heard me say that Robert isn't?"

I tried again. "She only wants to have an adventure. Is that so bad? Don't you think if she has adventures, Robert is the safest person for her to have them with?"

"On the contrary. All he needs is another half pint and he'll forget who she is, and what he shouldn't be doing with her. And if she doesn't keep her voice down, half the county will know who she is by the stutter. Damn—what was the matter with you? Don't you know what could have happened to you out on a night like this?"

"Yes," I responded promptly. "I could be ravished by an unconscionable libertine."

We began to move with the group in a straggling procession toward the bottom of the hill. Brockhaven spurred his stallion to the outskirts of the crowd.

"Your point," he said in my ear. I had the impression

189

that he was smiling, though there was an edge in his voice. "Is that what it was, Liza? Ravishing? You can be blunt. My head's cooler now."

No, I thought in my heart. I love you. But how could I say that to the complex, self-possessed man behind me? I was miserably aware of my own cowardice that wished to share the depth of feelings with him, yet dared not. What was left? For him to believe me a foolish adolescent, curious about my budding sensuality, eager for limited experiments in passion. Lord knows the man was accustomed enough to being the brunt of infatuation. Instead of I love you, I said in a polite voice, despising myself, "I don't know what it was. Perhaps you can explain it to me—you're the one with the experience."

"Oh, are we back on that theme again? I admire your resolution. When one considers that our last communication of *that* aspect of my life was marked by a certain want of cordiality, particularly on my part."

"Of course, you're right!" I said hastily. "I beg your pardon! I don't mean to sit in judgment."

"Don't sound so scared. I'm less of a monster than you think. Didn't your grandmother teach you anything about physical love?"

I thought it over and said, "She described for me the act."

"God forbid. The act? You're farther ahead than most girls your age. That is, if she told you all of it."

"Of course she told me all of it. There wouldn't be much point in leaving anything out, would there be, when one is forever seeing dogs mating, and other animals."

"As you say," he said. "They rather tend to give the whole thing away. Did your grandmother tell you anything else?"

"Only this—never make love with any man but your husband, and never refuse him." I twisted around to look at him. He was trying unsuccessfully to suppress a smile. "Well?"

"Well. I think someday you'll make a wonderful wife for some lucky fellow." He gave my cheek a flick with a long, careless finger. "Turn around." I obeyed him, facing front again, and he said, "It amounts to this, sweetheart. You are too tempting, and I am too temptable. The fox guarding the chicken. Which reminds me—d'you see Robert and Ellen?"

"There they are," I said. "Up ahead of the couple on the donkeys."

"Let's catch up to them, shall we? We'll get Robert to give us some of his wine."

The wineskin was empty, but had been replaced by a bottle filled with clear red wine, and I'm embarrassed to admit that I drank some too, right from the bottle, wanting to keep Ellen company. I swallowed too much, and the wine ran down my chin in sticky trails, and Robert laughed at me as he had done at Ellen. Brockhaven mopped me up with his handkerchief and said I was a disgusting brat. Ellen retorted that he was a terrible guardian with such cheerful stammering loudness that Brockhaven cringed and said, "Robert, make her keep her voice down. Not that way, idiot," as Robert tried to stop her mouth with a kiss. "What a foursome we are. Come on, let's not hold up the parade."

"Yes, let's go," chirped Ellen. "I want t-to watch them raise the maypole."

"Oh, no," said Brockhaven quickly. "No maypole. We're turning off at the first dark corner to get you both back to Edgehill."

Ellen looked at him with eyes already suspiciously bright. "I'm going to see the maypole, Alex. I'm going to see it, and if you t-try to stop me, I'm going to pull off my hood and my m-mask and start screaming that I'm Ellen Cleaver and that Lord Brockhaven is a fuddy-duddy, and that I've pleasured with Robert in the Edgehill wine cellar."

"You wouldn't dare," said Alex, his eyes narrowed.

"Yes, I think she would," said Robert. "She's drunk as a friar—I've never seen anyone pour wine down so fast in my life."

"I hold you personally responsible for that, Robert," retorted Alex in an exasperated voice. "What the hell's the matter with you, letting her drink that much? You can't expect an innocent chit to hold her liquor."

"I had about as much luck," Robert answered sweetly, "at preventing her from drinking too much as you're having persuading her to forego the maypole. Better to do as she says."

That is how we got to go to the maypole. We reached the village as the last vestige of black night had turned from the sky, to be replaced by strips of rose pink. Folk came spilling from their cottage doors and from the woods where so many hardy young had spent the night, and young and old began to greet the new day and the new spring with a raucous clamor of shouts, whistles, cheers, banging drums, and clanging hand-carried bells. Ellen blew earsplitting blasts on a cow horn provided for her by Robert. Young girls brought large baskets of flower garlands, passing them around, and soon I was draped with so many floral chains that I could barely move my chin without having my nose tickled in the petals. Aside from me, someone had given Ellen a small tiara decorated with stars, crescents, and wheels, the amulets to ward off witchcraft and evil.

Young girls ran to the field to bathe their faces in May's first dew, which it is said, is an infallible beauty charm. I had lost sight of Ellen, but Brockhaven groaned as he saw her led by Robert through the crowd, her cheeks smeared with wet grass.

The procession wound to the village green through cottages decked with green branches and birch boughs gathered last night in the forest. The ceaseless toll of May carols surrounded us as we rode behind the ten yoke of oxen, each with sweet nosegays of flowers tied to the tips of their horns, that drew the heavy maypole.

Children cavorted and scattered petals, and couples danced in wild leaps as the maypole was raised.

Nan, the girl who had been on the back of Robert's horse when we first came upon them, was crowned May Queen, wrapped in a blanket woven of bluebells and new

192

green leaves, and the dancing began in earnest, with the streaming, herb-laden ribbons on the maypole flying in endlessly changing patterns. Ellen took me by the hand in the singing, laughing crowd, and cried, "Dance, Liza, dance," and whether it was the wine or the gaiety around me, or the sweet freedom of anonymity, Ellen and I ran around the maypole, and danced like a pair of spirits. Someone, I believe it was Robert, stuck white willow wands wreathed in cowslips into my hands, and I waved them over my head and struck them together as the other girls were doing, and danced until I was dizzy.

I don't remember when Brockhaven plucked me from the crowd, but I vaguely recall being once again on his horse, his arm around my waist, and Ellen and Robert riding next to us, Ellen blaring on her horn for all she was worth. My eyes drooped, and I slept the rest of the way back to Edgehill.

Chapter Eleven

The next thing I knew I was waking in bed at half past two that afternoon with a splitting headache. I don't know how Brockhaven managed to get me unseen into my bedroom, or to get the horn away from Ellen. I don't know how he and Robert thought to ride out and find our horses, or how he guessed which farmer they should be returned to, nor do I know which maid he bribed to take our crescent crowns, and our soiled and wine-splashed dresses, and have the mess cleaned up with no one the wiser.

What I do know is that the second I woke up, I was summoned with Ellen to appear in Brockhaven's library. We sat with searing, biting hangovers while he delivered to us a lecture that could have cleaned the tarnish from the family silver, and warned us that if he ever saw either of us make the slightest attempt to rake it up again, he would take us by the scruff of our necks, and lay us, and the whole tale, before Lady Gwen. Opium-soaked meat—were we out of our minds? We must have been a fairly woebegone pair, because finally he laughed and gave us a dose of the powder that Robert used for his postindulgent affliction, sent us back to bed, and told Lady Gwen that we had indigestion.

The most amazing outcome of our escapade turned out

to be the change in Robert's attitude toward Ellen. In every tale one could read written for young ladies of virtue, any hapless young girl so lacking in self-control as to allow herself to behave in such a carefree manner would earn the lasting and incontrovertible disgust of any young man. Robert's reaction would have astounded the moralists. Instead of holding Ellen in disgust, he looked on her with new respect. He had never imagined there to be such a lust for adventure in this quiet, earnest little damsel.

He began to talk to Ellen about herself, and the more they talked, the more they discovered about each other; he began to call her Ellen the Lionhearted. Finally, to Ellen's delight, and far beyond her wildest dreams, he began to flirt with her, soaring her spirits to Olympian heights. I was glad for her sake, and it made things happy and exciting, an atmosphere that I sorely needed. My own spirits were plunged to the lowest desolation.

I dreamed at night of Brockhaven kissing me, touching me, and would wake up icy and sweating and twisted tightly in my bedclothes. When my guardian and I were together, mostly with Ellen, Lady Gwen, and Robert, I found that my gaze would catch and hold some random movement of Brockhaven's—the shaping of his long white fingers around the curve of a wineglass, or the way he would absently run the tip of a finger down the smooth, flat side of a knifeblade; and I would think of the deep, heady magic his fingers had made of my flesh. I found myself staring at the hollow at the base of his throat, and remembering how I had been close enough to feel the pulse beating there. I longed for him to talk with me and tease me as he had the day I walked on the stone wall. Deep within me there was a wish that he would tell me his secrets and emotions, and listen as I shared mine with him.

It had become so overpowering for me to be in his presence that speech was for me out of the question; I began to avoid him and was effortlessly successful. Perversely to my hurt, he avoided me. When we were thrown together unavoidably, in a room in which a third party was present and it would have been conspicuous if either one of us had left immediately, he was the same as he had always been—kind, yet distant and reserved, occasionally irritable. The shifting phases of his mood seemed derived from such things as the progress of planting and whether or not the new plow would arrive, rather than anything to do with me.

I couldn't imagine Lord Brockhaven asking any women for marriage and tenancy for life, because he seemed too whole and separate to have another person that close in his life. I couldn't imagine him feeling so strongly for a woman to want to marry her. What was left for me—to be his mistress? It was unthinkable that I should contemplate such a thing.

I was tempting enough to be kissed, provided I fell against him accidentally in a meadow or if he were to meet me incognito in a dark wood, but I had discovered that men can have that kind of physical contact with a woman and invest it with no affection; hence, Robert and Nan as we had seen them at the bonfire. It made me feel serious, sad, and hopeless. I could see a lifetime stretching ahead of me filled with unrequited yearning for Lord Brockhaven.

I realized how destructive it was to nourish my hopeless hopes, and spent hours undertaking what I fondly wished to be the expungement of Lord Brockhaven from my thoughts and my heart. I looked back in horror once the hours were passed, realizing that I had merely spent the time mooning over him.

Half of May was gone. The snowy apple blossoms had fallen from their trees, carpeting the earth underneath in plush ermine, leaving new green growth behind. Red campion had come to bloom, growing in the shady spots under the hedges. A pair of little wrens was nesting outside my window, and I watched them for long, reflective moments, two tiny feathery balls hopping and trilling not three feet from the sash. Ellen and I collected fragrant herbs and laid them in sand to dry to make sachets for her elderly nurse, who would be eighty years old on the seventh day of June. However much I did to keep busy, it remained nearly impossible for me to eat at the table when Lord Brockhaven was present. My energy began to wane, and I lost weight.

About this time, Ellen became afflicted with a spring cold, and was put to her bed with mustard packs and orders to sleep, and I realized how much I had depended on her company to keep me going. For the first time in my life I felt lethargic.

It worried Lady Gwen. On the third morning Ellen spent in bed, I was having breakfast with Lady Gwen and Robert. I had consumed what had become my normal pittance and then asked to be excused.

"My dear child," exclaimed Gwen. "Again you haven't eaten enough to keep a minnow aswim. If this continues, I fear we shall have to force feed you like a Christmas goose. I know I've asked you this before, and I don't wish to press you, Liza—but is there something troubling you?"

"No, dear ma am." I tried to smile. "Spring fever perhaps."

Gwen shook her head and took on a worried look. "I fear it's the change from the wandering gypsy life to this one, come so soon after the loss of your grandmother. So much to distress you! One would almost think, my dear, that you were pining."

When I said no more, she left with a troubled frown to visit Ellen's sickbed, after leaning over to tenderly kiss the top of my head. After she left, I glanced at Robert, who I thought had been reading the paper, only to find him staring intently at me. Meeting my gaze, he said quietly that he thought we ought to talk; not wanting to hear his questions, I pleaded a headache and left the room. I pressed my temples on the way out, feeling that the lie had actually brought me a real headache. I smiled ruefully, deciding that Grandmother would be forcing a tonic on me if she could have seen me like this.

Thinking of my grandmother filled me with a terrible longing, and I had to choke down a thick, unhappy feeling in my throat, and blink back tears. I went to the kitchen

and asked the steward for a glass of wine. He obliged, and
I took the glass to the garden and poured it on the earth
as an offering to my grandmother, saying, "May this be
before you." The familiar act of mourning and love lifted
my spirits, and in this mood of optimism, I decided I
would make myself a tonic.

I ran upstairs and changed into a high-waisted walking
gown of peach cotton trimmed with white velvet ribbons,
smoothed the high muslin neckruff, and went out in search
of bog bean.

A wonderful purifier for the blood is bog bean, a stim-
ulus to the appetite and a remedy for migraine. You'll find
it everywhere you look in Scotland, but in this area of England it only grows here and there. When it is discovered,
there is usually lots of it, so you're in luck. There was just
such a lucky spot bordering the garden at the dower
house. The dower house, a lovely small structure of
cream-colored brick, had been vacant for seventy-five
years. Ellen had told me that it was empty of furniture but
that the servants went through it twice a year and kept it
cleaned and in repair. Other than that, it was left alone,
except for irregular checks by the steward or Brockhaven.
The garden was in a picturesque state of neglect, the only
attention paid to it being a scything of the walkways at
midsummer. Tiny, fragile teardrops of lilies of the valley
grew along the garden path.

The day was quiet except for the song of the thrush.
Two squirrels chased each other across the overgrown trail
as I picked my way toward the bog bean, which grew, as
it does, in the small lake at the back of the garden. Thick
reeds, making a good recovery from winter frostbite, had
framed the lake with green whiskers. The surface of the
water reflected the blue sky, a surface shimmered and broken only by the pair of springs bubbling up from the bottom. A sheltering of yellow and orange azaleas shared the
bank with an occasional mound of dark rhododendrons,
while bluebells and Lent lilies were graceful partners with
lacy ferns. They danced to the slow, soft music of a long
spring zephyr which, as is the way with a truly beautiful

199

tune, was felt more than heard. A backdrop of dark yews bordered the setting from the rest of the world.

The bog bean was growing where I had marked it previously—in a patchy hummock about twelve yards from shore, nearly to the middle of the lake. One hand occupied by my straw basket, I gathered my skirts in the other, lifting them as high as I could, for this was one of the expensive dresses Lady Gwen had bought for me, and I didn't want to soil it. Silvery minnows darted around my feet as I touched the sandy bottom; it was a pleasant, rough feeling. The going was easy for about six of the twelve yards, and then there was a rapid descent where I could see it would be too deep to wade. I turned, and, accompanied by the minnows, went back to shore to remove the dress.

It was a little embarrassing to take off my dress out of doors, but I found the filmy gorgio dresses slight enough covering anyway. Besides, who was to watch but a pair of moorhens poking their black heads out to stare at me from behind the reeds? I still had on my chemise, its linen sides falling straight from the lawn frill at the drawstring neck to the top of my knees. The sun felt hot and good on my bare arms, and I thought how upset Goudette would be, and how she would make me wear gloves if my arms got brown. The breeze flirted with my hem a bit, whipping the chemise to my thighs, and I laughed aloud at the naughty sensation as I picked up my basket. My walk toward the water turned into a run, the basket, held over my head, bouncing up and down as I hit the water, causing two wide cascades to follow me into the depths.

To reach the bog bean I had to swim, a thing which I do not do well, yet good enough for the short distance I had to travel. My father had taught me in Greece when I was very small, to my grandmother's disapproval. She thought people who learned to swim were more likely to drown, being less afraid of the water, but still she had let my father have his way.

I picked my bog bean and swam back to the shallows, using wide kicks and trying to keep my basket above

200

water. The sun went behind a cloud at the same time that I stood up to leave the water, and the air felt so chill without the sun's direct rays on my wet skin that I threw my cargo on the bank and returned to the water, swimming backward with long, lazy strokes. When the sun came out later, I felt no strong inclination to leave my aquatic sporting.

I floated front up, and I floated front down. I treaded water and watched a tiny surface-skimming black spider with long, long legs go by not a foot from my nose. I dove under the surface after taking a deep breath of air, and opened my eyes to the fascinating underwater scene, a dizzy, blurry glimpse of sensuously waving weed and schools of sunfish fading into the murky blue distance; a ray of sunshine shafted through the water to light on an old sunken skiff. As my breath grew short, I broke to the surface, filling my lungs again, and found myself bobbing underneath a Lent lily growing from the hummock where I had picked the bog bean. I plucked it and slid the stem into the wet curls behind my left ear. Then I swam back to the shallows and stood plucking a bouquet of primroses as the water lapped at my hips, singing to myself a slow, sweet song in Romany about a dying girl who is turned into a swallow. One by one, I tore the petals from the primroses as I sang and watched them float toward shore like soft, pink sailboats. As my line of sight followed them toward shore, I realized that I was staring at the reflection of a man on horseback. At first I thought it was some whimsical trick of my imagination; then I looked up and saw him.

The man was backlit by the sun, a silhouette, and I tried to shield my eyes. I had thought I was alone. How uninhibited my actions had been. It was a shock to realize that I had been watched, and I didn't know for how long. I turned blindly and ran back into the water.

I heard the rider beginning to give chase, the hooves of his animal displacing huge, echoing splashes of water as they drew nearer to me. Somewhere in my overwhelming panic was the fear that I would be run down and

201

trampled. The distance was rapidly closed, and I cried out as a pair of strong hands plucked me from the water and lifted me to horseback. I struggled wildly.

"Liza, what in God's name is the matter with you?"

"Brockhaven!" I gasped. He had pulled me to the saddle in front of him, indifferent to my dripping wetness. His hand was laid on the side of my head, stroking the hair away from my face, his other hand holding me firmly by the shoulder. His expression held that maddeningly unreadable quality it often had when he looked at me.

"You're angry at me—aren't you—for being here?" I managed.

"I'm working on it . . . hard," he answered. "Anger, anger, where are you?"

Puzzled by his sleepy look, I said, "I don't understand—why is it hard?"

Murmuring, "Liza, my naive girl," his mouth came down on mine, his hands cradling my head, tangling in my wet hair. My lips felt ravaged and fulfilled, and seemed to spring back at the touch of his, and soften, and the sensation of our lips clinging and parting, meeting and separating, was overpowering to me. As he kissed me, he drew me closer, and the silken contact transmitted the diaphanous dampness of my chemise to the linen shirt he wore. I could feel him underneath, his muscles hard and shapely next to the softness and smooth hollows of my own body. I parted my lips the better to receive him, to understand the lesson he seemed intent on teaching me.

The sun . . . the sun was bathing us in its warmth, reflecting from the surface of the lake, making my head feel dizzy, warming the leather saddle beneath my thighs. I felt the heated water as it trailed down my legs, and Brockhaven's shoulder was on fire beneath my touch. His hands began a gentle odyssey over the wet fabric of my gown that left me weak, hot, and helpless. He moved his lips from mine, down my neck, to my shoulder where the cloth had slipped down, leaving me open to the sun, open to him. And then he tenderly slipped a hand beneath me, between me and the saddle, and lifted me to him, ever

202

closer, pressing the full length of my body to his. My arms were wrapped tightly around his neck, and he held me as though I weighed nothing, and again invaded my resistless mouth with his own.

"I've . . . gotten you wet," I said in a strangely husky voice that seemed not to belong to me.

"I know. It's not your fault." His lips were playing in the hair around my ear.

"You always say that," I said. I felt like a little wet monkey clinging to him, a little wet monkey that had fallen in the water by accident while attempting too dangerous a leap from vine to vine. The horse swished its tail across my bare legs as we kissed. "Alex—are you going to—to make me your mistress?"

He took the back of his hands and lightly rubbed my cheeks. "Is that what you want, Liza?"

I was too drunk on his love to cry out, no, and too filled with shame and pride to beg him to make me his wife. I could only stare mutely into the enigma of his blue eyes.

"Where's your dress?" he asked me finally. I weakly pointed, and he turned his horse to shore, and set me down. I bent over to wring what was left of the lake water out of the hem of my chemise. He smiled. " 'Too much water hast thou, poor Ophelia,' " he said.

It took me a moment to grasp his reference. "Oh—*Hamlet?*"

"Yes. Forgive me; the squire's quoting it all the time and put the whole parish into the habit. Liza, please don't look at me like that. We'll talk, but not right now. It's bad enough already. What's the matter?"

The sun had gone. The sky was nearly filled with great gray clouds, and a cool breeze had begun to blow. I wished so much for the heat to come back, and fiddled with shaking fingers at the hook and eye clasps on my dress. It was taking on the dampness of my chemise, and I couldn't see behind me well enough to tell the two apart. "I can't get my gown fastened," I told him.

He dropped from his horse and came to face me. Putting his hands on my shoulders, he turned me around. I

203

felt his fingers work with comforting efficiency as he closed the back of my gown.

Galloping hoofbeats came from the path by the dower house, and I looked to see Robert and Vincent riding around the far edge of the yews. Confused and alarmed, I spun my head back to look at Brockhaven and crossed my arms protectively over my wet bodice.

"That won't do any good, Liza," he said impassively. "They've seen us. Stand still and let me finish fastening your gown." He turned me forward, before I had time to guess at the emotion hidden behind his calm gaze.

There was nothing for me to do but watch apprehensively as the riders drew nearer.

Robert hung back as though he was in no hurry to reach us, his young face more troubled than I had ever seen it. Vincent spurred ahead, jumping from his saddle in front of us without waiting for his horse to come to a halt, his face a mask of scarlet rage.

"Curse you, Alex, for a cold-blooded bastard," he ground out through a rigid jaw, his clenched muscles popping up like white bone. "Poor romantic little waif, you had to seduce her, didn't you?"

"Oh, no," I gasped. "No, we haven't, we haven't. It's not anything like that . . . It's my fault—"

"Liza, be quiet," snapped Brockhaven. "Nothing is your fault."

"But it was I who took off my gown to . . ."

"Will you hush?" he said harshly, taking me by the shoulders. Then, more calmly, "Now hush. Don't say anything."

"But I want to tell them—"

"Don't tell them anything, do you understand? Don't tell them anything."

"But Vincent and Robert think—"

Brockhaven looked swiftly at his younger brother, a challenge and the shadow of an emotion in his eyes. "What does Robert think?"

Robert looked angry and in pain. He spoke slowly. "I think I'd like to hear a good explanation for why you're alone here with Liza's dress half off. Or else I think you should send her home with Vincent."

Brockhaven actually smiled. "You care so much? Good for you. But Liza will go home with Vincent over my dead body."

"Insolent puppy," Vincent rapped out. "Name your seconds."

The words were scarcely cold on Vincent's lips as Brockhaven snapped, "John Lennox and Dain Bredon."

"You've gone mad," said Robert with furious conviction, sliding quickly from his horse. "Both of you. Tame up! You can't duel over Liza without putting her name on the tongue of every rattle pate in the country."

"No. You're right," Brockhaven agreed, with a glance at his brother. "It would destroy Liza's fair name to fight over her. Let's use Isabella instead. Why not, Vincent? I've been cuckolding you for years."

His words were no less devastating than a rocket blown off in my face. I covered my eyes and felt Robert catch me in his arms.

"Liza!" he said, his voice tight with concern.

"Robert, please take me home," I whispered. "Take me to Edgehill."

His voice floated above me. "She's ill—can't you see it? I must take her home, but I can't leave the two of you here together. Vincent, if you care about this girl, you'll ride away so Alex can come home with us."

"Of course I care about her," said Vincent, suddenly weary. "Why do you think I—Why do you think it matters to me what Alex does with her?" I heard the creak of leather as he mounted his horse. "I withdraw the heroics. We can't fight over Liza without ruining her, and as for my slut of a wife—she isn't worth either your life, Alex, or mine."

In a mocking voice, Brockhaven said, "Here I thought you were such a devoted couple! What are you going to do about Liza?"

"Go to Cadal," was Vincent's reply. "He's an honest man, and the last thing he'll do is leave that child in the

205

care of a man who would see her corrupted before her nineteenth birthday."

The only words that were spoken on the way back to Edgehill came from Robert, as soon as we had left Vincent's earshot.

"He's right, damn it," he said. "This time Vincent is right."

Lord Brockhaven didn't trouble to disagree. As he helped me down from the horse at Edgehill, he said with a strained look, "Liza, were you planning to go out again? No? Good—I don't want you to leave the house. I'll talk to you later, I promise."

I nodded my drooping head and ran into the house, shoving open the heavy oak door without waiting for a footman. I had thought for nothing except attaining the privacy of my bedroom, so my foot was on the second marble step of the grand staircase before it penetrated my mind that the foyer wasn't empty. I turned. Before the half-open door to the long reception room stood a gypsy man being watched with edgy suspicion by one of the senior footmen.

The gypsy was young, perhaps eighteen, but for a gypsy that age is older than it is for a gorgio. At eighteen a gypsy is a man, probably married, and if married, certainly with children of his own. The maturity and confidence in the carriage of the youth said that it was probably so with him.

His hair was glossy, blue-black, and long. A faded ruby kerchief wound around his neck, its long ends falling to his chest, which was laid bare by a dirty, buttonless shirt. He had a handsome nose, like a hawk's beak, and eyes as soft and knowing as a swan's. He studied me with clean, unself-conscious interest. I lived in this house, making him the visitor, yet he had taken control of our exchange of glances, bringing it to an end by saying calmly to me in Romany. "God's blessing on you, little one. Do you speak the Ancient Tongue?" His voice was melodious, the words formal and polite.

"My fulfillment is in the Ancient Tongue," I answered, as it was the correct response.

He strolled toward me, his serene gaze wandering over my body without lust. "Does it fulfill you also to dress like an Outsider?" he asked.

Years of rejection for my mixed parentage had eaten away my self-respect, and it was more wounding to be spurned by a gypsy than by a gorgio, since I had always thought of myself as a gypsy. However gentle the youth's tone, my sensitivity read a veiled challenge in his question, and I put up my chin.

"I am half an Outsider," I told him with a pride that I was far from feeling, "and without a tribe. These are my father's people, and they have not turned their back on me."

The corners of his lips turned up in a slight smile. "Can you straddle two horses at once?"

"I can sit only the horse that is willingly ridden."

"Spoken like a Romany," he said approvingly. "The Mother of the Earth has given you a practical soul, lambkin. Look for me toward the outer door. Answer me. The man by the door—is he the great lord of this place whom the gorgio call Brockhaven? He has the look of one such."

I turned my eyes unwillingly toward the door, saw Lord Brockhaven there, and quickly faced the youth.

"Yes, that is him," I said, "but he can only speak gorgio languages—English, French, and Italian."

The youth gave me a smile redolent of grace and inner peace. Still in Romany, he said, "I also speak English." Then he made a hand sign that I knew well, for I had learned it at my grandmother's knee when my head reached no higher than her waist. It was a sign of dismissal and of fondness and one that meant "I shall see you again soon."

"May you remain with God, little one," he said as I turned in obedience and hurried lightly up the stairs.

In the room I had come to think of as my own, I sat down on the bed edge, winding my arms distraitly around my waist. Time slanted and stopped its endless sequence, and soon I felt I was alone in a limbo of mute, motionless suffering, drowning slowly in my bitter, shattering need for the man I loved.

Evening breathed its cold, fragrant breeze through my window, and in the spreading limbs of an elm across the park, the starlings began to settle in numbers. I could hear the sharp clamor of their clacking tongues.

Betty came to help me dress for evening, and was worried to find me sitting alone in the dark in the draft of the open window. I told her my stomach hurt, that I couldn't have dinner, and begged her to convey my excuses. She looked alarmed and spoke of fetching Lady Gwendolyn and the doctor and putting me into bed. I let her do the latter, to avoid the former, and agreed to have toast and warm tea, which the English think will cure anything. Before she left, I asked her if she knew where Lord Brockhaven was.

"Why, he's ridden off, ma'am, with a young scalawag of a gypsy. The gypsies have camped by the old ruins, and everyone's watching their washlines closely, I can tell you that." Misinterpreting my look of distress, she said, "Don't you worry your pretty head. Those gypsies haven't come here to try to steal you off! But if a one of them should try, he'd have his lordship and Master Robert to deal with 'em."

I smiled weakly and tried to appear reassured.

"No doubt the rascal came to ask permission for his tribe to camp, but I suppose Brockhaven's gone to drive 'em off prompt."

"I suppose," I said listlessly, rolling to my side and curling my knees under the bedclothes. Betty left and came back with the toast and tea. She watched me begin to eat before leaving again.

As soon as she was gone, I put the tray aside and crept back into my bed.

Lady Gwen came twice to my room, before dinner and again before she retired for the night, the first time to ask me how I was feeling and tell me with a worried frown that there was some kind of trouble between Lord Brockhaven and Robert. She had no idea why, except that she had heard Robert speak in a raised, angry voice to Brockhaven before Alex had left the house. She said Robert wanted to talk to me, but when I shook my head and looked at her pleadingly, she said she supposed it was nothing important and that she would tell him to wait until morning. The second time she came with the news that Ellen was doing much better and would be out of bed tomorrow and couldn't wait to see me. I asked her timidly if Brockhaven had returned.

"No, dear, I believe he has an invitation to Bredon's this evening, so I expect he'll be very late. You know what Bredon is," she said darkly.

He wasn't coming to talk to me tonight, then. He hadn't promised that he would come tonight; he had said "later." I couldn't wait, though, because the only words I could bear to hear him say to me were "I love you." Grandmother used to tell me that there's never been a body that died of a broken heart, but I knew, as I knew robins sing in May, that if Brockhaven told me he didn't love me, I would be the first.

It was not easy to write the note I left for Lady Gwendolyn upon my pillow that night.

I couldn't tell her about the burning need of my love for Brockhaven, nor of the brutality of the pain I felt that he could not love me back, no matter how much I willed it. I wondered if Mr. Cadal would come to her with Vincent tomorrow to tell her that they suspected Lord Brockhaven had taken me to bed, and I prayed that when they saw I was gone, they would say nothing, to spare her. It would be too much to explain to her in the note the depth of the ill feeling my presence at Edgehill had caused: Isabella's hatred of me, the flaring of the long-standing animosity between Vincent and Lord Brockhaven, and now even Robert estranged from the brother I knew he loved deeply. I ended my speculations and wrote little more than a thank you for all she had done for me, saying I was sorry. I also wrote a note to Ellen, and another to Robert begging him to believe Lord Brockhaven had done me no wrong. Then for the last time, I shed my gorgio shoes and climbed into the clothes I had been wearing on the day John Stewart had brought me to Edgehill as a poacher. I slid my father's medallion around my neck, quickly packed those of my possessions that would fit into the knotted square of my kerchief, and stole quietly from the sleeping house.

It hurt me to leave Kory and Yojo, but I didn't dare risk going to the stables for them. My only solace was that I knew Lord Brockhaven would see to it that they were well cared for, and I hoped that someday I would be able to send someone to get them for me.

As I walked, I considered the gypsy tribe that I would soon ask to join. Did one join a gypsy tribe? Never had I heard of such a thing. Admittance was strictly by birth or marriage. In the years I had traveled with my father and grandmother, our wagon had been avoided as Outcast, and the only hope I had of being received was the apparent friendliness of the gypsy youth I had seen tonight in Brockhaven's home. The young man's manner toward me had been warm, almost familial, and why I could not for the life of me guess, as it was in such marked contrast to the contempt that gypsies usually accord a half-breed, he had given me a love sign, one that indicated he would see me again. I might easily have misunderstood its meaning, though. He might be from another tribe; the sign might have different nuances. I half-smiled wryly. What if his sign had meant "go to the devil, she-fox"? He would be very surprised when I arrived at the wagon of his people, begging for sanctuary!

I knew it would be an imposition and an impudence to ask them to have me. What would they do with me, a young single girl? I couldn't marry. What elder would want his grandchildren tainted with my mixed blood? Perhaps there would be an older woman there, a widow crippled with gout, without children or sisters to do for her, who could use me to help her in her work. They might let me stay and do the heavy chores for her. And I could help take care of the young children and babies, make fires, and haul water. If I worked very hard and was always obedient, maybe they wouldn't care that I was another mouth to feed. I prayed and prayed that was how it would be, because if I had to be some menial, misplaced thing, it would be better among the gypsies, where at least I could be close to the wind and the road and the earth.

The full moon was encircled by a rainbow-tinted ring, and long white tendrils stretched from it to curl like pale fingers around the trees. The silver light laid a frosty border where it fell, and the world lost its colors, to be etched sharply in black and white. The tall grass in the meadows bent and rose in sections as though from the passage of unseen beings, with spiky weeds sticking up like sentinels. The day had been mild, but had now become cruelly chilly, with a close dampness, and I was glad for the warmth of my many skirts. Now and then I heard the rustle of the small, hunting night creatures disturbed by my human presence as I moved through the dark shadows of the trees.

The ruins were an hour's ride from Edgehill, if you didn't hurry, but were a long walk when alone in the dark. Goudette had done too good a job in softening the soles of my feet. The stones and weeds bit harshly into them. Many times I winced, and when I lifted my foot, I saw that it was wet with blood, little though I cared. It was nothing beside the mammoth emptiness of my longing for Brockhaven and those at Edgehill that I had come to think of as my family.

I wondered if Lord Brockhaven had returned to Edgehill from Lord Bredon's house, and if he'd gone to bed; and then I wondered how long it would be before I would cease speculating, at a given time of day, whether Brockhaven was eating, or sleeping, or riding. As time passed, would I wonder if he had married, and see him in my mind with children, bending down to scoop up a little boy to carry him on his shoulder, or kneeling to straighten the stockings of a small daughter with dark curls and haunting blue eyes like his own? I wondered if Ellen would tell them about me—the wild gypsy girl who had come to stay for a short while one summer—and pass on to them my legends and the Romany lullaby I had taught her, which she sang with such amusing pronunciation. I vowed to sing it every evening as the sun set, and remember our times together.

It was cold and quiet as I climbed the tree-lined path toward the ruins, and as I reached them, it struck me how cheerful they had seemed on May Day, and how desolate and lonely now. The charred logs from the bonfire lay in wide lumps of white ash and sand, and hiding among the weeds and rubble were scattered shards from broken bottles. A sharp pang in the bottom of my foot told me that I had stepped on one, and I sat on the edge of a broken wall to pick the dark, jagged glass from my heel.

As I sat, I listened for the noises from the gypsy camp. It was damp, and quiet, and peaceful, and any sound would have been audible, but there was no sound—not the distant creak of a wagon shifting on its axles, not the bark of a dog. The smells were not there either. The strong scent of horses would have carried far, and if there had been a camp within the mile, I would have smelled cooking grease and wood smoke. I fought panic that perhaps Betty had heard the wrong location for the camp, or that Brockhaven had indeed made the gypsies move on. If they were still here, they must be on the other side of the rise, where the bulk of the hill would conceal evidence of the camp from where I sat.

I stood up, limping from my sore foot, and walked through the ruins toward the brow of the hill. The sound I was listening for, in the darkest corner of my imaginings, was the strangled cry and heavy paw tread I had heard before in these ruins. But there was nothing, nothing at all, not even the fall of a leaf. The echo of my own step was muffled by a dark carpet of moss.

There was no real path to the hillcrest, only a twisting series of spaces where erosion had washed the hill to bedrock, covered lightly in places by a layer of sand. I left the moss, and the slap of my soles on rock was reassuring and solid, more like I was rooted in the world instead of floating in a misty limbo.

Toward the top of the hill, the rock gave way to a soft, acid sand that burned the bottom of my wet feet and waffled up between my toes. With dreadful suddenness, my next step plunged my foot ankle deep. I started, and my other foot came down hard in the sand, up to my ankle and then to my knee, sucking at my legs like the hideous mouth of a giant subterranean reptile. The rubble of sharp stones and dirt tore at my skin as the sucking maw of sand swallowed me to the waist. A scream of terror rose from my throat as the savage rupture took me down, and covered my shoulders. Sand was pouring into my nose and mouth, blinding me, trapping the air from my lungs, suffocating my screams for help.

Suddenly, I felt my feet below me fight free. I kicked them, struggling wildly. There was a crash of falling dirt, and I was surrounded by a hard floating stream of moving earth and stone. For a second I was dropping free through a dark band of still air, and then I landed hard on a jagged surface of rock, receiving on top of my bruised body a pile of debris from above.

Moments passed before I was able to begin to cry in an exhausted, futile way. Lifting one numb arm, I wiped feebly at the grit that clung to my eyelashes and pebbled over my face. Even this effort too greatly taxed my battered limbs, so I laid my arm back across my chest and lay, my eyes closed, in the quiet of this underground prison.

I sensed its black, nightmare presence before I heard it. The shadows were waiting, and I was not alone. My skin tingled with awe, and my teeth met as before a lightning stroke. I knew its voice before it spoke. Low and close to me, I heard the sick, hoarse howl that had so shocked my ears before by the Roman ruin. It was in here with me.

I lay in a terror deep and primeval with my eyes tightly shut, waiting for unimaginable horror, pain, and death. The blood rushed and pumped in my head as I heard the

213

sound of its rough, lung-wracking breath inhaling and exhaling in long, excited gasps.

I didn't want to see the creature, only to let it do its dreadful work and bring me quickly to oblivion, but it hung back so long, so inexplicably that at last it took more courage to keep my eyes shut than to make them open.

Above me was the long, forked rip that had been my entrance into this black cavern. Through it I could see the stars, and the sky shining purple against the gloom around me. My eyes drank in the starlight before I turned them to the side to gaze into the darkness, into a pair of slanting silver eyes that watched me with unwinking eagerness.

I became slowly aware of form and line, contour and texture, and at last I knew that the tormented creature that stood close to me in this hellish place was not a werewolf, not an underworld ghoul, but an aged and starving wolf. And mad; from its eyes I knew that some dreaded existence had left the creature insane. It moved with a sharp restless gesture of the shoulders, and when I heard the metal clank, I knew that it was chained.

On the heels of this discovery came another; there was a scrape of wood, and another starlight opening appeared far off in the gloom, followed by the lowering of a lantern. A pale light fell on an ancient set of stone steps. I was in a long-abandoned root cellar, from the looks of it, used only as a prison for the wolf since its Roman builders had evacuated their villa two thousand years before. The human keeper of the beast, who had made the poor animal into an instrument of murder, was about to descend into the chamber with me. I had a sudden fear that it would be Brockhaven—followed by a wash of sick relief when Vincent Randolph picked his way down the stone steps.

It was a long time before he saw me. He set down the lantern and came to stand before the wolf, feet apart, talking quietly. The wolf paced on its chain, rubbing nervously against Vincent's leg from time to time and whimpering. Vincent saw the hole in the roof first, his vision traveling down slowly to where I lay helpless in a pile of sand and rock. His quick shocked movement caused the wolf to howl and cringe pathetically. Indifferent to the beast, he came and crouched by me, lifting my head, and saying softly, "Liza . . . what's happened to you? Where are you hurt?"

My lungs were collapsing so rapidly that I couldn't find the breath to answer as his hands brushed gently at the sand and leaves in my hair.

"You've run away from Edgehill," he said, making the words a statement. "Were you coming to me, by any chance?"

There was little point in lying. I shook my head weakly, no.

"That's too bad," he said. The regret in his eyes was real. "It would have made things easier."

"I know about the wolf now," I gasped.

"Yes. It's a problem."

"Was it"—so great was my dread that I could hardly say the words—"was it this creature that made an end to Isabella's brother Frederick?"

The answer was an obvious one, and yet still I was surprised by his candor. "Yes, this one."

"You sent him after me, that day in the ruins . . ." I hated the whimper in my voice.

"It was the red riding habit that I made Isabella send you," he explained, his tone not unkind. "Red. Bella's favorite color. The wolf's been trained to kill anyone wearing it. I found you there, when I went to feed him. You were sleeping under a tree, your hair spread shining in the grass like black satin, your eyelashes dark against sleep-pinked cheeks, and your soft lips, so sweetly, so slightly open."

The dreamy detachment of his voice made it nonetheless frightening. "Caesar stopped him!" I said, to halt his slow catalogue of my features.

Placidly he said, "The wolf could have ripped Caesar to pieces. I called him back, because . . ." He placed his lips on my forehead.

I drew back, revolted beyond measure by his touch.

215

These wide-boned, graceful hands that touched me had for years fixed the chain that held the wolf, and had released that chain, once for Frederick, once for me. I lay cowering, staring at him, fearing him while he watched me through searching gray eyes.

"Is it Alex? You've fallen in love with him, haven't you?" he said with surprising compassion. "He'll never love you back, you know. He isn't capable of it. His own parents treated him brutally when he was very young, and mine were little better toward him. I could tell you stories—no, what good would that do? But he has a heart of iron. He can bring women to their knees—crazed with love for him—and hold them like that for years. Isabella has loved him since she was sixteen, and you see what it's turned her into."

I couldn't bear to hear more. In a pitiful scrap of a voice, I asked, "Are you going to give me to the wolf?"

"No—no, I'm not. Alex has been afraid of that, but he's wrong."

"He knows?"

"He suspects. But this place is so well-hidden, it has defied his every effort. Can you stand to be in here a few more moments? I'm going to take the wolf outside."

The thought of being alone in this cavern was infinitely less frightening than the thought of being here with Vincent and his pet.

"I'll leave the lantern here," he said, and untied the wolf, which followed him up the steps, heeling like a dog on its chain leash.

It was impossible that he would let me go, knowing the things I did about him. He had not let the wolf attack me, he had said, "because . . ." He had let the pattern of his lips and the well-regulated desire in his eyes tell me the rest. I had thought only minutes earlier that there could be no horror worse than to lay in the dark with the wolf, but I saw now that I had been wrong.

Standing on my feet, I would be no more of a match for the man than I was lying flat. I tried to get up anyway. Throwing myself upright, I let my feet take the weight of my body, but my right leg crumpled under me as though it were made of paper.

He had returned, probably having quickly tied the animal somewhere near the door. I suppose that he saw me fall, for his feet ran down the staircase, and he stood tall above me, looking down to where I lay in a pool of searing pain.

"You shouldn't have tried to get up," he said in a way much too matter-of-fact to be critical. "I'm sorry. Later, I'll have the injury in your leg seen to. I can't right away; there isn't time."

Kneeling beside me, he tried to slide an arm around me. Quailing violently from him, I brought up my knees and tried to roll on my side, over the dense, coarse rocks that littered the cave's cold floor, my heartbeats cutting like flint into the side of my chest.

"Liza, don't," he said. "Please don't! You'll hurt yourself! It's useless anyway, can't you see that?"

He caught my arms fast, holding them at the wrists as he leaned over me, gathering me to his chest. The cave's thick air hit my back as I was lifted. Vincent was carrying me toward the stone steps.

"I promised I didn't want to harm you," he said. "Even now, I mean it."

We reached the surface, and the fresh night air poured into my lungs, a deep relief after the stench under ground. Yet there was no relief from the horror of Vincent's hands spreading desolation through me like a cancer. I was set on earth against the smooth bark of a low bushy hazel, at the edge of a curtain of pale color from a second lantern. Ten feet before me was the wolf, his chain hooked to the cellar rim.

Vincent took my hand and I looked at him with tortured, aching eyes, as he said, "I know you're shocked and afraid. I hate to move you like this, but I have to get you out of here. It's better that you aren't here to watch what's going to happen. There's an inn not far from here, and the innkeeper won't ask questions. I'm going to keep you there for a while."

217

"Why? What's going to happen? What are you going to do?"

"I have to make it so we can marry, Liza. I have to be free; it's the only way. I didn't want it to be like this. But it must either be this, or you would have to die."

I didn't think then what he must mean by marriage and freedom. It never occurred to me that there might be a threat to anyone except myself.

"I'll give you the land—I don't want any of it," I said. "Please—I don't need it!"

"Liza. Liza. It's more than the land, my pretty one. It's you I want—" He caressed my cheek. My flesh felt discolored where his fingers passed. "And you I shall have."

Misliking a sound he heard in the distance, the wolf gave a strangled cry. Haunted by the fear that Vincent might try to kiss me again, I said, clumsily trying to distract him, "The wolf's voice—"

Vincent glanced to where he had tied the animal. "I bought him from a bankrupt menagerie. The trainer controlled it with a tight collar, and its voice has been damaged."

The crisp sound of horses' hooves interrupted him; it was an irregular noise denoting a hesitant rider. Vincent listened as the wolf cringed and slathered in the dirt at his feet.

"Damn," he said through clenched teeth. "She's early." He left my side, picked up the lantern, shuttered it, and walked out to the middle of the field, to stand under the boughs of a large single oak.

The horse and rider came into view and stopped at the forest line. The rider sat alertly, peering into the clearing, as the horse shied nervously and twitched its tail. Sighting the male figure under the tree, the rider slipped gracefully to the ground.

"Alex!" It was Isabella's voice. She half-ran joyfully across the clearing, and halted in the open, as if not believing her good fortune. Vincent left the shadow of the tree. They looked like silhouette figures in the dark, inconclusive human shapes, tentative in the moment of misunderstanding and deception. He advanced on her until he was close enough for her to recognize him as her husband. She gave a soft cry of surprise.

"Vincent, it's you! But why? I've come here to meet—"

"I know," he replied. "I sent you that note. It was one I intercepted years ago, and kept for just such an occasion."

"Al-Alex isn't here?" she whispered, her voice cracking.

"No, he isn't. I would imagine he's happily asleep at Edgehill. And here you are, so early, so eager. And dressed with such care."

"You've done some cruel things to me, Vincent, but this is the lowest. I'm going home." She whirled, her skirts billowing out, and started to march back to her horse, but he grabbed her and viciously turned her about.

"My cruelty seems to be the only thing that affects your indifference toward me. You're here for a reason, my love. There's something I want to show you." He had left the lantern shuttered under the tree, and turned to pick it up. "Follow me," he commanded his wife.

She stamped her foot in irritation, though there was a note of unwilling curiosity in her posture as she looked at her husband. "Oh, all right," she agreed pettishly. "I warn you, though, I'm in no mood for your games tonight!"

As they started to walk toward the wolf, Vincent said, "This one you may find exciting." When they were so close that I could hear the movement of her long skirt, Vincent set down the lamp, and drew the shutter. An oval of dim light swept over the wolf and Isabella gave a stifled shriek.

"What in the world is that?" she demanded, staring at it, grasping his arm.

"Think, Isabella," he said. "Think."

She must have been suspecting for years, because it took her such a short time to come to the right conclusion.

"You killed Frederick," she breathed. "It was you—you and this accursed beast." I expected her to cry out with rage and bitter sorrow. Instead she began to laugh in delighted misbelief.

It seemed at first that this terrible knowledge had disor-

219

dered her reason; then I realized that her laughter was a genuine expression of glee. If she had loved her brother, if she regretted his death, those emotions were eclipsed by an admiration for Vincent's murderous cunning. Though I knew my useless leg would never let me get far, I tried to drag myself away. That is when she saw me.

"Why . . . why, it's Liza!" She came closer, the mature lines of her figure moving smoothly under the expensive military cut of her crimson riding dress.

The wolf was becoming increasingly agitated. Isabella seemed not to notice as it lunged at its chain and growled with deadly concentration. "And you've hurt her!" She ran to Vincent and kissed him, like a child presented with a toy, and slid her arms hungrily around his neck. "Oh, Vincent. And I was such a shrew to you! She's going to die, isn't she?"

A half smile curled on his lips. He set her back from him. "You'd like to see that, wouldn't you?" He went to kneel by the wolf, his hand on the clasp of the chain. The animal flattened its ears and slathered. "Shall I let him go, Bella?"

"Oh, yes, do," she said.

The pieces jumped together in my mind like a macabre living puzzle. Isabella's riding habit, a red habit like mine had been, though the style of hers was more severe—had it been a gift to her from Vincent? Now I knew how Vincent meant to give himself the freedom to marry me. My words were sobs.

"No, Vincent," I cried. "Please don't! I'll do anything. I'll give you anything, I promise you. Don't let the wolf go!"

"So now you're pleading for your life, you wretched fortune hunter," snapped Isabella contemptuously. "You would have stolen my land from under my nose."

"Oh, Isabella, no . . ." I gasped.

"It's no good to beg," she hissed. "I hate you. Vincent's told me about finding you with Alex. You may think Alex is taken with your false innocence, but he's had a string of pretty sluts like you. I'm the only woman he cares about!"

"Isabella, please get on your horse and ride out of here. You don't understand—your life is in danger . . ." In my anguish for her, I became incoherent, and Isabella looked at me with loathing. I tried to stand, to push her away; ignoring the searing pain in my leg, I managed a half-crouch.

"Stand away from the girl, Bella," said Vincent with ominous calm.

She obeyed him, looking at me gloatingly as she backed into the starlit clearing.

"Farther," said Vincent. She did as he told her.

The wolf was ravening, its growls and barks drowning my cries to Isabella to flee. Vincent unclasped the chain, a smile on his lips.

In an ugly blur, I saw the wolf lunge at Isabella. Her screams of disbelief mingled with the throaty growl of the wolf as it closed the distance between them. Vincent grabbed me and shoved my face into his chest.

There was a gunshot, and the scene was ended, like a never-to-be-finished book slamming shut. Vincent slackened his grip, and I twisted violently to see Isabella with her hand over her mouth, staring at the trees, where Brockhaven stood next to the young gypsy I had met at Edgehill, who was lowering a musket. A puff of blue smoke was wafting on the breeze. The wolf was lying on the grass not five feet from Isabella.

Brockhaven clapped the youth on the shoulder, and strode toward us.

"Take your hands off her," he snapped at Vincent, "or I'll take that musket and blow your damn head off."

Vincent paused, and began stroking my hair. "She's had a bad scare, and I think her leg is broken. Try to curb your martial instincts."

Brockhaven motioned for the musket, and began to load it, staring at Vincent the while.

"You were ever an impatient young cub," said Vincent. "Shoot me if you want to—I'm going to set her down gently." He helped me to a large gray rock, the hard coldness a relief after the prison of Vincent's arms. I looked at Brockhaven.

"Is the wolf dead?" I asked him.

"Shot through the heart," he answered. "He didn't suffer."

"He suffered for years," I said, my voice breaking, covering my face in my dirty hands.

Brockhaven removed his greatcoat and laid it on my shoulders; it felt warm from his body, and good.

I gazed up at him protestingly. "No—you'll get cold."

"Never mind," he said, and buttoned it under my chin.

The youth came up behind Brockhaven, studied my face for a moment, and said to Brockhaven in painlessly articulate English, "If you like, I'll take care of the blond woman. She can return to her home, eh? Stay here. I'll bring back a horse for the little one. I see she can't walk."

He left without waiting for an answer, his hard, bare feet striking off to where Isabella stood, weeping hysterically, at the edge of the woods.

"Poor Isabella . . . I should go to her," I said uncertainly.

"To hell with Isabella," said Brockhaven. "As far as Chipping, one could have heard her screaming at Vincent to turn the wolf loose on you. It wasn't easy deciding whether to shoot her or the wolf. What's this about a broken leg?" His tone was abrupt, even angry, as though he was irritated that I had been a nuisance. But he had come to me first, not Isabella.

It seemed so long since I had seen his dearly loved face—Brockhaven, my love, whom I had thought never to see again. I was unable to keep myself from gazing at him in what he most surely must have thought of as mawkish adoration; I stamped in my mind the way his ebony hair curled into the chiseled contours of his face, the way his skin glowed golden in the lamplight. In that moment it didn't even matter whether he loved me or not. It was enough simply to be near him. I wanted to reach out and touch him, to ask him to hold me in his arms, in spite of Vincent, in spite of everything.

"It's my right leg," I said.

He ran his fingers gently up the affected limb, tracing the damage. "What happened?"

Sitting as I was, amid the bittersweet joy of being so close to him, and in the ruin of my plan to leave Edgehill, I found it suddenly difficult to answer his direct question. What had happened, he meant, to bring me to this place and in this condition, when he had told me directly not to leave home, for any reason. The throbbing pain in my leg began to grow, and I felt sick to my stomach; my head swam, my eyes ached. The task of explaining became a labor of Hercules.

Vincent moved as though he would have put an arm around me, but Brockhaven uncoiled from the ground beside my leg with the lean, supple haste of a striking panther.

"Don't touch her," he snapped in a voice as hard as I had ever heard him use.

Vincent withdrew; his face became cold, dark, and controlled. "She was running away from home; why to here, I don't know. The ground collapsed under her, and she fell into the old root cellar where I've kept the wolf. I found her in there half an hour ago. I don't know how long she'd been in there with the beast, but her injuries are from the fall."

"Are they?" Brockhaven asked him. "If she's been harmed by you in any way, Vincent, I'm going to kill you."

"If I couldn't hurt her that first time when she was alone by the ruined villa, why do you think I'd be able to now?" retorted Vincent.

Brockhaven looked at him sharply. "It *would* be easier to see Frederick die than her."

"Naturally," said Vincent softly. "Don't be a fool, man. We may have a penchant for desiring the same women—but this one, I begin to love."

"Go to the devil, Vincent. If she'd been a hag, you'd have killed her on the spot."

"If she'd been a hag, you wouldn't have seduced her. At least I mean to marry her."

"And you keep a convenient wolf to eat up your present wife," replied Brockhaven. He smiled, like a person watching a farcical play. "I'm curious, Vincent. If you don't think I plan to marry her, what do you think I have in mind?"

Vincent leaned back against a tall, moon-silvered boulder, his legs casually crossed, his eyes heavy-lidded. "Such a pleasure to speak frankly, isn't it?" he said. "I think you intend to sleep with her, get her with child, and marry her off to Robert."

Brockhaven laughed. "And waste the years I've spent trying to pair him with Ellen Cleaver? Come, Vincent, you can do better than that."

"God knows, then, I don't. There's no need for you to marry her when you've got control of her money."

"No need at all," agreed Brockhaven amiably.

"Especially if I were to be out of the way and no longer contending for her guardianship. That's why you tried to push me into a duel. Poor boy—too honest to kill me on the sly. But Isabella was a poor weapon to have chosen, because I know you haven't been cuckolding me for years."

"Really," said Brockhaven with a sardonic smile. "What did the jade do, confess?"

"Yes, last week in a frail moment. She admitted that it only happened once between you, a few months after our marriage, and that she practically had to rape you. It's clear that you've no taste for adultery, much maligned youngster that you are."

It was irrational that Vincent's words should make my heart beat faster. It didn't mean that Brockhaven cared more for me, the less he cared for Isabella. I rubbed my arms under the coat to keep them warm and thought how painfully sweet it was to look at Brockhaven, like trying to drink thick honey.

"Ridiculous, isn't it?" said Brockhaven. "Especially considering the passion you've expended in a slow burn about it."

"Once was enough," Vincent replied. "But I told you already, not enough to die for. Of course, there were times when I've been hit with a mood—when Bella's spared no effort to throw herself at you in public, for example—and I did reflect that I might not be desolated to hear that you'd broken your neck." He gave Brockhaven a crooked smile. "So much for that. We have to think of Liza, don't we? Here she is, with a broken leg, and we're at a standoff, neither of us trusting the other with her."

"Why a standoff? I have the firearm," Brockhaven reminded him suavely. "What do you have to hear from me?"

Vincent shifted against the boulder. "Have you dishonored her?"

"No."

"Tell me you won't," said the older man.

Brockhaven's hand came to rest on the back of my head. "You have my word on it," he said, his fingers moving down the length of my hair, then in a slow circle on my back. The mood became contemplative, silent, with both men staring at the ground. I was so tired, and Brockhaven's thigh was so invitingly close to my cheek that I let my head droop against him, realizing far in the back of my mind that it was a rather shocking thing to be doing. He made no objection to it, though, just continued to stroke my hair, and when some moments had passed, he spoke to Vincent again.

"So. What do you think we should do about you?"

There was a short hesitation before Vincent replied, "I think, go to America. The New World. Land of Opportunity. Would that be far enough for you? It will take me a few days to make arrangements—get a draught from my bank, meet with my man of business. I'll cut things to the bare minimum, of course. America."

"A good place for you. You know what will happen, if you come back to England?"

"Terrible things," said Vincent. "You really don't need

225

to enumerate them, my dear." His gaze dropped to me. "Would you let me kiss her good-bye?"

"No. Good-bye, Vincent. Farewell."

"Good-bye, Alex." He was still looking at me. "God bless you, little one." He turned and disappeared quietly, wraithlike, into the night.

Alex lifted his hand to the back of my neck, continuing his massage. "Still alive down there?" he asked me.

"Yes," I said and looked up at him.

"You know," he said, "I think he's really in love with you."

"He's a very strange man," I said. "Do you understand him?"

"Oh, yes . . . too well. Don't be afraid. If he says he's going to go, he's going to go."

"Yes, I know that. I can't help feeling sorry for him."

"I suppose not," he said, smiling. "Maudlin wench that you are. Do you hear that?"

I lifted my head, and looked toward the forest to see the gypsy youth emerge from the foliage riding bareback and without a bridle on a white horse with an exotically long mane and tail. Reaching us, he slid agilely from the horse and said to Brockhaven, "The man has gone— Vincent?"

"Yes. He won't be back. What did you do with his wife?"

"I took her to the camp. One of our women will see her home." The youth's lips tightened. "A barbarous thing. If she were my woman, I would never have let her get so bad that I'd have to feed her to a wolf. What ailed her husband?"

I could see that Brockhaven was amused by the youth's worldly air, though he didn't show it with a smile. "He was too indifferent to her to care. She touched only his pride."

"Some men are like that," said the youth. He shook his head, and his long hair moved smoothly in the black breeze. With a gentle movement of his hand, he indicated me. "Does she know yet?"

226

"No," said Brockhaven. "I waited. I thought your father might want to tell her himself."

"Not he," said the youth, shaking his head and smiling. "He would weep too much. He'll weep anyway, when he sees her." Bending down to my level, he said to me in flowing Romany, "Liza, I'm the son of your uncle. My name is Trenit. Two years ago, this man, Lord Brockhaven, came to the camp of my father and asked if we knew what had become of a young man, Charles Compton, heir to the Marquisate of Chadbourne, who had eloped many years past with a young gypsy woman. The young lord told us that he wished to find Compton because Compton had become the owner of a great property, and if that property went unclaimed, it would remain in the pocket of Compton's niece and her husband, who were exploiting the peasants there to starvation.

"There was nothing my father could tell your young lord, for we too were without knowledge of what had become of Charles Compton. It began before my memory, Liza, when your mother came before the elders of the tribe eighteen years ago and told them she would marry Charles Compton. There was a great dismay because your mother was much loved. The future they saw for her with the spoiled son of a wealthy gorgio was one of heartbreak and abandonment. Your mother had great pride and anger toward the elders, anger that those who claimed to love her would have so little faith in her judgment. She said she would leave, and no one believed her. Her mother, afraid of the foretold bitter ending, went with her. It was a heavy blow for the tribe, and most of all for my father, who lost at one time both his sister and his mother.

"For many years, the tribe searched for their missing daughter, but your mother and her husband had gone to Europe, and the wars of Napoleon came, and it became impossible to trace their path."

"I thought no one cared," I cried out wretchedly. "So many years . . . I was sure that my mother was rejected by her tribe."

"It was a stupid disharmony, Liza, not a rejection. The

227

elders meant to show love and protection in telling your mother not to see Charles Compton. It was a great misfortune that they were blind to his high character, blind to your mother's adult intelligence. You must forgive them, dear. It is hard for the older ones to see their babes grow up."

"Yes," I said softly, thinking of the years I had together with my grandmother and my father, of the love Grandmother had given to me and to my father, and the sadness she had kept locked inside her, parted as she had been, from her people and from her son. Having to choose between son and daughter, she had sacrificed everything to aid the most needy.

"I don't say these words to make you cry, lambkin," said Trenit. "Scratch not your open wounds."

"I shall try not to," I said, wanting to win his respect with a show of courage. Hardly daring to hope it was true, I asked him, "Did you come to Edgehill because of me?"

"Two years ago," he answered, "before the young lord met with us, he had talked with other tribes, and after we left he was to talk with many more. He made a pact with my father to communicate anything either of us learned about your family, and we are here because Brockhaven has kept his word."

Chapter Twelve

In my childhood I had had a rare, lovely dream that I would be found by my mother's tribe and accepted. I had never believed that such a thing might be possible, and yet tonight it was as though I had entered that dream. Logic and time had lost their pretense of importance. The black nightmare of the wolf's cellar melted into the prickling happiness of being led into the camp on the white horse, and being set down into the loving arms of my uncle Pulika.

What a man he was! An immense spirit, with hands so wide that each could have lifted a good fat hen, and yet they held me as with the maternal tenderness of a young mother. His hair was shorter than Trenit's and more straight; a kerchief pulled it back from his broad, supple-skinned forehead. Best to me were his eyes, for I had seen them for so many years on my grandmother. They were oval, piercing, and incisively humorous, and he shut them frequently, or sometimes opened them wide to add emphasis to things that he said.

Before I even said "Greetings, Uncle," he had scooped me up and was showing me off to the crowd of gypsy men and women who gathered around us, grinning and exclaiming. My uncle beamed like a proud father displaying his firstborn son and asked everyone, even those too young to remember, if I wasn't the image of my mother. I caught a glimpse of Brockhaven standing quietly while Trenit translated the turbulent gush of Romany to him. My guardian was smiling, and I wondered if he was thinking that Lady Gwendolyn said so often that I looked exactly like my father.

The wife of my uncle was tall, and important, which is the gypsy way to describe a beloved person's heaviness of frame. She kissed me, pinched my cheeks, and right away gave me one of her heavy gold bracelets before she made Uncle Pulika set me by the fire so she could cover me in blankets, pour water over my hands to get them clean, and give me food.

I asked her not to trouble herself but was overborne, and my uncle and I talked while a heavy iron cauldron was set on a tripod over the flame, and the air thickened with sizzling fat and the scent of garlic. The noise and the smells awakened the chickens, who came to cluck irritably in the glow of the fire and the old half-lame rooster strutted underfoot, looking as if he were not sure whether or not he should go stand on the wagon tongue and do his duty for the tribe by crowing.

Trenit's wife was a girl no more than sixteen, with pretty, delicate features, a determined chin, and a well-advanced pregnancy. She came to pat my hand, offer me the use of her own bowl and cup to eat from, and call me sister. She would have sat down at my side, but a cry from her wagon stopped her. Off she went to fetch her son and Trenit's, plunking the howling toddler on Trenit's lap with a wink and a smile at her mother-in-law, while she came to help chop onions into the cauldron.

There were so many things to say that I had no time to be shy, and to wonder if I was making a good impression or whether I was talking too much or too little. Lord Brockhaven had told them a great deal, and I was glad I was spared the awful task of telling my uncle that my grandmother had died. We were left with the happier things to ·discuss—where we had traveled, how we had lived, and the places we had visited. I told about Edgehill, and Lady Gwendolyn and Ellen, the girl who loved gypsies, and everyone agreed that she must be very smart and admirable. Through it all, I had the fun of seeing Trenit, with Lord Brockhaven's help, trying to keep amused the cross, sleepy baby.

We talked about Vincent too, and I was surprised how much Lord Brockhaven had confided in my uncle, for Brockhaven seemed to have told him even that he had fears for my safety. I learned that it had been the wolf's howl that had brought Brockhaven and Trenit to the hilltop to investigate. It had been decided that two men, walking quietly, would be less likely than a group to scare away the creature, if it were free, for Brockhaven had been still here at the camp, talking with my uncle.

To eat was a stewed goose, seasoned with sage, thyme, and marjoram, and mixed with apple bits and currants; on the side were cold nutmeg meatballs and paprika on mashed chick peas in sesame oil. Poor Brockhaven! My aunt was too hospitable to let him go unfed, and I saw that he knew too much about gypsy etiquette to do anything so boorish as refuse her, so he had to eat. This couldn't have been made any the easier for him, because he had surely seen the way Aunt had cleaned out the cauldron before cooking in it—one wipe with a piece of old bread. The baby had been playing horsie on Brockhaven's knee and the little thing gave an angry shriek when Trenit pulled him away so that Brockhaven could take his food. With amusement, I watched as Brockhaven made the baby happy again, fishing in his pocket and producing for him a pocket watch in a gold case.

After the meal was not such a good time for me, since everyone began to talk of my leg and seeing that it was set. Brockhaven wanted me to have a gorgio doctor; my uncle held that it would be better handled by old, yellow-eyed Santinia Smith, their medicine woman; and I wanted no one to touch it at all. It was my leg, but as you can imagine, it was my opinion that was the least regarded. For ten minutes Brockhaven was firm. I was going to see a doctor, and that was that, though my uncle hollered and railed and said that he wasn't having a stupid hulk of a gorgio doctor making hocus-pocus over his niece and probably leaving her with one leg shorter than the other in the end. Members of the tribe began to roll up pantlegs and pull up sleeves to show this arm and that limb that Santinia had treated and see, it was perfect and straight, wasn't it?

I'm not sure whether it was the drama of this testimony that convinced Brockhaven, but he finally agreed to let the medicine woman fix my leg. With many expressions of pity and concern, I was carried to a thick pile of eiderdowns before a wagon set well off from the cluster. I don't remember much of the bone-setting except that it was very painful and, while I have always felt sorry for people with broken legs, I could afterward say that my sympathy increased tenfold. When Santinia was satisfied that the bone was laying just as it ought, she bound the leg with knitbone, made me a reassuringly foul-tasting infusion, and left me to rest by a small fire while she went back to report to my uncle and Lord Brockhaven.

I watched sleepily from the distance as people heard the news that I was doing very well, and in twos and threes began to return to their beds. The camp grew quiet, the chickens settled back to roost in the wagon spokes, and Trenit's wife tenderly picked up her baby son, who had drifted off to sleep on his father's shoulder. Trenit got wine, and sat with Brockhaven and Pulika and several of the elders by the fire. My eyes shut, and the lullaby of night noises from the forest courted my weary soul into a light sleep.

It was still dark when a gentle pressure on my forehead called me back from slumber.

"I didn't mean to disturb you." It was Brockhaven's voice, and I rolled on my back to see him sitting on the eiderdown beside me, settled as though he'd been there for some time. He said, "You were so restless that I was afraid you might have a fever. Your skin's cool, though, thank God."

I blinked and rubbed my eyes. "My uncle?"

"He lay down to try to get an hour or two of sleep."
He drew up his knees, and rested his arms across them. A small fire still glowed in a shallow pit beside us, and reflected in the sensuous curves of Brockhaven's hair with long red tears.

"I never knew," I said, "that you owned a pocket watch. A pocket watch. Imagine."

I could see I had taken him by surprise. "Dear me. What's wrong with a pocket watch?"

"It seems so—"

He grinned. "Go on. It's too late to back off."

I smiled drowsily at him, wishing he was sitting closer. "Middle-aged. Staid. It's not the kind of thing one thinks of as belonging to a shocking sort of person. Where did you get it?"

"The squire gave it to me when I came into the title. Woe betide me if I forget to carry it too. Every time the man sees me, he asks me peremptorily what the time is— and if I don't have the watch to pull out, his eyebrows shoot to his hairline. Are you in much pain?"

"Terrible. I think I'm going to have to bite on your handkerchief."

"Too late. The baby's kept it after playing hide the watch."

My lips curled into a rather silly smile. "Light-fingered lot, we gypsies. We start young too."

"I'll say you do. Good Lord, your cousin Trenit and that—child he's married to. Do you know that your uncle considers you an old maid?"

"I'm sure he's right. I'm feeling quite past my prime tonight. Is this Santinia's wagon? Is she asleep inside?"

"Yes and no. It's her wagon, but she took her eiderdown and a shriveled potato half—"

"That's a lamp. You take an old cotton bit from an apron and soak it in lard—"

"Well, it wasn't soaked in rose water, let me tell you." When I had finished giggling, he said, "Anyway, off Santinia went to sleep in the forest near the ruins. She says she wants to listen for the mandrake."

I made a wise expression and put up one finger. "For the chest!"

"So she said. Tell me about the mandrake; or is it something too esoteric to convey to the weaker gorgio intellect?"

"No. But would you mind? The position of my leg has become uncomfortable and I'd like to move it over—oh, thank you. That's much better. You have such a gentle touch, my lord. Let me see. The mandrake."

"It's some kind of a root, so I gather."

"Quite right. On the surface of the ground, mandrake has a small flowering vine but its potency lies in the root. The adult mandrake root has the exact shape of a human body."

"Really? The exact shape, you say?"

I sighed. "Try to explain anything to a gorgio. I'm not talking off the top of my head, you know. I've *seen* them. Lord Brockhaven, what are you thinking about, whenever you stare at me like that? I've wondered about it a lot."

In a perfectly normal tone of voice he said, "When I stare at you like this, I'm thinking about what a marvelously beautiful girl you are. Don't heed it a bit. The mandrake?"

It took me a moment to find my tongue and then I stammered, "Y-y-yes. Well. The mandrake root—the male mandrake root, that is—"

"Do they come in sexes? How rash of them. But pray, continue."

"I'm trying to! The male root sends out tentacles that run vinelike through the ground in search of a female mandrake. It often takes a long time. Years, in fact."

"Shy creatures, are they, the females?"

"Very shy. When the male does find a female, their vines begin to intertwine, and the male and female move through the ground until they are close together, and then they mate, just as humans do. Sometimes you can dig them out of the ground in that position and . . . will you stop laughing? It's the truth! Just because you haven't any experience in the matter is no reason to— Oh, please

234

don't! Everyone will wake up! If you think I'm funny, what were you, eating gypsy food? I'll bet you fed it to the dogs when no one was looking!"

"Not at all," he retorted genially. "This wasn't the first time I've eaten with your people, you know. You're probably thinking that I object to the kettle's only being cleaned with a bread crust? That doesn't bother me in the least! If I might be permitted one tiny criticism—it would be nice if your uncle hadn't used that particular cauldron to water the horses."

Indignantly, yet mindful of keeping my voice low, I said, "Why not! It's perfectly acceptable for a man to take his food where a horse has drunk, as long as the horse is healthy. It's not like it was a dog or a cat. . . ! My lord?"

"What is it, sweetheart?" He lifted one of my hands where it lay on the quilt and placed it between his own, his thumb stroking lazily over the curling lines of my palm.

It was not easy to speak with him touching me and calling me sweetheart in just that voice.

"Have you really been wishing Ellen and Robert would marry? Could that be why you invited Ellen and Lady Gwendolyn to come to Edgehill?"

"Partly," he admitted. "Gwen knew, of course. My brother and Ellen are the kind of headstrong, passionate children who would be ruined by marriage to the wrong partner, and I'm afraid that the wrong partner would be anything less than each other. Robert's finally begun to fall in love with her, have you noticed? He doesn't know it yet, perhaps, but soon."

I gazed into his face, and into the finely shaped eyes that seemed to me the most intelligent and the sanest I had ever seen. There were so many things he cared about—he, a man who had never been taught to care. He gave so much kindness in his own way, though he had received so little when he had been very young and vulnerable. His manhood and the graces of his character had been hard-won in the preying teeth of the corruption and the cruelty that he'd known.

He left me to stir life into the sullen red coals of the fire. Coming back to the blankets, he said thoughtfully, "Let's send Isabella to Italy. What do you think? She has a pair of great aunts from her mother's side living in Florence."

"Do you think she'll agree to go?"

"She'll have to after tonight. Santinia left you a—God knows what it is! She said I was to give it to you if you woke. Would you like it?" He stretched out his hand to the wagon steps, half hidden by the high grass, and picked up a tin cup. I heard the splash of a thin liquid as he brought the cup to his own lips, and took a sip. He grinned.

"Brandy. And French, at that."

He put the cup in my hand and I sat up, turning the cup around in my hands in what I hoped was an inconspicuous movement, so that my lips would rest on the same spot his had. I knew the taste; my grandmother had given it to me whenever I had a cold, and though I hated the flavor, I took two gulps of the burning fluid, and then a third. I gave him back the cup, and said plaintively, "I'm cold."

He set down the cup and put my arms under the quilts, pulling it high around my neck and tucking it under my shoulders. I waited until he was finished before I said, "I'm still cold."

He touched my cheek, then started to get to his feet. "I'll go to your uncle and see if I can find you another quilt."

"I don't want another quilt."

He accepted this calmly enough. "Shall I build up the fire?"

"No."

He stared at me, and said in a light, pleasant voice, "I'm sure you must be feeling terrible. What a time you've had! I'll fetch Santinia. She can make you something stronger."

"I don't want Santinia, I don't want something stronger. I want you to hold me . . ." I turned coward and dropped

236

my head to the side, away from him. "Underneath the quilts."

The silence stretched very long before he said, "Liza, I don't think that would be a good idea."

"I don't care about good ideas and bad ideas, Alex. I hurt, and feel sick. I've felt sick all afternoon and all night, and my leg aches like an anvil's been dropped on it and—"

"Hush. Hush now. Please don't exhaust yourself any more by crying. There, Liza. Softly now, darling. My love, please stop crying. Will you stop if I hold you? Here. Move a little. Is that better?"

I was so enamored with his comforting that I might well have forced myself to keep crying if it were not made impossible by the joy I felt as his arms enfolded me, as strong and hard as they were. His hand came up behind, and cradled the back of my head, and pulled me to him, and I felt his warm, moving chest beneath my cheek.

His hair smelled like a gypsy's, soft scents from the fire smoke and the night forest, and I felt the graceful curves of muscle and bone as his body sought mine. I sighed all over from contentment, but Brockhaven said unromantically. "A *very* bad idea."

"Don't worry, my lord. If we hear anyone coming, you can quickly jump out from under the covers."

"Oh, I can, can I? Thank you very much. A pretty spectacle I'll present."

"Well, if you're going to get grumpy . . ."

"I'm not grumpy." He raised on one elbow, looking down at me with a grin. "What do gypsies do, if they catch young folk together like this?"

"Make them get married," I answered him readily.

"Mmm? As long as I'm not to be ceremonially bisected, or something—" His fingers spread on my forehead, stroking away the wandering strands of my hair.

Daringly, I laid the flat of my hand against his chest. "You were angry . . ."

"When?"

"Tonight. When you found me with Vincent."

237

His smile was crooked, and heart-stoppingly sweet. "Did I seem angry? Lord. Anger is a pallid creature compared to the emotion I felt. Liza, all I could think of at first, was that you had run away from Edgehill because you were afraid of me."

"You know now that I am not," I reminded him in a small voice. "Alex, why didn't you ask me to—to become your wife?"

His arms tightened around me, his lips moving softly on the surface of my cheek. "How could I, dear one? It was bad enough, in honor, to have kissed you with me as your guardian, and you so alone in the world without a single responsible relative to protect you. Liza, I knew that the announcement of our engagement would be the one thing that would make Vincent move to take your life."

He shifted a little, and my fingers slipped, quite by accident, between the buttons of his shirt and came to rest against the bare skin on his chest. I gasped, and said I beg your pardon, and would have pulled them away, if he had not shook his head and covered my hand with his own.

"You might have told me—that you loved me," I whispered.

"Yes. I'm sorry. I would have, if I had realized that you didn't know. It seemed to be pouring out of me by the bucket until I was afraid I would drown you in it. It wasn't until much later that I knew I should have said the words, and made sure that you understood." His lips came to mine, and pressed them, and then whispered against my mouth, "I love you, Liza." My lips parted under his questing kiss, and I felt the leisurely stroke of his hand on the curve of my back.

Carefully, because of my leg, he turned me on to my back, still kissing me, still with one hand underneath me.

"You know, dear," he said, "one thing our cultures have in common is the button mechanism." His mouth covered the fullness of my lips and lingered there while he said, "You know how to do it. Why don't you?"

"Do you mean that I should—your shirt?"

"Yes, that's what I mean." His lips touched the hollow

238

at the side of my neck, below my earlobe. "Yes. Yes. Liza, are you going to marry me? Say 'of course, Alex.' "

"Of course, Alex," I could only whisper. "Am I doing this right?"

He laughed shakily. "It would seem so. Talk to me, Liza. What possessed you to swim this morning in the dower house pond?"

"It was the bog bean. I wanted to make a tonic for my loss of appetite."

"Really. An appetite tonic." His lips seared over mine, washing my being in a hot, shuddering wave of pleasure. "How does this compare with bog bean?"

His wonderful touch moved lower and my flesh hummed with delight under the subtle movement of his hands. Love-giddy, I said, "Better. Ever so much better. But then it's been a long time since I've had bog bean tonic." It was heady, soul-deep enchantment to let my hands explore the uncovered skin beneath his shirt. Marveling that my awed, bashful touch could stir him, I laid my worshipful hand over his heart, and learned the hard echo of its rhythm. It was on this beat that my very life drew breath. I whispered to him, "I suppose you disliked it excessively to find me at the pond like that?"

"Did you think so? You'll be surprised when we're married, and I make you do it every day."

"Fine," I said. "I'll include it in my memoirs, 'The Misadventures of Countess B.' "

He laughed in that happy, perfect way he has when he's relaxed and completely at peace.

"Indeed, m'lady, we had best start behaving ourselves or the first chapter will be titled 'Before the Gypsy Wagon,' instead of 'On the Night of My Wedding.' " He stroked his finger down the line of my nose. "Say 'I love you, Alex.' "

I pulled him fiercely to me. "I love you. I adore you. You're the only man I'll ever love."

He placed his hands on my cheeks, and with a rapt honesty that would shed forever my doubts, he said, "And you're the only woman I'll ever love."

He kissed me, long and hard, on the lips; and in a light

239

movement, was on his feet, straightening his shirt.

"Where are you going?" I asked him.

"To wake your uncle, my dearest love, and ask for his blessing. Not that I imagine it will come as a surprise to him! A very perceptive man, your uncle. What do you think, Liza—for our honeymoon, shall we take your wagon and travel with the tribe?"

My throat was too full with happiness to speak, but I smiled my love to him and gave him my hand. He bent over to brush it with a gentle kiss, and then covered me with the quilt.

The flaming shaft of the early-morning sun was beginning to slant through the trees as he gave me an intimate little wave. I leaned back, smiling at him, my hands clasped behind my head to watch him walk with clean, quick strides across the field to the gypsy camp. He stopped halfway across, and came back to me, to pick me up, still wrapped in the quilt, and together we began our journey.